A Kary Turnell Mystery

I Knew
You When

MARK OKRANT

OAK MANOR PUBLISHING, INC.

Designed and Published by
OAK MANOR PUBLISHING, INC.
603-860-5551
www.OakManorPublishing.com

Mark J. Okrant 1947 -
Mark Okrant/I Knew You When
Murder Mystery 1.The Mount Washington Resort
2. Historic resort

ISBN 0-978-0-9791757-5-6   First Edition

Dedicated to
the late Ethyle Okrant, Shirley Chatzek, Lucille Godbois,
and to those who continue
their campaign against cancer.

I knew you when you were lonely
I knew you when you were only
A girl all alone without love
I knew you when.

Billy Joe Royal,1965

PROLOGUE

As they tooled north along Interstate 93, Dana Cerone was in a terrific frame of mind. "Can you believe Charles actually gave us permission to do this?"

"I was shocked," replied her colleague and best friend, Maya Lassiter. "Funds are usually so tight at CNHS, just like every other public high school. For Charles to find money for both of us to be there, cover our registration fees, plus spring for two nights at a resort—I can't believe it."

"And don't forget the subs; they must be costing a hundred and twenty apiece."

The two women had taught together at Crawford Notch High School since the mid-eighties. Maya, an Italian teacher, and Dana, who taught the Natural Sciences, had instructed their respective Advanced Placement courses for several years. Despite being regarded as two of the best teachers at CNHS, they were well aware of economic realities. So it was little wonder they could barely contain their excitement when Principal Charles Barker approved both requests to spend three days and two nights conferring with other AP teachers at the elegant Mount Washington Resort in New Hampshire's White Mountains.

"Three days of pampering myself!" Dana nearly howled.

"You're forgetting something *cara mia*," Maya reminded

her friend, "We're here to attend a conference, which means detailed reports to Charles, not to mention revised lesson plans. Besides, I'm vice president of NHTAP, so I'll be stuck in board meetings half the time."

"But I won't!" Dana laughed as she smacked her friend on the arm.

"Ouch, Dana, that hurts! Are you trying to make me wreck this car? I wouldn't even be driving this stick shift if you weren't here to help me." The two women had rented a red, five-speed, Ford Mustang convertible to celebrate the occasion or, if truth be told, because Maya's SUV was spending more time in the Draper Garage than in her own driveway lately. Because the two women had rejected the Enterprise agent's recommendation to get temporary auto insurance, the last thing they needed was a car wreck, especially on teachers' salaries. Maya was extremely uncomfortable driving the fast, standard shift car but, when they were only five miles from the resort, finally acquiesced to Dana's insistence that she get behind the wheel.

"Sometimes you're too damned aggressive for your own good, Dana," Maya said.

As the two women entered the long spiraling driveway leading toward the grand resort, they had no way of knowing how prophetic Maya's words would prove to be.

PART I
CONSTERNATION

1

His name is Kary Turnell. During his clear-headed moments, he teaches sociology and criminology at the brick and mortar campus in Plymouth, just south of the White Mountains in New Hampshire. These days he was putting the finishing touches on his second murder mystery which was based on an actual case he had solved up north at The Balsams resort. When the telephone rang, he was in his office advising a beautiful redheaded student. His sister-in-law Maya, the last person from whom Kary ever wanted to hear, was on the other end of the line. She didn't sound any too pleased, or coherent for that matter.

"Kary, it's Maya. Nya told me I had to call you."

Nya and Maya! What had their parents been thinking when they named those two? Kary pondered.

"Well, you have," Kary replied curtly, "so you can hang up now."

"I'd like to but I can't." Now that was the old Maya Kary had come to dislike. "I can't because she's in the bushes." And with that Maya began to wail so loudly Kary involuntarily covered the ear piece with his hand.

"Who's in the bushes?" Kary asked as the erstwhile redhead looked at her professor with large, green, inquiring eyes.

Trying to make light of the matter, Kary moved his hand to cover the receiver and said, "There's no problem, Shauna. It's my sister-in-law. Her friend's in the bushes." Sensing this would be a good time to be anywhere else, Shauna rose and gathered her things. As she retreated quickly from Kary's office, she called over her shoulder, "I'll come back some other time, Dr. Turnell."

"Oh, great!" he thought aloud, his hand still covering the receiver. "My sister-in-law is out of control and now my best student thinks I'm some kind of whacko." Maya still was in no condition to provide Kary with any details and he had a Sociology class waiting for him. He had to find out whether this telephone call was really something he needed to act upon, and quickly.

The fact that Maya had called him was almost newsworthy. They had barely spoken to one another in years, and that only happened at family gatherings on those rare occasions when they found themselves in a confined space with no one else within ear shot. Maya didn't think her sister Nya should still be married to him. For ten years, Nya had endured Kary's acute case of writer's cramp and everything that went with it. Following the success of his first novel, he wasn't able to write a solid paragraph. It wasn't long before it became evident to Kary, as well as to everyone else, that something was dramatically wrong. Random House was the first to comment publicly when he continued to miss deadline after deadline. For reasons Kary never understood, he had developed a prolonged, seemingly incurable case of writer's block. He began to believe all of the nasty stories in the media when he was described as a one-book wonder. As Kary became obsessed with writing another best seller, Nya paid the price, enduring his foul attitude. What was worst for Nya was his inattention to her in the physical sense. When her frustration had reached its zenith, she confided in her twin sister Maya. Following the case at The Balsams nearly ten months prior, Nya and Kary were once again madly in love, the whole shooting match. But, still, Maya was not convinced that Kary deserved to be with her sister. At the height of his marital difficulties, Kary realized it was in his best interest to have as little as possible to do with his sister-in-law. Nothing that happened since Nya and he rekindled the spark in their marriage convinced him to reconcile his differences with Maya.

Kary was beginning to think that his sister-in-law would never stop bawling. His left ear felt like it was going to explode. Finally she blurted, "Dana is dead! They found her body in the bushes an hour ago." He knew what was coming. Maya was going to ask for his help. She really didn't want it. And he wasn't thrilled about giving it.

2

Despite the strong contrasts in their personalities, Dana and Maya were friends for more than twenty years. They met as rookie teachers at Crawford Notch High School in the White Mountains. Maya had introduced the first AP Italian course to the high school, in 2000, and several years later, Dana introduced AP Chemistry.

"You know what's pretty cool," Dana said to Maya, "the way we're able to discuss teaching techniques, even though we teach such different subjects."

"That's for sure," and despite the insecurity she felt behind the wheel of the Ford Mustang, Maya smiled over at her best friend. "I don't know what I'd do if you didn't teach at CNHS." Over time, their friendship had extended beyond the high school, as the two women and their husbands became inseparable.

Dana and Maya enjoyed more than their share of success in teaching the Advanced Placement courses and were thrilled to learn the regional AP conference was being held so close to home, and especially at such a beautiful and historic place. For three days and two nights, the teachers had an opportunity to work, eat, and sleep in rooms that had hosted the United Nations Monetary and Financial Conference in July of 1944, leading to the establishment of the International Monetary

Fund. Over the years, the resort had accommodated leading figures from the worlds of entertainment, politics, and sports, and was about to provide both women with an opportunity for a little adventure away from school.

Maya and Dana loved their jobs, especially their students. As they drove along, the two talked non-stop about the same thing they always did, namely the high school. They hit all of the usual topics.

"It's been another good year at school. Despite a few yo-yos, I've seen real progress in my first year students," Maya offered.

"Me, too; and, the little Wong girl has the potential to be my best student in years," Dana said.

"I had her older sister, Jen," Maya contributed. "She's at Columbia now, doing really well, from what I hear."

"Of course, then there's the Muddle boy!" they shouted out in unison, then howled that they'd had the same thought.

"That poor kid," Dana said.

"Poor kid, my foot!" Maya laughed. "If he'd stop looking at girls and pay attention in class, he'd do just fine."

Dana laughed. "His hormones are working overtime, that's for sure."

As they drove along, more war stories were discussed, as was a rumored affair between the physics teacher and one of the new administrators.

Until about twelve years earlier, Maya and Dana harbored a deep concern for students who were having problems at home. It was remarkable to them how many students living in a seemingly idyllic place like northern New Hampshire were practically destitute. As a result, it had not been uncommon for Maya or Dana to take such a student under her wing, spending hard-earned money to pay for anything from a notebook to a good meal. But, that was before "The Incident," a subject they promised themselves not to discuss, under any circumstances, ever again.

3

Laureli Hopkins long anticipated her return to the Mount Washington. She'd made her last drive up the resort's long, twisting entrance way during the summer before her senior year at Portsmouth College. Laureli was the daughter of the long term maitre d'hotel, so the old hotel was like a second home to her. But this trip to the Mount Washington Resort was for a very special reason.

"I worked every summer at that old place for five years, so this decision is a no-brainer," Laureli told her husband of two years, Bob Hopkins.

Laureli was in the midst of a twelve-hour whirlwind tour to announce her intention to seek the Democratic nomination for U.S. Congress, representing New Hampshire's second Congressional District. It came as no surprise, therefore, when she told her husband and her campaign manager, "The Mount Washington just has to be the third place where I make my announcement."

Early in the morning of May tenth, Laureli arrived at Poor Boy's Diner in Londonderry. Poor Boy's was a traditional place for candidates in her district to make such declarations over breakfast with the locals. From there, she moved on to the capitol building in Concord. Rather than stand on the capitol steps, she elected to make her announcement at the base of the statue of native son Daniel Webster, with the statue and the building's familiar gold dome and granite columns as her back drop. After an interview with state and regional media, she attended a lunch in her honor at the Barley House across the street from the capitol grounds.

From the Barley House, Laureli's small entourage traveled several miles to the Concord airport where the new candidate boarded veteran pilot Bob Jenks' single engine Cessna for a flight to Twin Mountain.

"I still think flying in small planes is too dangerous," Laureli's husband Bob Hopkins scolded, but neither he nor their campaign manager, Mandy Tompkins, was able to dissuade her from making the flight to Twin Mountain.

"Listen, Bob, this airplane trip was donated by a campaign supporter, and I have no intention of insulting a benefactor, no matter what Mandy and you say about it."

Upon arriving at Twin Mountain, Laureli met her mom and sister, Lucy and Sara Dutton. Laureli's father Armand Desmoreau had been estranged from his wife for more than two decades. After the separation, Lucy adopted her family's surname, and her older daughter followed suit. Therefore, while Laureli was having some quality time with her mom and sister, Armand waited at the Mount Washington for his daughter to arrive. Meanwhile, Mandy and Bob made the tiring ninety minute drive to Bretton Woods, then met with staff at the resort to ensure the announcement went off without a hitch.

Once Laureli was airborne, Mandy turned to Bob and said with a sigh, "We'd better hit the road right away, Bob. It's going to take at least an hour and a half to get up there in your car." The plan designed by Mandy called for Bob and her to return to Nashua immediately following Laureli's announcement. Their job would be to keep the momentum of the campaign going. Meanwhile, Laureli was to remain at the resort as a highly visible participant in a two-day summit on the region's economy. Laureli Hopkins was no fool; she knew this issue would separate her candidacy from any competitors within the Democratic Party, and it had been a blemish on the Republican incumbent's track record.

4

Paul Grandhomme was back at his job and, whether he thought so or not, he was fortunate to still be working at the Mount Washington Resort. May 10th, the day of Laureli Hopkins' announcement, was Paul's first day back to work following an involuntary absence of a month. Paul had an IQ below 90 and was regarded as a strange person by his fellow workers, who had given him the moniker, "Pothead." The nickname had nothing to do with using marijuana. It came from the fact he was never seen anywhere on the resort grounds without wearing a two quart sauce pan as a hat. Paul wore it on his head with the handle facing backward, much like the contemporary fashion of wearing one's baseball cap with the bill facing toward the rear. He began doing this several years earlier in response to a large section of decaying ceiling tiles that were falling on his head. At the time, his fellow kitchen staff had celebrated Paul's choice of protective gear. Since it was the first occasion he wasn't the object of cruel verbal and physical taunts at the hands of his fellow kitchen workers, Paul felt this would be a good way to remain in the limelight. Of course, had the younger men in the kitchen known about Paul's heritage, they would have made it impossible for him to continue working at the resort, but that was a secret the general manager and Paul's family guarded closely. At first, his fellow workers chuckled when they saw Paul hadn't removed the pot; then they ridiculed him. After a few days, despite the fact virtually everyone returned to treating him as they had before the pot incident, Paul kept wearing the utensil on his head. His behavior might not have seemed quite as strange if his only station was in the kitchen; however, Paul's job called upon him to set up for parties, meetings, and other events in virtually every corner of the resort. He loved the fact that most of the resort staff and even the regular guests recognized him, some of the latter even called out to him, "Hey, Pothead, how's it going?"

It was an incident involving one of the gardeners that earned Paul his hiatus from the resort grounds. One day, while carrying a load of desserts from the kitchen to the patio area of the resort's outdoor pool, Paul slipped and fell on top of a tray filled with cream pies and tarts. When he arose, he was a creamy mess, from his pot to his shoes. Bobby Lane, who had been tending the nearby ferns, was the first staff person to see what the resulting commotion was about. In an earnest attempt to make light of the situation, he called out, "Pothead Grandhomme, ladies and gentleman, his next performance will be at 4 this afternoon!" Perhaps Paul was having an especially bad day, or maybe it was because he'd fallen down right next to two beautiful young women whom he was ogling at the time, but he lost it. Removing the pot from his head, he struck Bobby square in the face using a backhand motion that would have made Andy Roddick proud. The sight of Bobby's front teeth and a sizable quantity of blood streaming from his mouth produced screams from the two women and sent Paul scampering away.

Tom Capstone, the resort's general manager, was not a happy person when Paul appeared in his office in the north wing of the grand resort hotel building. Surrounded by pictures depicting the resort's construction, Tom's demeanor was as stolid as his surroundings.

"Mr. Grandhomme, I am very disappointed in you. I've looked the other way although you've insisted on wearing that silly pot on your head. By the way, please don't wear that in my office. You've been a good, reliable worker or I'd fire you on the spot for what you did to Mr. Lane. I'm giving you this one chance. I'm going to suspend you for one month with pay. However, it will be your responsibility to pay for any dental work that isn't covered by the parent company's insurance. Do you understand?"

"Yes, sir, Mr. Capstone," Paul replied. As he turned to leave, he'd glared back over his shoulder and said, "Thanks a lot!"

Tom Capstone didn't know exactly what to make of the younger man's comment, for the tone Paul used was unclear. Tom thought about calling him back into the office for a clarification. Instead, he decided to make a notation in Paul's file, "He exhibited aggressive behavior that bears watching once he returns from his suspension."

5

The Mount Washington Resort was nearly as beautiful and famous as the great granite mountain for which it had been named. Despite the fact that Maya and Dana lived in the North Country for two decades and drove past it twice each day on their way to and from high school, neither had ever spent a single night in the resort. In fact, like most other residents of northern New Hampshire, neither had stepped foot inside since it was renovated more than a decade earlier. Upon reaching a point three miles west of Crawford Notch, Maya turned left into the entry road and pulled over so the pair could drink in the view.

Having used a glacial ridge jutting out onto a green plateau and traversed by the Ammonoosuc River as his pedestal, Joseph Stickney had sculpted his hotel as one would a work of art. From a distance of one mile, the Mount Washington Hotel resembled a large luxury liner moving slowly along a sea of green.

"Oh my," said Maya, "don't you just love the way the red roof tiles contrast with the white stucco."

"I only have eyes for the mountains," replied Dana. Indeed, the resort was built with Mount Washington, the tallest peak in the northeastern United States, as its backdrop. The farther they proceeded into the property, the better they could tell how really large and magnificent the hotel was.

"It must be as long as a football field."

"Longer, I'll bet." The women said nothing further as they continued winding their way up the drive. It was fortunate that Maya didn't hit any of the expensive automobiles they passed along the way, so focused was she on admiring the elaborate Italian Renaissance Revival architecture with its lengthy piazza, intricate balconies, and paired columns. Finally, she pulled up beneath the porte cochere where they were greeted by a valet parking attendant who looked like a Greek god.

"My name is Andreas. May I help you ladies?" His words flowed through a set of perfect white teeth and betrayed a decidedly Mediterranean, probably Balkan, accent.

Avoiding a more tempting retort, both women smiled and Dana replied, "We're here to attend a conference and we need to check in, Andreas."

"Welcome to the Mount Washington Resort. You may go right inside where you will see the front desk to your left. We will unload your luggage. Would you like us to park your car for you?"

"Yes, please," Maya replied. She was in no mood to drive the car any more. Besides, she wasn't about to say no to this unbelievably handsome young man.

Andreas gave Maya and Dana his biggest smile, handed Maya a small, green ticket, and informed her she could telephone for their automobile by referring to the number he had given to them. Andreas would have loved to put the Mustang five-speed through its paces. He knew, however, that would be akin to filling out his own pink slip. So he drove carefully back down the driveway to the valet parking lot while Maya and Dana walked onto the porch leading into the hotel.

Entering the hotel, Dana and Maya were immediately

enraptured by what they saw. The floor of the huge lobby was covered with a rich, woolen carpet with a reddish hue and a floral pattern. Looking to their left, they spotted the concierge's desk and saw the registration desk situated just beyond it. Along the east wall, Dana eyed a gorgeous grandfather clock. Two parallel sets of columns ran much of the length of the lobby and plush chairs with high backs were positioned strategically. A huge stone fireplace dominated the lobby's east wall just beyond the ornate clock.

"There is so much to explore here. I just hope I have the time," Maya said.

"Oh, I will," Dana replied with an expression reminiscent of the Cheshire Cat.

"Let's register, then maybe we both can look around." Maya was doing her best to ignore Dana's comment, but without much success.

Registration was handled with great efficiency and the two friends soon found themselves being guided by their bellman into an old fashioned Otis elevator hand-operated by a tall, elderly man.

"Are ya' staying with us long?" the bellman asked.

"Two nights. Is our room nice?" Dana wondered aloud.

"Dana! I'm certain it's lovely," Maya scolded. Sometimes her friend was like a bull in a china shop, but Maya loved her dearly.

"Trust me, you ladies will really enjoy yer room," the bellman replied. His accent was decidedly Manhattan.

Exiting the elevator, Dana and Maya were guided to the right and up a slight incline that led to their room. The bellman showed them in with a flourish of his hand. "Voila, ladies."

The bellman was correct. They were immediately impressed by the accommodations. The bedroom was enormous, nearly as large as Dana's classroom. Two queen beds with carved mahogany two-posted headboards were nearly lost in the large space. The bedspreads, thick-pile carpet, couch and twin high back chairs all had a similar floral pattern. An oval, mahogany coffee table contained several magazines as well as a book displaying information and a photographic history of the resort. Brass lamps adorned both mahogany end tables. An ornate fireplace with a white wooden mantle dominated the front of the room. On either side of the mantle were two large windows that faced the formal front entrance of the resort. Between these windows was a tall colonial style mahogany cabinet that held a large television and three dresser drawers.

"This is just lovely," Maya said, now wishing privately her husband Stan could have joined her. "It's too bad I'll be too busy to spend much time up here."

"But I won't," Dana chided her. In truth, once the actual conference began Dana would be as busy as Maya, but not during their first day at the resort.

Sighing aloud, Maya said, "Let's get unpacked, take a walk around, and register for the conference, shall we?" The two finished unpacking then, deciding not to take the elevator, walked down the several flights of stairs leading to the lobby. They made their way through the increasingly crowded space to a set of tables set up in front of the great stone fireplace. A sign on an easel indicated this was the registration area for the New Hampshire Teachers of Advanced Placement (NHTAP).

Spotting no one ahead of them in line for the moment, Maya said, "Oh good, this is a perfect time to register."

As the two walked up to the table, one of the NHTAP members, a short, buxom blond named Mabel Murphy who was working at the registration desk, cried out when she saw

Maya, "Madam vice president. Welcome to the beautiful Mount Washington hotel!" All the while, Mabel barely acknowledged Dana's presence.

Maya smiled and embraced the much shorter woman. "Well, it's a pleasure to be here. And how have you been, Mabel?" Maya was relieved the other woman was wearing her name tag because, truth be known, she had no idea what her name was. Mabel was one of those people who made herself visible at the NHTAP conferences year after year without imprinting on anyone. Then, remembering Dana, Maya turned and introduced the two women, who immediate shook hands.

"Ouch!" Mabel cried out.

"Oh, I'm sorry," Dana said in a tone that Maya recognized as insincere. Once Mabel handed the two women their packets, both immediately checked to see if the all-important receipt for their conference payment was included. Next, not seeing anyone else they recognized, they walked toward the Conservatory on the east side of the hotel, the side facing the Presidential Mountain Range.

As she scanned the materials, Maya asked Dana, "What was that all about?" She knew perfectly well.

"Oh, I must have squeezed her hand a little too hard," Dana replied.

Knowing her friend reserved that treatment for people she didn't like, Maya said, "You don't even know Mabel. Why do you feel compelled to do things like that?"

Before Dana could reply, Maya spotted two items in her packet that had captured her attention. Dana knew her friend's preoccupied look all too well.

"Um, Earth to Maya, Earth to Maya. Come in, please!"

"Huh? What? Oh, there's a note here that says the NHTAP board will be meeting in the Lafayette Room at 2:45. Yet another curve ball from our madam president," Maya said sarcastically. "This means I need to find the room and get down there. I can't afford to be late."

"For chrissake, Maya, that's fifteen minutes from now. You don't always have to be the first one in the room."

"Oh, come on, Dana. We've been friends for how long? You know I'm an early freak. I've gotta go."

"Not before you tell me which other item in our packet was so interesting."

"Look at your packet. There's something in there about a political candidate making an announcement."

"A candidate? How cool is that?!" Dana was nothing if not a celebrity junkie. She couldn't resist the opportunity to see someone who was famous, or who might become famous in the next twenty years or so. Rifling through the NHTAP materials, she dismissed item after item quickly. Finally, she found the flier that read, "Laureli Hopkins, Democrat from Nashua, will announce her candidacy for U.S. House of Representatives from the Second Congressional District. Please come to the Ballroom at 3 p.m. today. Refreshments will be served."

"This is too perfect. Maya is going to be in board meetings until dinner and I needed something to do before my pedicure, anyway." In keeping with NHTAP tradition, there were only board meetings on their first day at the resort. In truth, Dana could have arrived at the Mount Washington a day after Maya. With her travel paid by the school there was no way she was going to miss out on an extra great meal and night in a beautifully furnished guest room. Focusing her attention on the flier, she asked herself, "Who the heck is Laureli Hopkins? I've never heard of her, and here she is running for the House. Her name sure doesn't ring a bell."

6

With Maya in her meeting, Dana was somewhat at loose ends. The candidate's announcement wasn't for another fifteen minutes. While she loved political announcements, over the years she had become the anti-Maya, preferring to arriving late to being early. However, the ballroom was filling fast. She recognized the reporter from her local newspaper as he went rushing by to find a space to stand in the front row. Then she saw Maya flash across the hotel lobby. Maya appeared to be searching for someone and, judging by the look on her face, she wasn't happy. Dana had been standing near the entry way to the ballroom where the announcement was to take place, but she immediately backtracked when she saw her friend.

"Maya! Hey, Maya! What's going on? You look like someone just kicked you in the stomach."

Upon seeing her friend, Maya immediately broke down.

"What is it? What's happened? Is Stan all right?" Dana asked.

"Stan's fine. I asked Sara to send these to me as soon as they arrived." With that, Maya handed Dana a memo handwritten on resort stationery. It was a list of the results of the AP Italian test. Sara, the principal's administrative assistant had called the results in to the resort and requested they be given to Maya. Having arrived at her board meeting, Maya had learned that the start of the meeting would be delayed by fifteen minutes. So, the dedicated teacher she was, Maya took a walk to the front desk to find out if she had received any messages.

Dana read the note aloud, "News not as good this year. Only three of your seven students passed the AP test." Dana knew this was devastating to Maya, who always worked tirelessly to prepare her students for the exam. There was also the matter of constantly having to convince skeptical administrators about the value of the AP program. After all, this was money that could be spent on the CNHS championship baseball team.

Dana hugged her friend. "First of all, these scores are no reflection on you as a teacher. You're one of the best teachers at Crawford Notch. You just had a bad group of kids this year. Hell, Maya, last year all nine of your kids passed. That's never happened to me. And the second thing is—"

Maya knew what her friend was going to say, so she beat her to the punch.

"I know. We're away from school, so why on earth did I have the scores sent to me? You're right. Of course, you're right. I'm just worried that the French and Spanish kids did better on their tests than mine did."

"You're damned straight I'm right! Listen, I have the same seven kids in AP Chemistry. They're not going to do a damned bit better for me than they did for you. So let it go, Maya. Let it go!" Dana sounded like she was lecturing her friend and maybe she deserved it. Dana had a revelation.

"I have an idea. Skip your board meeting and I'll forget about this announcement? Then we can—"

But Dana never finished. A resort staff member dressed up like Benjamin Franklin called out in a loud voice, "Ladies and gentlemen, please come to the ballroom at once. Our candidate will be making her announcement followed by an opportunity to sample a fabulous array of beverages produced here in New Hampshire."

"Forget about that, let's just go off by ourselves and play," Dana said as she held Maya's hands.

"No, I'm all right now, Dana. I'll go to my board meeting where everyone will be staring at me and thinking, "I'll bet her students didn't do so hot on the Italian AP exam.""

"Maya, cut that stuff out!"

"I'm kidding. Honest, I'm kidding. I really am fine. Besides, I know better than to keep a politics junkie away from her fix. Go see this new hotshot and tell me all about her during dinner."

7

The day wasn't about to get any better for Maya. When she returned to her board meeting in the Lafayette Room, Priscilla O'Neal, the organization's president, had a disapproving look on her face.

"Where were you, Maya? I needed to talk with you."

Maya felt her stomach flip over. As much as she believed in the AP program, she often rued the day she became involved with this board. The board labored long and hard over a number of things Dana mockingly called minutia. Things hadn't always been this bad, but once Priscilla ascended to her throne, the meetings had become agonizingly long and fruitless.

"That chick doesn't know how to get out of her own way," Dana had once said. And she was right.

"Oh dear, what's the problem, Priscilla?" Maya tried to use as solicitous a tone as she could muster.

"What isn't the problem is more like it. Claudia isn't at the conference."

Maya really liked Claudia, the NHTAP membership chairman. "Oh, is everything all right with Claudia? I just spoke—"

But Priscilla just waved her hand as if to say, "Don't interrupt me."

"We don't have a current list of our members here at the hotel," Priscilla sniffed.

Carmel Silva, the board secretary, had overheard their conversation. She interjected, "Is that really a problem, Priscilla?"

"Of course, it is. Don't you see that anyone could crash our conference and we wouldn't know if they were a dues-paying member or not."

Yeah right, Maya thought to herself. Legions are doubtlessly waiting to crash our meeting so they can steal secrets about teaching AP. She wisely didn't antagonize the president any further. Instead she said, "We'll just have to work together to cover for Claudia." Then, just to stress out Priscilla, she added, "I do hope Claudia is okay."

Priscilla shot Maya one of her infamous nasty looks. Then she continued her diatribe. "There's even more bad news. Pam's laptop just blew up and all of our financial records went with it."

"But she must have had a back up."

"Sure there is, but the CD is all the way down in Keene." Priscilla appeared ready to explode.

Maya instinctively knew this was one of those times when the president needed an ego boost. While Maya knew almost anyone else could easily deal with these problems, it was obvious Priscilla needed calming or she would go right off the deep end.

"What can we do, Priscilla?" she asked in a tone that suggested she, too, was desperate.

"Well, fortunately for this organization, I have things under control. Obviously all of these problems will slow things down. So, I have asked the resort to set up a special dinner meeting. We'll meet here in the Lafayette Room until 6. Then we'll take a break to change for the evening and we'll gather again at 7 for a working dinner."

Maya groaned to herself. She knew exactly what this meant. She would be busy until the wee hours with NHTAP board activities. There was no way she'd be having dinner with Dana and there wouldn't be time to meet with any of her old association friends. Most annoying of all, knowing how much Dana loved politics, Maya was anxious to debrief her roommate about the candidate's presentation in the ballroom, but this was going to have to wait, all because of Priscilla's incompetence.

8

Dana was kicking herself. By sticking to her pattern of being the last person to arrive at anything—a meeting, a concert, a hockey game—she wasn't able to get a clear view of Laureli Hopkins. At 5 feet 2 inches, Dana wasn't built for viewing from the back of a crowd. She wished that Maya had come to listen with her. Had that been the case, they would have arrived well before the caterers and been standing in the first row. Dana couldn't understand why the candidate didn't elect to stand on the stage to announce her candidacy with the audience seated before her. Had Dana been the candidate, she would have stood on the stage while people remained seated so she would appear taller. Dana also would have had the resort staff open the curtains behind the stage because there was big picture window behind the drapes which offered a terrific view of Crawford Notch.

"I suppose there's some type of image building going on here that escapes me. She probably wants to appear like she's one of the people."

Dana thought she had been talking to herself and was surprised when an elderly gentleman standing next to her interjected, "My daughter is just plain folks. She doesn't want it to seem like she's looking down on anyone."

Dana smiled to herself. Of all the people in the crowd

to be standing near, she had found the candidate's father. It was a good thing she hadn't been saying anything derogatory under her breath.

All of a sudden, there was a hearty round of applause. Dana could see camera flashes going off, but nothing else. Then came the announcement, "Ladies and gentlemen, may I present Laureli Hopkins, candidate for the United States Congress from the Second Congressional District of New Hampshire."

Following a second loud round of applause, the candidate began to speak. She sounded confident and strongly versed in the usual issues espoused by Democratic candidates. Her speech was filled with the standard political pabulum about bringing change and representing New Hampshire values in Washington. Next, she reminded her audience that the second district had never before elected a woman as their U.S. Representative. During the remainder of her comments, she painted a picture of how her character and values differed from those of Samuel Trout, the sitting U.S. Congressman, who she would be running against. Not surprisingly to Dana, she stressed the need for new leadership and a new direction.

"Sam Trout is a nice man, but he's been in office for sixteen years and can no longer see things the way those of us who live out here in New Hampshire's villages, farms, and woodlands do. We need a new set of eyes and ears in Washington, eyes and ears that can see and hear today's problems aren't the decades old issues Sam Trout is still supporting. I stand here today, in this time honored inn, as one of you. And I ask that you cast your votes in November to send me, Laureli Hopkins, to Washington."

Laureli's speech didn't generate as much sustained excitement as she had hoped. After all, she was one of them...

a local girl who had made something of herself. Following several minutes of sustained if somewhat subdued applause, she concluded her comments. "I promise you all, right here and right now, that I will bring your voice, not the voice of a Washington insider, to our nation's capital. Thank you for coming out to see me today and the Lord bless you."

Dana moaned to herself, "Why do these candidates always have to play the religion card? If it isn't religion, they're waving the flag." Then she caught herself. What if the candidate's father had overheard her? She'd have been totally embarrassed. But Dana need not have worried. Prior to the conclusion of the speech, the elderly man had moved away from her side and immediately pushed through a group of news people and well wishers toward his daughter.

As she made her own way toward Laureli Hopkins, Dana eavesdropped on a conversation between two middle-aged men. One of them, a short, balding man dressed in a hounds tooth sport coat, reminded Dana of the late Heywood Hale Broun. Based on the blazer the second, taller man was wearing, she figured him to be one of the resort's executives.

The shorter man, who was addressed as Bernie, said, "Well she certainly knows how to create political theater, I'll give her that. The decision to announce here was very clever. The political pundits tell us that location says as much about a candidate as the content of her speech. I thought the choice to have her stand among us while she was contrasting herself with Congressman Trout was well conceived, yes, well conceived indeed."

But the taller man, Mark, wasn't quite as ready to anoint Laureli as his Congresswoman, yet. "I didn't feel she did a good job of making the link between this location and her issues. For that matter, what are her issues, Bernie?"

Bernie just chuckled at his acquaintance's comment.

"Time will tell, Mark my friend, time will tell. I still say it was all first rate political theater. She and her people must have learned how to do that somewhere. They want us to think they're not insiders, but I wonder."

"Just what is her background, Bernie? I follow New Hampshire politics pretty closely and she seems to have appeared out of thin air. Has she ever held an elected office?"

"Not that I know about. But there's no law saying someone needs to go from one elected position to another. The only related law I know is a rule against "double-dipping"— holding more than one government position at one time," Bernie replied.

"So, Ms. Hopkins, doesn't have to be an elected official, be it a state senator, legislator, or city council member, to be a congressional candidate, eh? You know something, Bernie, given the lay of the political landscape these days, it may prove beneficial that she hasn't held an elected post because it means neither the politicos nor the press has anything on her. Since she hasn't offended anyone in an official capacity, the lady has no track record to attack." Mark continued, "Answer this for me: how does someone like her achieve a high enough political profile without having held elected office?"

"It's easier than you may think, Mark. She could achieve a high profile status and gain credibility by working for someone else's political campaign. I'll bet good money that young Ms. Hopkins was the brains behind either the governor's last campaign, or maybe Mel Dormund's recent run for the U.S. Senate."

"Yeah, but Mel lost by twenty points," Mark replied.

"True, but remember the media raved about how Mel went from being completely off the map to finishing respectably. You want to bet our young candidate played a major role in that?"

"So what you're telling me is she's developed a whole bunch of political capital by contributing to other candidates' campaigns. Do the parties really ascribe to the rationale that, if someone like Hopkins does a good job strategizing and campaigning for someone like the governor or a congressional candidate, she'd also do a good job in Washington?"

"That precisely what I'm saying, Mark."

"My word! Does such a thing happen often?"

"Not that often, but it does happen. Ironically, it's true democracy in action," Bernie said.

"How's that? I'm not following you."

"From what I understand, Laureli Hopkins is not a woman of financial means, at least not enough to bankroll a congressional campaign. And we're both pretty certain she hasn't held any prior political positions, at least not in New Hampshire. So, you'd expect this Ms. Hopkins would stand about as much chance of being backed as a political candidate as a Muslim would of being elected Pope. But, by earning her stripes as a staffer—first as a gopher then gradually working her way to the status of top dog—this is how she could earn recognition as a viable congressional candidate, all the while remaining sheltered from public scrutiny. Laureli Hopkins has becomes associated with success because of her role in someone else's campaign. But, to take the next step, she has to have a lot of ambition and cojones."

"What do you mean?"

"Playing such a role isn't enough. She must be able to convince others in the party, based upon what she's done for another candidate, that she has the stuff to get herself elected and actually accomplish something in Washington."

"Now I get it. And by good fortune, this is the perfect year for an unknown like her to grab the limelight. The other potential candidates in the Democratic Party are a bunch of bottom feeders and Sam Trout is really vulnerable."

"You aren't kidding; it seems everyone but Sam knows he's finished."

Coincidentally, as Dana stopped eavesdropping on the men's conversation, the media finished its questioning of Laureli Hopkins. So, the crush of people, including the candidate, her husband, campaign manager, and father moved en mass toward the row of doors separating the ballroom from the hotel lobby. Dana was too much of a political junkie to allow Laureli Hopkins to leave the ballroom without getting a good, close-up look at her. The problem was, at her height, she couldn't see over all of the hangers-on. In an instant she saw her opportunity when a family, who had cozied up to Laureli, said their adieus. Without hesitation, Dana began to push her way toward the candidate whose profile was now in full view. But her forward motion involuntarily ceased when she was no more than six feet from her target. Laureli had turned in her direction. The two women locked eyes for as many as ten seconds. Neither of them said a word as Dana continued to stare at Laureli, but avoided moving any closer. It was as if she had a ball and chain around her ankles. Suddenly Laureli's husband broke the spell, as he led his wife by the arm with her entourage in tow through the ballroom's doors and into the lobby. Dana was left to wonder what she just witnessed.

9

His coworkers called Denny Dupont "boss" to his face, but referred to him as "The Cowboy" when he wasn't within earshot. The resort's food and beverage manager was tall, a few pounds overweight, and bald save for a fringe of dark hair that extended from one temple, around the back of his head, to the other side. Because he'd been at the Mount Washington for more than two decades, and was well versed in all nuances of operating the resort, Denny's influence extended to every corner of the property. Denny's demeanor was generally akin to a male cheerleader. He loved the Mount Washington and looked forward to coming to work each day. He was well aware of the Cowboy moniker and quietly reveled in it. Why wouldn't he? In everything from his appearance to the way he ran things, Denny Dupont was a cowboy. When not operating in one of the public spaces, he could be found at his desk wearing a plaid shirt, bolo tie, and a pair of size 13, black, Dan Post teju lizard cowboy boots. Only during those rare occasions when he was able to get away to play golf at the resort, did he remove his boots in public; however, this was offset with a size 8, black, Palm Leaf cowboy hat, similar in style to the one worn by his childhood hero, Hopalong Cassidy.

Only if a worker failed at a task because he or she didn't

listen, or if two section heads were disagreeing just to be ornery, would Denny use his loud voice and intimidating size in a manner that was anything but pleasant. Unfortunately, for Denny and most of the resort's staff by association, May 10th was to be one of those exceptions. He had arrived at his desk situated in the lowest level of the resort feeling like his usual chipper self. But, within minutes, he was forced to endure a shouting match among Candy McLee, the group booking coordinator, Len Banker, the banquets manager, and Barbara Rubstone, the ice carver. At first, Denny tried to get them all to calm down and discuss the issue in a calm, rational manner. The Mount Washington was no different from any other resort. With a staff of several hundred people working and, in some cases living in close proximity to one another, passions were bound to ebb and flow from time to time. When this happened, Denny was usually the man they sought out, first because of his normal easy-going manner, and secondly because the last thing they wanted to do was face Tom Capstone, the resort's general manager. An appearance before Mr. Capstone always resulted in everyone receiving a verbal reprimand, and sometimes a written one was placed in their permanent records. As everyone was aware, three written reprimands could mean dismissal from the resort staff.

So the three were taken aback when Denny stood up from his chair and roared at them, "You three aren't about to listen to reason, are you? Then do me a favor—get the hell out of here. When you're ready to talk civilly you can come back. Or, better yet, why don't you take your argument to Mr. Capstone. Maybe he'll be amused."

Facing the latter option, the three were already beginning to negotiate in a more reasonable tone by the time they reached the hallway outside Denny's office.

That quick glimpse of his colleagues' sudden change in

have been enough to improve

look down at the memo on his

a list of the meetings and events

that day. Denny expected to see

ics group, the Advanced Place-

the candidate's announcement.

day was not an unusual occur-

formed about the presence of a

ts Repatriation League. If there

didn't enjoy in his line of work,

rstood why his colleagues were

the morning. This news defi-

hood.

vboy said. A pop up was a last

at the resort with very little

tacted the conference service

n occasion at the resort. Pop

h time to react the way they

all kinds of space, time, and

nouncement," he said aloud

gly in something he'd once

politicians: 'The Cowboy is

boy's chief concern is the

the next election.' Denny

through his mind a couple

enny hated hosting politi-

"Something always goes

lar. And somehow he was

those times.

10

Dana plopped down in one of the plush chairs that were placed throughout the south end of the lobby. She was disconcerted and knew it had something to do with Laureli Hopkins. Dana felt pretty certain she'd never met the candidate before. Something was awfully familiar about her. The feeling reminded Dana of the time she'd attended her twenty-fifth high school reunion. It was the first and the last time she'd gone. Maya had advised her not to go. "Why dredge up a bunch of old memories?" she warned. But, Dana hadn't listened and it took her a full week to stop feeling she'd aged overnight, and had taken twice that long before the lingering pangs of nostalgia passed.

The feeling she had now wasn't based on nostalgia and, up until a few minutes earlier, Dana hadn't felt this good in ages. If truth be told, Dana started to feel like a young woman right after she'd colored her naturally dark brown hair to a golden blond, and that was nearly two years ago to the day. She had to smile when she thought how her husband Ben couldn't stop touching her hair, or anything else for that matter. Of course, Ben never could keep his hands away from Dana, and he still couldn't despite the fact that both were well into their fifties. Before long, the warm thoughts she had for Ben displaced the strange feelings she was having. So, she stood up, crossed through the still-crowded lobby, and made her way up the stairs to her room.

When she arrived in the room, she immediately noticed the blinking, red light indicating a telephone message. Pushing the button to retrieve her messages, she learned there were two. The first message was from Maya.

"Hi honey, it's me, Maya." Then sighing, Maya had continued, "Don't count on me for dinner. Priscilla, per usual, is going to stretch out our board meeting. It looks like we'll be meeting through dinner and dessert for that matter. This may go on 'til past 10. I know how you love your beauty sleep, so don't wait up. Do me a favor though, please leave the bathroom light on, so I won't have to disturb you when I come in. Arrivederci."

"Nuts," Dana said out loud. "Just when I need a sounding board, that jerk Priscilla has to pull another of her marathon meetings."

Then the electronic voice on the phone said, "To hear your second message, press 1 now." But, when Dana did, there was nothing but dead space on the other end. She waited for the sound of the telephone being hung up on the other end, but there was nothing for about fifteen seconds.

"Hmm, I wonder what that was about."

Dana lay down for a power nap, pulling down her bed covers so as to avoid lying on the bed spread. After a few winks, she spent the next half hour getting ready for dinner. She took a quick shower, dressed, combed her longish blond hair, and put on a dash of blush powder. Dana was usually too much of a tomboy to use makeup, but decided to make an exception for reasons not even she understood. Then, grabbing the Dooney and Bourke purse Maya gave her as a fiftieth birthday present, Dana opened the door to leave. Just as she was about to pull the door closed, the telephone rang again. She rushed back into the room and picked up the receiver.

"Hello," she said brusquely.

"That's a nice telephone voice you have there, Dana."

"Oh, sorry, Maya. I, er, was expecting someone else."

"Really? Who were you expecting?"

"It's a long story. Say, I have a bunch of stuff I really need to talk with you about."

"Oh, Dana, I'm so sorry. You know I can't wait to hear," Maya said without much conviction in her voice. I'm just calling to tell you my meeting in the Lafayette Room will be going on until around midnight. The first vice president from AP National is coming to talk with us about some of the proposed changes in testing regulations. I need to hear this guy so I can report to the general business meeting on the 12th. The good news is I won't have any meetings tomorrow. So, we're free to talk as much as you'd like during coffee breaks and meals.

Dana was resigned to the fact she'd have to mull over things on her own until the next day. Besides, she could tell her friend's mind was already in the Lafayette Room, so any further conversation would be fruitless. "It's okay. What I have to tell you will keep, but your time is mine tomorrow, signora."

"It's a deal. Sleep well, you lucky dog."

"You too—eventually," Dana said with a smile.

After Maya hung up the telephone, Dana replaced the receiver and headed for the door again. Before she'd taken five steps, the telephone rang again. Dana raced back into the room and picked up the receiver on the second ring.

"Did you have a change of heart already?"

But there was no response. And, because there was no dial tone, Dana was certain someone was still on the other end of the line.

"Who is this? This isn't funny." Then she paused. "Who is this? Hello. Hello."

Dana wasn't easily spooked, but this was becoming creepy. She hung up the telephone and waited. When it didn't ring after a minute or so, she again grabbed her purse, opened the door, and left to have dinner on her own.

11

Laureli watched from the porch outside the ballroom as Bob and Mandy walked back down the driveway toward the car they had driven to the resort only hours earlier. She looked for signs of any behavior out of the ordinary, not that she knew what she expected to see. Bob and Mandy were spending a great deal of time together, and Laureli couldn't help but wonder if their mutual interest was completely directed at the campaign, or whether they were working a little scheme of their own. Laureli's marriage to Bob was not based on mutual love and affection. Rather, Laureli had found Bob's influence and his money irresistible and she was prepared to use any—absolutely any—means to get what she wanted. And what she wanted, for now, was a seat in the U.S. Congress. For his part, Bob was attracted by the idea of making love to a woman who was twenty years younger than his first wife. The excitement of feeling her smooth, youthful skin against him had been irresistible, and Laureli allowed him to consume all he wanted during their second clandestine meeting. To the casual observer, they appeared to be very much in love, but neither Bob nor Laureli saw it for anything other than what it was: a form of barter.

By the end of April, Laureli had been too consumed by

her rise within the Democratic Party to notice whether anything was changing in the relationship between her campaign manager and her spouse. But, she began to notice that Mandy and Bob had developed a comfortable repartee that far surpassed anything Laureli ever enjoyed with her husband. Laureli considered all of this for several days. Then, rather than find ways to keep the two apart, she began to devise ways to keep them together. Whether this was out of naiveté, or calculation on Laureli's part, her concern about the status of their relationship was consuming what few free moments she had.

Even if Bob and Mandy were having an affair, they were both too worldly to make any slipups while walking in the resort's driveway, where the two were never far from the scrutiny of the departing media, arriving guests, or Laureli.

Once Bob and Mandy were out of view, Laureli went directly to the Ammonoosuc Room where the regional economic summit was being conducted under the watchful eye of the state and regional press. As Laureli sat there, she was filled with thoughts of the woman who had approached following her announcement in the ballroom. But, Laureli had come too far to allow a distraction to stand in the way of her goal. Getting her head back into the meeting, she made a point of expressing her views on the need for New Hampshire's rural areas to have a voice in economic planning. Much like one of Dr. Phil's television sermons, Laureli's comments were a classic example of stating the obvious. Nevertheless, she knew it was vital to be perceived by the media as having a strong opinion on this important issue. Ten minutes after the last member of the Fourth Estate had left the Ammonoosuc Room, Laureli quietly extricated herself from the meeting, not to return.

12

Dinner that night was a study in contrasts. While Maya endured the endless haranguing of Priscilla O'Neal and countless reports that epitomized the trite expression *deja vu*, Dana allowed herself the luxury of a spa pedicure then met a delightful group of AP teachers from Portsmouth during dinner. The four women and one man consumed a bottle of California Pinot Noir and enjoyed a sumptuous meal, delicious dessert, and much laughter. Normally Dana preferred to be in her pajamas by nine o'clock, but things were still going strong at ten. Best of all, she'd been able to put the circumstances of her peculiar afternoon out of mind. Finally, at fifteen minutes after ten, she rose to leave.

"Do you have to leave, Dana? The evening's still young," Benton Horn, the sole male in the group said.

"Yes, I'm afraid I do. This is way past my bedtime. Besides, I've had a bit too much to drink."

"In that case, I insist on taking you to your room," Benton replied.

"Oh, Dana, you'd better watch out," one of the women, Cindy Cole, said. "He's a bit of a player, you know."

"I am not, Cindy. Now you stop that!"

"Thanks anyway, Benton, but I'm sure I can find my own way."

Dana said her good nights one more time. When she was about half way across the dining room, Benton arose and told the remaining three women, "I might as well head up, too."

When he was out of range, Cindy asked the others, "Do you think he's going after Dana?"

"I wouldn't put it past Benton, the others replied in unison.

***

Finally, thankfully, Maya's meeting reached it's conclusion at 11:45. She had learned more than she ever wanted or needed to know about AP regulations changes, and endured Priscilla's incessant whining for much longer than she would have thought possible. As she exited the elevator, her chronic ankle problem reappeared and her feet were swollen and purple.

"Of course," she said to herself, "you've been sitting down for hours." Without an opportunity to put her feet up periodically, the swelling in Maya's feet and ankles were as inevitable as death and taxes. Maya couldn't wait to take off her shoes and stockings, put on her nightgown, and get into bed. Her first concern would be gaining entry to the room without awakening Dana, but this necessitated using her key to open the noisy, sometimes uncooperative lock. Unlike a number of resort hotels that had transferred over to an electronic key card system, the Mount Washington gave its guests the same brass room keys that were in use for more than half a century. She hoped the lock wouldn't stick. "But what if Dana has double locked the door; I guess I'll just have to knock and wake her up," Maya said to herself. However, she needn't have worried, as Dana had not thrown the safety bolt, and the door lock opened smoothly.

When Maya opened the door to the room, the shades were drawn and it was pitch black. "Damn," she thought to herself. Dana had forgotten to leave the bathroom light on as Maya asked. Having left her pajamas on the foot of her bed, Maya easily found them in the dark and tiptoed to the bathroom. There was just enough ambient light from the lamp posts situated outside along the driveway to guide her there. She entered the bathroom, closed the door, and turned on the light. Once the door was closed, Maya removed her shoes and dress, then closed the lid of the toilet seat and sat down. From a seated position, she slowly worked her stockings down, massaged her aching feet, and removed the rest of her clothing. She considered taking a quick shower, but decided not to risk awakening Dana. She paused for a minute to look at her naked image in the mirror. Deciding that most of her body parts were still where she'd left them, Maya pulled the night gown over her head, turned off the light, and opened the door. She realized her mistake in not allowing her eyes to become accustomed to the dark room at the instant she'd stubbed her toe. Tears welled in her eyes, but she was determined not to cry out. The room still appeared pitch black to her. So, moving slowly and with great effort, she felt the way to her bed. Within minutes of placing her head on the pillow, Maya was fast asleep.

13

At first, Mandy Tompkins was not exactly elated to be point person for Laureli Hopkins' campaign. She worked closely with Laureli on the governor's reelection campaign and was impressed by the younger woman's focus and ambition. As someone who herself knew how to recruit and organize volunteers and to attract media attention, Mandy was amazed by Laureli's learning curve. It had been rumored for several months that someone from inside the party, someone without a political track record, was being considered as the next congressional nominee. "It has to be me. Who else could it be?" Mandy understandably figured. After the initial shock of being passed over for a thirty year old with less experience, Mandy decided her only course was to remain loyal to the Democratic Party; and, it wasn't long before she jumped into Laureli's campaign, firing on all cylinders. "It's my duty," she told a long time associate. "Besides, no one in New Hampshire is better than I am at running a political ground campaign, not even Laureli. I know the landscape and I can strategize with the best of them." So, Laureli appointed Mandy as her campaign manager. Like any qualified go-to person, Mandy took immediate control of the campaign staff, quickly impressing Laureli in the process. "Wow, Mandy, you're a whiz," Laureli told her. "You're in total control; you rule in the conference room and it's great watching you shift gears on the fly!" Mandy was truly a competitive force. One time, unbeknownst to Mandy, a campaign worker arrived early and caught her practicing her posture and facial expression, while shaking an imaginary hand in front of the full-length mirror in campaign headquarters.

Within six weeks of joining the campaign team, Mandy had growing concern about the younger woman's candidacy. Having worked closely with Laureli and Bob Hopkins for several weeks before the date of the formal announcement, Mandy noticed her candidate was certainly cut-throat enough to win an election, but found her to be less than trustworthy. On several occasions, she caught Laureli distorting the truth, even to her own husband. But, there was a second, and larger, problem. Mandy was falling in love with Bob Hopkins. It hadn't been intentional. The first moment Bob looked at her with his wonderful, gray eyes, she was smitten. The fact that Bob, who, at fifty, was twenty years his wife's senior, was closer to her age of forty-one, may have been a factor. Mandy had been married to a political activist, but they parted company fifteen years earlier. Since that time, she had a number of affairs, mostly casual, but considered herself beyond the stage of having another serious relationship. That was before she met Bob. By late April, Mandy began to wonder whether she could stand seven more months of working for a candidate she didn't entirely respect, especially when that same woman was sleeping with a man she coveted. That was before Laureli began to pull her numerous solo acts, where she would travel alone to a meeting while insisting that Mandy, as her campaign manager, and Bob, as her chief financier, travel together to those sessions. The more time the two spent together, the closer she could feel their bond growing. Finally, a week prior to the May tenth announcements, Bob drove Mandy home, following a full day of recruiting campaign contributions. When they reached her door, he took Mandy's hands in his and turned her toward him. Looking deeply into her eyes, he said, "I really care about you, Mandy." With that one remark, Bob kissed Laureli Hopkins' campaign manager on the lips. It wasn't a passionate kiss, but wasn't without meaning either. It was enough to convince Mandy to remain in charge of Laureli Hopkins' campaign, despite her misgivings.

14

The judge in Maya's dream wouldn't stop pounding his damned gavel. The sound was incessant and annoying. Maya awakened from her dream with a start. It took several seconds to realize someone was knocking on the door to her room.

"Dana, can you get that please?" Maya called over her shoulder toward the bed that was closer to the door. When Dana didn't respond, Maya sat up and looked toward her roommate's bed. It was empty. Dana must have awakened early and gotten up. She even pulled up her covers. Then remembering her friend might be in the bathroom, she called, "Dana, can you answer that? I'm not dressed." But there was no response and this time the knocking was accompanied by an insistent man's voice.

"Ms. Lassiter, may I speak to you please. It's urgent."

Maya called out, "Just a minute." She quickly went to the closet and put on her robe. Tying the cord around her waist, she called, "Who's there please?"

"Hotel security, ma'm," was the reply.

Maya quickly opened the door, ignoring the fact she hadn't fixed her hair or put slippers on her feet. The man standing before her looked to be about her age, mid-to-late fifties. He was about six feet tall, with medium brown hair, a receding hairline, and was wearing a white dress shirt, dark green tie, and a name badge.

"Ms. Lassiter?" he queried.

Even in her confused state, Maya remembered the instructions from a television program warning that she should always ask for a police officer's identification. The white, plastic badge on the man's chest indicated his name was Boyd Brown and he was chief of security for the resort.

"How can I help you, Chief Brown?"

"May I come in for a moment, please?" was all he said.

Maya was not comfortable about this. Where was Dana anyway? Her friend was small in stature, but would do a lot better dealing with this situation, in case Chief Brown wasn't who he said he was.

"Oh, um, sure. Will you please tell me what this is all about?" Then looking at the clock next to her bed, she groaned, "Oh my goodness, it's 3:00 in the morning. Can't this wait until later?"

Officer Brown replied, "I'm afraid I've come bearing bad news, Ms. Lassiter."

"Bad news? Has something happened to my husband Stan? Is that why you're here?" Maya felt her knees going weak.

"No ma'm, I'm afraid there's been an accident involving your roommate, Dana Cerone."

"Dana, why she's— Where is Dana?" Maya cried out. Her mind raced as she realized for the first time Dana had not slept in the bed next to hers. Losing control, she began to whimper.

Then the inevitable news came, "I'm sorry to tell you that Dana Cerone was found dead at two o'clock this morning."

15

Maya felt as though she'd just been kicked in the stomach. She ran to the bathroom and threw up. She tried to return to the bedroom but vomited again. After several minutes, she washed her face and slowly returned to the room where Chief Brown was still standing in the same position he had been.

"Do you think you can answer some questions for me, Ms. Lassiter?"

"I—I—think I can," she replied weakly. "How did this happen? Dana was supposed to be sleeping in that bed." As she looked over at what was supposed to be Dana's bed, Maya once again began to weep. "How could Dana have died at an expensive resort like this?" was all she could think to say. Clearly she was in shock.

The chief could empathize with Maya's reaction, but he also needed to get some information from her.

"I'd be grateful if you could answer those questions I mentioned, ma'm. I know this is a terrible time for you. So why don't we sit down on these two chairs by the window."

As soon as they both sat down he began, "There are some things we need to know. May I ask how long you'd known the deceased?"

Deceased! That word sounded so strange when used to describe her dear friend. At his mention of the word, tears again began to stream down Maya's face. Seeing her reaction, Chief Brown stood up and walked briskly to the bathroom. When he returned, he was carrying a box of tissues, which he handed to Maya.

"More than twenty years. We teach together at Crawford Notch High."

"So she is the same Mrs. Cerone. Both of my kids, Bill, Jr. and Mary, had her as their Chemistry teacher."

Maya smiled in spite of the way she was feeling.

"Of course, I had both of your children in class, too."

"Yes, I should have remembered, Mrs. Lassiter. My kids loved both of you."

"Dana was a terrific teacher," Maya said. Not only that, she was also my best friend. Everyone in my family is going to be crushed about this." And then Maya began to sob uncontrollably. Chief Brown sat patiently. He had been through this kind of thing before, but that was before he retired from the Carroll Fire Department in 1992. When he accepted the security chief position at the resort, he hoped he would never experience anything like what just transpired.

Maya willed herself to stop crying. She needed to be strong. And later, she would need to be there for Ben, and for Dana's two grown children. She couldn't bear to think of their grief. Maya was a strong woman. She needed to draw on all of her inner strength to compose herself. "I think I'm ready to answer your questions now, Chief."

For the next ten minutes, Maya patiently told Chief Brown what time they had arrived at the resort, when she last had seen Dana, and what she believed Dana did last night while Maya was at her meeting. My damned meeting! Suddenly Maya was filled with rage. Had Priscilla O'Neal been in the room at that moment... well, she couldn't be responsible for what she'd do to her.

When Chief Brown concluded his questioning, Maya had some of her own. "Can you tell me where Maya... Dana's body... is? I'd like to see her."

"Her body was found in the shrubbery. Paul Grandhomme, a member of the resort staff, was out walking last night when he discovered her."

"I would like to see her, please, Chief Brown. Besides, don't you need to know if it's really her... body, I mean... that you've found?"

"Yes, we do, but this is highly irregular. While I doubt Ms. Cerone's death was anything but an unfortunate accident, the police may decide it's a crime scene."

"You mean, it's possible someone killed Dana?"

"Anything is possible until the police have ruled it out, Ms. Lassiter. The police have been here for nearly an hour and they aren't talking like it's a homicide."

"I'm going to throw on some clothes and come downstairs. Where did you say Dana was found?" When Officer Brown responded, Maya said, "I'll be down there in ten minutes."

Once the chief left the room, Maya got dressed. Normally a morning ritual she relished, the simple act of selecting something to wear was proving painful. She didn't worry about make-up and ran a comb through her hair without even looking in the mirror. Steeling herself, she was now a woman on a mission. As she left the room, Maya prayed this was some terrible case of mistaken identity, but in her heart she was certain it wasn't.

16

Maya emerged from the elevator. She had avoided the one normally operated by a staff member, as it was well after hours, but her knees were still too weak to walk down the stairs. Looking around, she discovered an elevator that was situated around the corner from the one most patrons knew about. When the doors opened at the lower level, Maya took a left turn and headed down the long corridor leading to the indoor and outdoor swimming pools. Much to her chagrin, all of the doors on the east side of the hotel were locked and posted with security guards. She had tried to reason with one of the officers, but was politely rebuffed. However, Maya would not be dissuaded. She went to the nearest stairwell and walked up a flight of stairs until she reached the porch. Walking outside a set of doors on the west side of the hotel, she proceeded around to the east side, but was met there by a line of police tape and a Town of Carroll police officer.

"Will you please tell Security Chief Brown that Ms. Lassiter is here? He's expecting me."

The officer stared at her for several seconds. He pushed the button to his two-way radio.

"Yeah, Sergeant, there's a Ms. Lassiter here. She says Chief Brown has given her permission to come to the area where the vic was found."

Because the officer had set his radio on speaker mode, Maya could hear the sergeant's response clearly. "I don't want anyone unauthorized down here. Do you copy, Rattner?" Before Officer Rattner could relay the message to Maya, the radio came back to life. "Belay that, Rattner. Hold on a minute." There was a thirty second pause during which the line was quiet. "Rattner, please escort Ms. Lassiter to the outdoor pool area. She's agreed to ID the vic."

"Roger, Sergeant," Rattner replied. Then, turning to Maya, he said politely, "Please follow me Ms. Lassiter. I'll bring you downstairs." Led by the officer, Maya retraced her steps to the door nearest the pool entrance. At their approach, another officer rapped on the locked door three times then unlocked it from the inside. When the door swung open, she immediately noticed a maze of yellow police tape strung all around the resort's lower patio and out to the farthest corners of the outdoor pool. Bright lights on portable poles had been set into the ground and were illuminating a fifty-by-one hundred foot area.

Officer Brown stepped forward with a very large, dark-haired man. The light was so good she was able to clearly read the patch on the latter man's baseball style cap, "Town of Carroll Police Department." The three stripes on his arm indicated he must be the sergeant to whom Officer Rattner had been talking.

"Ms. Lassiter, I'm Sergeant Joe Crandall from the Carroll Police Department. I'm terribly sorry about this. I understand you were a friend of the deceased."

Deceased, there was that word again. Maya felt she might gag. She quickly and, she hoped, seamlessly regrouped.

"Yes, Sergeant. If that is Dana Cerone, she is... was... my best friend."

"Come this way please, ma'm.

Where were they going? Maya didn't see any sign of Dana. But she followed blindly and numbly along the smooth, gray concrete path. Before she took more than a few steps, Sergeant Crandall advised her to walk exactly in his footsteps. "We have some disturbed stonework along the path. Probably nothing, but we don't want to move anything, d'ya understand ma'm?"

"Yes, I understand, Sergeant." In the illuminated area adjacent to the resort's lower patio, she could see a triangle-shaped arrangement of smooth stones. It appeared they had been disturbed and there was what looked like a two-inch depression, about the size of a quarter on its outer edge. Given the circumstances, Maya's powers of observation—which were always excellent—were especially keen.

"Please come this way." They walked along the south edge of the path leading toward the gate to the outdoor swimming pool. But where was Dana? Walking a few yards farther, they reached two very large ferns; each was at least five feet tall and the same width. Then she saw a woman's shoe with a slender three inch heel. It had been nearly camouflaged at this distance, even with the extra illumination. How could the resort's staff person possibly have noticed this? Maya's head was spinning. She wondered for an instant: could the man who reported Dana's body actually have been the one who killed her?

"Ma'm, are you all right?" The sergeant's voice brought Maya back into focus.

"Yes, officer. I'm just a little shaky."

"I'm going to need you to step on the board that my officers laid down for the ME."

Maya looked down and saw a long two inch by eight inch piece of lumber that had been put in place for the medical examiner to view the body.

Once Maya mounted the board, Chief Brown inquired, "Are you sure you're ready for this, Ms. Lassiter?"

"Yes, please, let's do this." Maya's voice was firm, but she felt like her knees could give out at any second.

The sergeant gently pushed aside several of the fern's fronds and shone his flashlight on Dana's face. Maya recoiled at the sight of her dear friend, but then forced herself to look down again. Dana's head lay at the base of a large boulder. Blood from what appeared to be the back of her head stained the granite's surface.

"Oh," was all that escaped from Maya's lips. Her knees began to buckle, but the officers were prepared for that likelihood. Taking her firmly by the arms, they walked her backward off the plank. Once she was back on the main path, she willed herself to gain control of her legs again.

"Is that your friend, Ms. Lassiter?"

"Yes, Sergeant, that's Dana Cerone."

There was no conversation from the time they left the path until Chief Brown walked her to the door of her room. Finally, Maya broke the silence.

"Do the police really feel this was an accident, some kind of fall?" she asked.

"Well, Ms. Lassiter, there doesn't appear to be any signs of a struggle," the chief replied.

"Then how do you explain the nasty gash on her head? And what was she doing out there in the first place?"

"Ma'm, I don't know. That's something you'll need to take up with the police, but not this morning. Take my advice. Try to get a little rest, then go back home. My guess is Ms. Cerone's family will need you."

"This has all happened too fast," she said. "I need to figure out what to do next. Has anyone called her husband, Ben?"

"We couldn't do that until we had a positive ID. Now that we do, Sergeant Crandall will have that unfortunate task. Could you please give Officer Rattner her husband's telephone number? We'll need to inform him about his wife's death and coordinate with the family about where they want Ms. Cerone's body sent."

Maya just nodded at the chief's last remark. All she wanted to do was lie down; the world was suddenly spinning too fast. Dana's dead. Body needs to be delivered. Funeral. "Good lord, why did this have to happen to Dana of all people?" she cried.

17

When Chief Brown returned to the pool area, Sergeant Crandall seemed very quiet.

"What's going on, Joe? You seem awfully quiet."

"I'm not sure what we just did was a good idea, Browny."

"I don't see where it can do any harm. Besides, she was insistent on seeing her friend's body."

"Yeah, but we probably should have waited until the body was at the morgue... if we let her see it at all. She isn't next of kin. Besides, what if the Cerone woman was murdered and your lady friend is the perp?"

Chief Brown smiled at that idea. "Look Joe, I think I'm a pretty good judge of character, and that lady is no murderer. I'd stake my job on it."

"You may have just staked my badge and your job, old friend."

Just then, their conversation was interrupted by Officer Rattner. The officer pulled his sergeant aside and the two men talked animatedly just outside of Chief Brown's earshot. Their conversation continued in this manner for several more minutes. When he returned to Chief Brown, Sergeant Crandall was muttering aloud.

"Something wrong, Joe?"

"You could say that."

"What's happening?"

"Do you know Paul Grandhomme very well, Browny?"

"I wouldn't say I know him very well, but we've both been working here for a pretty long time. I went to school with his mother. So, I suppose you can say I know him. Why?"

"Paul Grandhomme was the one who reported finding the Cerone woman's body," Crandall said.

"Yeah, I know it was Paul. Look, Joe, Paulie's a bit slow but he's basically a good kid. So what's your beef with him?"

"No beef... he's missing."

"Missing?"

"Yeah. We asked him to hang around in Stickney's Restaurant until we could talk to him some more. We waited on account he was pretty upset about finding the lady's body. Besides, we were pretty busy 'round here. It must have happened while Officer Rattner took down the vic's contact information. When he went into the restaurant to find your Mr. Grandhomme a few minutes ago, he'd taken off."

"Like I told you, Joe, he's kind of slow. Maybe he misunderstood and just headed for home."

"Don't I wish? We've checked there already. His mother hasn't seen or heard from him since he left for work this morning. She sounds pretty angry about it."

"That is a problem."

"He's a young man with a lot of explaining to do."

18

Maya lay sprawled out on her bed. She was so distraught about Dana's death she'd forgotten to remove the bedspread before lying down, something she normally would never forget to do. She had just slipped out of her clothes and collapsed on the bed. It was nearly four hours since she first learned about Dana's so-called accidental death. Dana had been in excellent shape and there were things about the scene where she died that made no sense. For the moment, Maya decided there was no point pushing the authorities about the cause of her friend's death. "Not unless they refuse to consider how else it could have happened," she said aloud.

At promptly 7 o'clock, there was a knock on the door. "Who is it?"

"It's me, Ms. Lassiter, Chief Brown."

Rising and pulling on the robe over her bra and underpants, Maya looked through the peephole to be certain, then opened the door.

"May I come in for a minute, Ms. Lassiter?"

"Of course. And please call me Maya."

"Maya, I have news that I think will please you."

"Really, what is it?"

"The medical examiner has given a preliminary assessment of the vic, that is, Ms. Cerone's death."

"And what did he think, Chief?"

"He's tentatively ruled that an accidental blunt trauma to the back of the skull was the cause of death."

Maya just sat there staring at Chief Brown.

"I thought you'd be pleased by this news."

Maya thought carefully before speaking. "In a way. In a way I am. But there were a couple of issues I'd love to be able to discuss with the sergeant."

"Look, Ms... Maya, I know how you must feel—"

"Do you, Chief?"

"Yes, I've lost a friend in an accident, too. It was a long time ago. At first, I felt the same way you did, but after a time I came to accept that the ME knew what he was doing."

"But what if the police missed something?"

"Look, Maya, the police are keeping an open mind on this. They'll keep the area taped off and will rope off the east side of both the porch and lower terrace for a couple of days."

"And what about Dana's body? Has it been moved?"

"Yes, her body is in the morgue. Before they removed it, er, Ms Cerone, the scene was photographed from every conceivable angle."

"So what do think will happen next, Chief?"

"My guess is they'll look carefully at your friend and unless they see something they haven't already, they'll release her body to the Cerone family."

"And what happens then?"

"At that point, it will be 'case closed'."

Maya was not satisfied by what she'd heard, but her complaint wasn't with the man sitting before her. She might still have a beef with the Carroll Police, however. After Chief Brown left the room, she sat for several minutes thinking over what she just learned.

"I can't just sit here and do nothing." While Maya had been in shock and collapsed after seeing Dana's body, she was a very resilient woman. "I need to talk with someone, but who?" Her natural inclination should have been to immediately call her husband Stan as soon as she first learned of Dana's death, but she hadn't been thinking straight. Now there was nothing to stop her. She reached for her cell phone and began to speed dial her home telephone number, when she remembered something.

"Shit! There's no cell phone coverage up here." For a moment, she considered the option of having the valet deliver the Mustang so she could take a ride to Twin Mountain where there would be phone coverage. She rejected that idea, wanting no part of wrestling with the standard shift, especially in her present frame of mind. Her second option was to obtain some change at the registration desk and make a call from the bank of pay phones.

"I suppose that's what I'll have to do," she sighed. So she quickly dressed, brushed her teeth, combed her hair, grabbed her purse and room key, and headed for the same elevator she had used earlier. When she reached the lobby, she changed three dollars into quarters and headed to the pay telephones. But, much to her chagrin, a book salesman was using the middle of the three phones while his paperwork occupied much of the rest of the counter. Worse, he was talking loud enough to be heard in Boston without using the phone. Maya considered looking for another phone bank when she heard him say, "I really need that stuff sent to me overnight, Frank. Yeah, yeah, please do. Talk to you later." With that he hung up the phone, gathered his materials, and walked away without looking at Maya.

As he rounded the corner, Maya muttered to herself, "There is a heaven after all."

It had been years since Maya made a telephone call on a pay phone. Rather than use all of her coins at once, she decided to place a collect call to Stan. While the operator placed the call, Maya tried to compose herself. Maya was weeping by the time her husband agreed to accept the charges.

"Maya, is that you, sweetheart?" Stan asked. In stressful times, Maya always was able to turn to Stan for comfort. He was her rock.

"Oh, Stan, I have such horrible news."

Knowing how seriously his wife took her position on the NHTAP board, he attempted to cheer her up. "What happened, did Priscilla blow another gasket?"

"No, Stan," she was all she could say before the flood gates opened again.

"Jeezus, Maya. You're scaring the hell out of me. What's happened?"

"Dana is dead, Stan."

"What did you just say?"

"You heard me, Stanley. Dana is dead."

"When? How? Was there an accident?"

"I'm not sure," Maya was bawling by now. "The police say it was an accident, but...."

"But what?"

"Some things just don't seem to add up."

"Look Maya, you're upset, and you should be. You've just lost your best friend. But that doesn't mean you should immediately suspect funny business. Please come home and let the police do their job."

"I can't leave, Stan. I need to stay."

"Why, for heaven's sake? You're traumatized."

"I want you to come home, Maya. I'd drive up there right now, but you know I have to be in London for that meeting tomorrow evening." Stan knew he was fighting a losing battle. He had been married to his wife for more than thirty years, so was well aware that nothing he said was going to change her mind. After about twenty seconds of silence he said, "Look, you do what you need to do. Just be careful. In the meantime, I'll send some flowers and a huge fruit basket to the Cerones. Then I'll stop and see Ben and explain that you'll be home in a couple of days."

"What if he asks why I'm still up here?"

"I'll tell him that you're an emotional wreck and that Nya has gone up there to stay with you until you're feeling better."

Nya. Her sister Nya was her closest confidant besides Stan. Nya had been there for her before, during or after every crisis: when she had cold feet about marrying Stan, when they needed advice after the house had flooded, and for virtually every important decision she made during her lifetime.

"That's a terrific idea, Stan," she said while wondering why she didn't think of that earlier. "I'll call Nya as soon as we get off the phone." Maya was beginning to regain control of her emotions. Neither of them was in a rush to hang up, so they talked about the one subject that was on both of their minds, Dana, or rather how to help Ben and the Cerone children deal with this. The news would be devastating for all of them. When she finally hung up the phone, Maya wished she had committed her sister's cell phone number to memory. But that was never necessary, as Nya was number two in her speed dial. "I hate being without my own phone," she said, and silently vowed never again to stay at a hotel without cell phone service.

As she reached into her purse to retrieve several of the remaining quarters, Chief Brown happened to walk by.

"Hello, Maya," he called to her. Maya was pre-occupied with her search for change, so he said, "Actually, I was just coming to look for you. It looks like you can use some help."

"You're looking for me? Here I am. I was about to call

and ask my sister to come up here and stay with me."

"Oh, is that so? I hoped you were going to check out and head for home. In your place that's what I'd do."

"I'm not leaving just yet, Chief. I owe it to Dana to stay."

"Somehow I'm not surprised to hear that. In that case, there is something I need to tell you."

"And what's that?"

"You need to move out of your room."

"What?!"

"Sorry, it's SOP. Just in case the Carroll Police decide to treat your friend's death as something other than an accident, they need to close off your room and impound your automobile temporarily. I wouldn't concern yourself, you'll be moved into another room and your car will be returned in a few days. This is all just a precaution."

"Does this mean I'm a suspect?"

"Oh, my goodness, no. I do need to ask you to remove your belongings without disturbing Ms. Cerone's. A female staff person will accompany you whenever you're ready. I've already obtained the keys to your rental car from the parking valet."

These guys are thorough, she thought. They already know I'm not driving my own car. Maybe I've been too hasty to judge them. "If you can give me a few minutes, I need to make a phone call." Then realizing that there were several dozen people wandering past the pay telephones, she added, "Although I wish I had a bit more privacy."

"Well, since I can't permit you to go back to your room alone, how about if I allow you to make your call from my desk?"

"Are you sure that's okay, Chief?" When he nodded, she smiled and thanked him.

19

Maya accompanied the chief to his office in the lower level of the hotel. Chief Brown's office didn't reveal very much about his character. The walls of the office, unlike elsewhere in the lower level, were covered with the kind of cheap faux pine paneling that became popular in home basements during the 1960s. A bulletin board with several current and a few dated notices dominated the long wall behind the chief's desk. Two gray, industrial desks filled up much of the floor space. The desk that Maya presumed belonged to the chief was pushed toward the far corner while a cocoa-colored portable room divider afforded the chief a modicum of privacy. There was paperwork everywhere on Chief Brown's desk. A few empty soda cans were used as paperweights, or just hadn't been thrown away. In the right corner of the desk sat three framed photographs. Each had been faded by exposure to light indicating to Maya that these must have been brought here from some other location. There was a picture of a woman who looked to be about thirty. Maya presumed it was given to the chief by his wife a long time ago. A colorized black-and-white photograph of a teenage girl, and one of a boy flanked his wife's photo.

"This must be your family," she said.

He laughed. "Yeah, from quite a while ago. That picture of my wife, Marge, was taken on our tenth anniversary, and we've been married thirty-six years. The two kids you had in school are both in their thirties. My daughter Meg has two kids of her own. Brad is the assistant basketball coach at Concord High School."

"I remember Brad Brown and of course I see the resemblance to your wife. You both did a great job raising those children, Chief."

"Thank you. We've always been very proud of them both." Then the chief excused himself. "I'm going to give you some privacy. I'll tell my dispatcher why you're here so she won't disturb you either."

"You're very kind. Thank you."

Maya opened her cell phone to the directory. She scrolled down to her sister Nya's name. Using a yellow LePage pencil she'd found on the desk, she wrote Nya's cell phone and house phone numbers on a piece of scratch paper from Colebrook Office Supply. She was sure the chief wouldn't mind that she borrowed a sheet from the coffee-stained pad. She dialed Nya's cell phone. There was no way Maya was going to risk calling Nya's house unless she absolutely had to, because she didn't want to risk talking to her brother-in-law. The phone rang five times. Maya was about to utter an expletive when she heard Nya answer.

"Maya, it's wonderful to hear from you. I'm in New York attending a meeting with a bunch of big deals. So I only have a second to talk."

"This is terrible timing," Maya mumbled.

"I can tell by your voice that something's wrong. I thought you were up at the Mount Washington at a conference."

"I am. Only, something terrible has happened." Before her sister could interrogate her, Maya blurted, "Dana is dead, Nya!"

Nya was stunned. She and Kary had known the Cerones for years. They'd watched one another's children grow up. Nya hadn't been close to Dana the way Maya was, but always appreciated her aggressive, take-no-prisoners personality. In fact, once during the time Nya and Kary were living like strangers in the same house, Dana had advised Nya to "grab him by the nuts and tell him to use 'em or lose 'em." Of course, that was over a few glasses of wine. Both Maya and Dana always had been outrageous with a little wine in them. The difference was that Dana became a little too aggressive when she'd been drinking.

"What are you going to do now, Maya?" her sister asked.

"I was hoping you could come up here and stay with me for a couple of days. The police are saying it looks like an accident. If you saw where Dana was found you'd have your doubts, just as I do."

"So, let me get this straight, you're planning to stay at the resort for a couple of days and interfere with a police investigation. Am I hearing you correctly?" Nya was incredulous.

Maya recognized that tone. Since the time they were small children, whenever Maya did something that seemed like a senseless, ill-conceived idea, Nya's voice betrayed a certain level of—shall we say—dismay.

"Well, that is what I was thinking, big sis." Despite the fact the women were twins who had been born an hour apart, Maya always referred to Nya as the older one, especially when she was pushed in a corner by her sibling.

Nya ignored her sister's dig. "Even presuming I supported this hair-brained idea, I can't come up there. I'll be trapped in meetings until the 13th. I wish I could help… wait a minute… I can help you!"

"You can?"

"Well, not me personally but…. "

"Wait a second, Nya, you're not going to suggest what I think you are, are you?"

"Do you want help or not, little sister?" Ouch, that hurt, thought Maya.

"After all that's gone on between your husband and me during the last ten years, I can't believe you think I'd ever ask Kary Turnell for help." In truth, during the time when Kary had supplanted his responsibility as one-half of a conjugal pair with booze and terrible behavior, Maya became his principal detractor. It wasn't that Maya and Kary never got along, quite the contrary. In fact, Maya had been thrilled when her sister brought home such a handsome, cerebral guy. However, blood being thicker than water, as Kary continued to make Nya more and more unhappy, Maya increasingly withdrew from him. By the time of Nya and Kary's last-ditch effort to restore their marriage at The Balsams, Maya was openly critical of Kary, especially to his face.

"Well, suit yourself, dear sister," Nya replied.

Maya could tell from the tone of Nya's voice that her big sister was growing impatient. Nya continued, "Look, my sister, above anyone else in this world, I can appreciate why you've been pissed at Kary. For a long time he deserved it. Kary has changed. You know better than anyone that I was this close to ending our marriage, but he has been wonderful for the last six months. And I don't see that anything is about to change in that department."

"I'm really happy for both of you, sweetheart. I really am. But, how can I—"

"Just call and ask him. I can't prove this, but I think he'd love to be able to mend fences with you," Nya said. "Listen, I have to go. Give Kary a call. I don't know what his schedule looks like. If there's any way he can help you, he will."

When her sister had hung up the phone, Maya tilted back in the chief's chair and uttered an expletive.

PART TWO
COMPLICATION

20

Kary was actually awaiting the telephone call from his sister-in-law. Five seconds following her conversation with Maya, Nya quickly hit speed dial and talked with Kary about the impending call from his antagonistic sister-in-law. After his initial disbelief passed, Kary listened while his wife told him it was way past time for Kary and Maya to patch up their differences. Nya told him about Dana Cerone's death. She purposely omitted the circumstances surrounding Dana's death.

"Excuse me, sweetheart," Kary said, "but if anyone has been the offended party here, it's me."

"No, actually, my love, you're speaking to the offended party, remember dearest?"

When Kary didn't retort right away, Nya knew she had him. "Look, all I ask is that you listen to what Maya has to tell you. If you keep an open mind about this, I think you'll be more than willing to help her."

"I'll listen... but only because of you. Besides, I really liked Dana. In fact, I liked her more than Maya."

"That's not funny, Kary. Now, will you please see what you can do to help Maya? If you do, I promise I'll do something nice for you in return."

That offer made Kary smile, not to mention salivate. "Okay, okay! You've appealed to my humanitarian spirit. I'll try to help you're sister."

"Somehow, I thought you might see it my way," then added in her sexiest voice, "Go get 'em, Tiger."

"Grr," Kary said as the connection was broken.

While Kary advised a student early in the morning of May 11th, he was anticipating the call from Maya. After all the problems between the two, he wasn't about to let Maya know that he'd already been recruited. Kary considered telling Maya she was at the bottom of his expected calls list, but was determined to take the high road—well sort of. When Maya led off with, "Kary, it's Maya. Nya told me I had to call you." Kary couldn't resist replying curtly, "Well, you have, so you can hang up now."

"I'd like to but I can't," she replied. Now that was the old Maya he'd come to dislike. "I can't because she's in the bushes." And with that Maya began to cry.

"Who's in the bushes?" he'd asked. Nya hadn't said anything about bushes. "Tell me what this is all about."

He hoped Maya could remain calm, but the dam was already broken and she continued to sob into the receiver. "Dana is dead! They found her body in the bushes five hours ago. I can't get anyone to talk to me. I don't want to leave until, until."

Kary couldn't believe it but, despite everything that had transpired between Maya and him, he was genuinely feeling sorry for the woman on the other end of the conversation. Even knowing what hell she'd put him through during the time when Nya and he were so close to calling it quits, he couldn't ignore Maya's plight. Enemy or not, Maya was his wife's sister.

Once she gained control again, Maya gave Kary the abridged version of the events that had transpired since the time of the friends' arrival at the Mount Washington Resort the previous day and earlier that morning. Kary listened intently and even scratched a couple of notes on a blank note card that he kept on his desk for such purposes. When Maya finished, his advice was direct.

"Look, Maya, your theory that Dana's death wasn't accidental may be one hundred percent correct. My bigger concern"—he couldn't believe he was actually saying this—"is for your welfare. I suggest you get into your car and drive down here. Then we can sit and talk about this. Let's put a day and a few miles of distance between you and this awful thing. Then if you and I agree that there's something that needs looking into, the two of us can drive up there and talk with the authorities."

Maya began to sob again. "I can't drive home!"

"Why not?"

"The police have impounded my car. Besides, it's a standard shift and I can barely drive it."

So much for Kary's sensible plan. Within minutes of hanging up the telephone, he informed both his administrative assistant and the department chair about the death of a close family friend. He told them he needed to cancel his classes for a couple of days. Then Kary put on his sport coat and grabbed the overnight bag he had kept packed since the height of his troubles with Nya, and strode out of the office building. By the time his car reached I93, Kary was hoping he wasn't getting in way over his head.

21

As Kary drove the fifty mile route from Plymouth to the Mount Washington Resort, his mind set was already transforming. It was a beautiful sixty-five degree May morning. He had lowered the top of his dark green Chrysler Sebring convertible. Unlike his sister-in-law, Kary found the process of driving a standard shift car meditative; he was truly one with the road. Kary talked to himself as he drove, ignoring the noise of riding in the open convertible. When he left Plymouth, his head was full of thoughts like, "Why me?" and "How did I let Nya talk me into this?" As he neared the resort, though, he was already formulating a game plan. Kary didn't particularly relish the idea of driving back to Plymouth from the resort in the same day, for he had a problem that he'd self diagnosed as MDS, Motion Deficiency Syndrome. Simply put, he had a tendency to become drowsy in a moving car. That's the reason he decided to stay overnight in the area. No way was he going to pay several hundred dollars for a night at the main resort, especially without Nya in the room with him. Instead he called ahead and reserved a room at The Lodge at Bretton Woods, the ever-expanding motel on steroids situated across the way from the grand hotel. "Not a bad place and what a view for ninety-nine bucks," he told himself. Kary's golf clubs were in the trunk of the Sebring, just in case.

Kary checked into The Lodge, put his belongings in the room, then drove across Route 302 to find Maya. The day was crystal clear and Kary marveled at how beautifully the Presidentials framed the massive resort. "I'd forgotten how huge this place is. It has to be longer than a football field," he thought aloud. He was temporarily distracted when a pair of golf carts, each bearing a man and a woman, cut across the access road. The men appeared to be Kary's age, late fifties-to-early sixties, while the two women couldn't have been much older than thirty. Kary imagined several scenarios and each of them made him smile. As he neared the final bend in the driveway, he headed straight into the visitors' parking lot, deciding that a brisk, uphill, quarter mile walk would help clear his mind for what lay ahead. Had he known what actually awaited him, he'd have walked from Plymouth.

By prearrangement, Kary met Maya in the Conservatory, just off of the main lobby. Maya greeted him wearing a yellow cotton dress. While not Nya's identical twin, the familial resemblance was unmistakable. The truth was that Kary regarded his sister-in-law as the second sexiest woman on the planet, after Nya, of course. It was apparent neither of them thought about how to greet the other. Eschewing an embrace, they simply exchanged a firm, but ambiguous handshake. There was little small talk. Neither asked how the other was doing.

"So what's the latest, Maya?"

"Er... nothing really. I've been lying low as you suggested. I attended the plenary session of my conference."

"Wow, that took courage." Kary meant what he'd said. He couldn't image being able to do that himself under similar circumstances.

"I had to, Kary. Rumors are flying all over this resort. I asked Priscilla... she's our president... to allow me to say a few words. So I told everyone what has happened."

Kary wasn't able to disguise his reaction to this piece of news.

"What's the matter, Kary, did I do something wrong?" Maya's tone could best be described as one of impatience.

"No... well, yes. If you're correct and there has been some form of foul play, the less information you give out the better."

"But why?"

"Did it ever occur to you that an AP teacher may be the one who attacked Dana? You may have just tipped off the culprit." Maya's eyes instantly welled with tears, so Kary quickly redirected the conversation.

"I'm operating in the dark, here, Maya. I need your help to identify the best person from the resort to talk with, and the sooner I do this the better. I have to tell you, it's entirely possible no one will be willing to talk with me. I'm sure Nya has told you these resorts operate like little communities. They're closed shops—there's them and then there's us."

"I don't follow you."

"The staff here regards us as a necessary evil. They're hired to serve us, to make our stay as comfortable as possible. We're not their friends. If anything, we're the enemy."

"I would never have believed that."

Most people don't. I only know about this because Warn Barson, who used to be the GM at The Balsams, let me in on that little secret. The fact remains, unless I can find someone who will place his or her trust in me, we're not going to get anywhere today."

"Nya told me how you solved the case at The Balsams. That must count for something with these people."

"Think about what you're saying, Maya. Imagine you've just been hired to teach Italian at a new high school. Your former colleagues had liked and trusted you. Now you're dealing with a whole new group of teachers. Are they going to accept you right away? Does your reputation go with you?"

"Well, no, of course not," Maya said. Unless one or two of them know teachers from my old school, I'm starting with a clean slate."

"Well, it's the same thing here, only worse, actually."

"Worse. Why?"

"Because, when you walk into that new school, you're still a teacher just like they are. In this situation, not only am I not one of them, I'm not even a registered guest here. In fact, you could be looking at the first man to be hauled bodily out of here, cold sober."

"I don't think Chief Brown will do that to you, Kary," Maya said. "First of all, he likes me."

"There's no accounting for taste," Kary replied with a grin. But Maya wasn't amused, so she ignored him.

"Second, while I only have my instinct as a reader of people to go on, I don't think he's completely convinced Dana had an accident either. I don't have any way of knowing that for certain. I'm just basing my belief on years of reading students' faces."

"Well, it appears we'll be putting all of our eggs in your Chief Brown's basket then. But I want you to realize something up front. If he tells me to shove off, I won't have any choice but to leave," Kary said. Secretly, as he still hadn't seen any evidence to support Maya's suspicions, Kary almost hoped he would be told to leave the hotel. "Let's go find the chief and hear what he has to say."

22

As Kary and Maya wove their way through the crowded lobby, Maya decided it was necessary to clear the air with her brother-in-law. "Listen, Kary, I want you to know these last several years have been difficult for all of us. It wasn't easy calling and—" It was immediately apparent that Kary hadn't heard a word she was saying.

"Huh? Did you say something, Maya?"

"I was just trying to."

Sensing what Maya might be planning to tell him, Kary cut her off. "Listen, Maya, you're a terrific sister, okay. But right about now I need to focus my attention on the problem at hand." Then in an effort to soften the situation, he added with a slight smile, "If I can help you figure this out, maybe there's still time to become a terrific brother-in-law."

Maya didn't say another word until they were nearing the chief of security's office. She suspected in that moment that she'd done the right thing by asking Kary for help.

When they arrived at the chief's office, the door was slightly ajar. Knocking first, Maya stuck her head inside the doorway and asked the security officer sitting at the desk nearest the door if the chief was available.

"No ma'm, I'm afraid he's upstairs meeting with the general manager."

"Oh, that's too bad. Are you expecting him back soon?"

"Hard to say. GM's a hard man to predict." Then reaching for a pad and a ballpoint pen, he asked, "Can I take a message?"

"Yes, please. Will you tell him that Maya Lassiter and her brother-in-law would like to talk with him." Then looking back at Kary for approval, she added, "We'll wait for him in the Conservatory."

As the two started to retrace their steps, Kary asked his sister-in-law, "How close can you get me to the place where Dana was found?"

"It depends. Do you want to look straight down on the scene or go down to the lower level where she was actually found?"

"Let's go to the same level where she was found. From what you've described, the police were here for several hours beginning around 2 a.m. The natural light at that time of day wouldn't be helpful. If they already were convinced Dana had an accident, they may not have searched the area thoroughly in broad daylight."

As they reversed direction, they were joined by Chief Brown. "Maya, I see you're still here. My security officer said you'd dropped by. Can I help you with something?"

"You can, Chief. I'd like you to meet my brother-in-law, Dr. Kary Turnell. He's a professor...."

"Kary Turnell... Kary Turnell. I know that name from somewhere." Then, after thinking a few seconds, his face lit up. "I know; you're the one who solved that murder-missing persons case up at The Balsams, aren't you?"

Kary was nonplussed. "Guilty as charged, Chief. But how on earth did you know that? Warn Barson was very careful to keep that story out of the papers."

"Do you remember working with a fellow named Bill Norman?"

"Bill? Of course, I do. He was a huge help in working things out, and a great guy to boot."

"Well, it was apparently a mutual admiration society, because he had nothing but good things to say about you and how you put your ass on the line to do things discreetly."

Kary was very pleased to hear about Bill's comments. What was more important at this juncture was the possibility of having the chief on his side. They may have just stumbled upon the break Maya and he needed. He was curious. "I'm surprised Bill would talk about that whole business. You must know him very well." It was a statement intended as a question.

"Bill and I are first cousins. We've been best pals since we were in diapers. Trust me, Professor, I doubt Bill even told his wife about what happened."

That was a relief to Kary. He needed to get some answers and clearly he was talking with the best person to provide them.

"I'm wondering if you'd mind if I did some clandestine nosing around?" Kary asked.

"I'm afraid I can't allow you to do that, Professor." Pausing, he added, "I may be able to do something better, though. I hadn't said anything to Maya before this, but I have my doubts about the 'accident' assumption the police are stuck on. Why don't you hang loose for about a half hour. I want to catch the GM before he leaves for a meeting. Would you be willing to work with me on this?"

"Are you kidding? I'd be honored," Kary responded.

"I'm going to see what he says. If he agrees, I'll need to talk with Sergeant Crandall from the Carroll P.D. I'm sure you'll want a look at Ms. Cerone's effects."

"Do you think he'll agree to let us look around, Chief? After all, this is still a police matter, isn't it?"

"Not as of eight o'clock this morning. That's why I was upstairs talking to Mr. Capstone, the GM. The police think Maya's friend was the victim of an accident. That's that as far as they're concerned. Carroll P.D. doesn't have the resources to devote to a dead end. So, I'm pretty sure Crandall won't mind if we do a little asking around, as long as we keep things quiet."

"Discreet just happens to be my middle name," Kary smiled.

"Okay then, why don't you two grab yourselves a cup of coffee and I'll be back ASAP."

Once the chief departed, Kary turned to his sister-in-law and said, "Maybe you should go back to your AP meeting. I'll hang out with the chief for a while. Hopefully the two of us can pull some information together."

Maya wasn't happy about being pushed out of the investigation process, and she still wasn't completely comfortable with Kary. After all, the two had been anything but on friendly terms for more than a decade.

"Come on, Kary. Dana was my friend. You wouldn't even be up here if it weren't for me."

"You're right, Maya. But, assuming we're able to get permission to do some detecting, two is company and three is a crowd in this kind of situation. I never involved Nya in my work at The Balsams either. People will talk with one or two people. They start becoming really uncomfortable if the group gets any larger."

Kary was making sense, of course. Maya was resigned to the fact she wouldn't be allowed to follow Kary or the chief around, but she wasn't done negotiating. "Okay, I'll go back to my meeting, but on one condition."

Kary groaned. He could see negotiating with Maya was similar to bargaining with Nya. "You sisters are peas in a pod, aren't you?"

"Why, Kary, I think you just paid me a compliment," Maya beamed.

"The highest kind," Kary smiled. "What's that one condition?"

"I'm sure the chief thinks I'll just be in the way, too. I expect you to keep me completely informed of what's going on. Deal?"

Kary sighed in feigned defeat. In actuality, he liked the idea of having another intelligent party off whom he could bounce ideas. "You have a deal. Just remember, we have to be very careful. See if you can learn anything from your AP friends. Just don't discuss what we're doing. Then bring your information directly to the chief and me." It was his turn to ask, "Deal or no deal?"

"Deal." The two shook hands. This time Kary could sense that there was much more warmth than their earlier handshake.

23

Paul Grandhomme was terribly confused. He'd never remotely been involved in anything like this before. Sure, he had seen something like it on TV and in movies: the speed with which the woman had flown through the air, the hard thud of her skull striking against the rock. He'd been frozen in fear while he crouched in the dark, trying to make up his mind what to do next. He wanted to go and see if the lady was all right. But, in his heart, he was certain she was dead. How would he ever explain this to Mr. Capstone or the police or, he sobbed, to his mother? He wished he didn't come down here to the pool this time. He had gotten into the habit of coming here each time one of the resort staff was particularly mean to him, and one of the chef's assistants had pulled down Paul's pants right in front of that new waitress. Why did this woman have to show up here, and why tonight of all nights? Paul wished he'd left as soon as she'd arrived.

From the time he was in his mid teens, Paul was drawn to do things by small voices in his head, and those voices had caused him to make some bad decisions. The worst happened at the age of fifteen. He'd pushed that bully Roger into the gully and Roger had nearly died from the fall. When Paul confessed to his mother, she had beat him with his own belt. From that time on, Paul tried without much success to ignore what the voices told him to do. Each time he yielded and did the bidding of the voices, he was careful not to let his mother know. "She'll beat me for sure," he muttered as he crouched hidden under a tall shrub, the twin of the one that caressed the woman's inert body.

Paul was not a man to formulate plans. He was incapable of proactive thought. He acted in reaction to the voices and to the suggestions and actions of those around him. As he sat in the cool night air, he weighed his next step by remembering what the actor in his favorite crime show had done. The episode he needed flashed through his brain and just stuck there. He remembered it was a story about a small boy and his dog. The dog had attacked a vagrant who was trying to hit the boy with a stick. When the dog jumped at him, the man fell and struck his head. As Paul remembered the story, he mumbled to himself, "The boy helped his dog." In the story, the boy showed the authorities where the man was lying, then took his dog and ran away so the animal wouldn't be put to death. While there was no dog in Paul's own dilemma, he realized he must show the authorities the woman's body, then run away as soon as he could.

****

Lori Dark was not lacking dreams for her future. She knew in her heart she was going to be somebody someday, she just didn't know where or how to get there. Nor was Lori lazy. She couldn't stand the thought of being dependent upon her mother for the money she needed, so she took a job washing pots and pans at the Mount Washington Resort to earn spending money. The job was rough on her smooth skin and put a damper on the relationship she hoped to have with Billy, the center on the high school basketball team. At night, while she lay awake in bed waiting for sleep to come, she wondered to herself whether Billy's size thirteen sneakers and huge hands translated into anything else. "Before I graduate from here, I'm going to find out," she said aloud, as the red glow on her face nearly illuminated the dark bedroom.

Lori hated the time when she was at home alone. Worse than having absentee parents and siblings away at school, Lori's teen years predated the availability of cell phones. She came to depend on the land line in the house as her sole means for communicating with the outside world. You can imagine the shock, horror, and anguish she felt during the second half of her junior year when her mother announced, "I ain't payin' for no house phone anymore. I ain't never home to use it and we can't afford to pour good money down the toilet."

That had been a milestone moment in the life of young Lori Dark. It was at that very instant that Lori felt the loneliest she ever had in her entire life. It didn't matter that she was popular with her peers at school. Now there was a huge hole in her life. It was a hole that had been left by her parents, each absent in a different way. One night, as she lay in her bedroom surrounded by nothing but darkness, Lori devised the scheme that would change everything.

24

When Chief Brown returned from the general manager's office, the look on his face was anything but encouraging.

"I guess he wasn't very supportive of the idea, eh Chief."

But the chief hadn't been listening, so immersed was he in his own thoughts. "I'm sorry Kary, what did you just say?"

When Kary repeated himself, the chief stared at him for a moment before responding. "No, no, that's not it at all, Kary. In fact, the GM is on the phone postponing his trip but wants to talk with us right now."

The chief's demeanor and the news that the general manager wanted to see the two men had Kary mystified. While he half expected the chief to return with orders to show Kary off of the property, this development was completely unexpected. It was understandable the GM might want to judge Kary's character for himself. A face to face meeting was the best way to do that. But why was he postponing his travel plans? Kary was eager to meet the man and find out.

"Mr. Capstone, this is Dr. Kary Turnell, the man I was telling you about."

"Tom Capstone," the general manager said. "It's a pleasure to meet you, Dr. Turnell."

"Please, Tom, call me Kary." While Capstone was nearly a foot shorter than Kary and slight of build, there was nothing delicate about his handshake. Kary was immediately impressed by the man standing before him. Tom Capstone's friendly but confident demeanor gave him the bearing of an ideal general manager.

"Please sit down, gentlemen. I don't know whether the chief has told you yet, Kary, but we're in a quandary."

"The chief hasn't saind anything to me, but his expression tells me something must be amiss. My guess is general managers don't make a habit of cancelling important travel plans on a whim," Kary replied.

"You're very observant, Kary. It may prove to be very opportune that you're here. You are, of course, aware that the body of Dana Cerone was found on our property early this morning." Kary nodded. "What you possibly didn't know is that we have a candidate for the U.S. Congress staying with us."

"I heard something about her announcement on the radio early this morning, but wasn't aware that she was staying here."

"Perhaps I should say," Tom Capstone corrected himself, "we think the candidate is staying with us."

"I'm afraid I don't follow you, Tom."

At this point, Chief Brown interjected, "It seems our congressional candidate is missing."

"Missing?"

"Missing," both men replied in unison.

"Isn't this a matter for the police?"

"Not necessarily," the chief said. "We could be looking at a situation where the candidate simply left without telling anyone. Her room charge has been paid by her campaign. So, before we push any panic buttons, I'd appreciate it if you'll assist the chief in making some discreet inquiries. I've been assured by Chief Brown that you're quite good at that."

"Thank you."

"I'm glad you're willing to help with this, Kary. You'll find the good chief here is more than capable of making discreet inquiries."

The chief added, "Two heads may be better than one. If this turns out to be more complicated than meets the eye, it will be good to have such an experienced hand to fit some pieces together."

"Discreet inquiries are one thing, gentlemen, but are you suggesting there's a relationship between our victim in the bushes and your missing candidate?"

The general manager and the chief looked at one another, then stared at Kary. "We'd believe almost anything at this point," Capstone replied. "A death, accidental or otherwise, and an unexpected departure, those things don't happen here. And I particularly don't like them happening in such a short period of time."

"I'm not a big believer in coincidences, Kary," the chief sighed.

"Me either, Chief."

As the chief and Kary stood up to leave Tom's office, the GM's intercom buzzed. Capstone picked up his telephone receiver, listened and said, "Show him in, Alice." Then turning to the two men, he said, "You'd better stay here for a minute. Things just became a little more complicated."

A man dressed from head to his ankles in kitchen whites knocked then entered Tom Capstone's office. As he entered, the man removed his white kitchen cap. "Thanks for seeing me, Mr. Capstone."

"That's no problem, Dave. I think you'd better tell these two gentlemen what you came to tell me. You know Chief Brown, of course. This gentleman is Dr. Turnell. He's helping me with a special project. Kary and Dave shook hands.

Despite the fact that Dave's hands were strong and well cal-
loused, his handshake was weak and indifferent.

Dave Riley was clearly uncomfortable being in the general manger's office, especially in the presence of the resort's
chief of security. Sensing this to be the case, Tom Capstone
encouraged his employee once again to tell his story.

"It's about Paul Grandhomme, Mr. Capstone."

Capstone shook his head. "Don't tell me Paul is in trouble
again. He just returned to work yesterday."

"Oh yeah, that's right. Paul smacked that other poor kid
with his pot," the chief said.

Kary, who had planned to say nothing while Dave was in
the office couldn't contain his curiosity. "Did you say 'pot'?"

Capstone looked at Kary. "Yes, Paul Grandhomme is
what we used to call slow. He's been wearing a cooking pot on
his head for some time now. One of the other employees embarrassed him in front of a couple of guests and got smacked
in the face with Paul's pot for his poor judgment."

Kary grimaced at the thought of this. "Is this Paul often a
violent person?" In the back of his mind Kary wondered why
Paul Grandhomme had been hired and how he had been able
to keep a job at such a prestigious resort.

"No, not at all. Paul's actually something of a pussy cat.
He mumbles to himself a lot, but he's never done anything
to harm anyone as far as I know. And his employment record
has been spotless—that is, until last month."

"Last month?" Kary replied.

"Yes. I ordered him to take a month off with pay as punishment for what he'd done. I was hoping he would behave
himself when he came back. He loves this old resort, prefers
it to home, actually."

Then remembering the other man in his office, Capstone
asked, "So what's the latest on Paul, Dave?"

"He's still a no-show, Mr. Capstone."

"In that case, it makes his disappearance cause for concern," Kary offered.

Tom Capstone thanked Dave Riley then sent him back to work. Once Dave was gone, Tom turned to Kary and the chief. "This is getting curiouser and curiouser, gentlemen. First a dead body, then a missing candidate, and now an AWOL employee. Please, do me a favor and figure out one or two of these situations for me."

Kary replied, "We may be looking at one situation, Tom, and there's only one way to find out, isn't there?"

As the two men left the office, the chief said to Kary, "What's our first plan of attack?"

"I want to catch up with Maya. She may have overheard something that can help us. I promised I'd keep her in the loop."

"Do you think that's a wise idea, Kary?"

"Look, Chief, Maya's pretty traumatized right now, but he's tough and she's smart. Besides, she's my wife's sister."

"I don't follow."

"My wife Nya has an incredible gift of common sense. She's the Yin to my Yang, the one who provides grounding to my flights of fancy."

"So you think Maya can help, huh?"

"I do. Besides I owe her that much."

The chief looked at Kary expectantly.

"It's a long story. Mostly she knew Dana better than almost anyone. Since Dana's life was apparently as routine as anyone's, the answer to her death may lie in the past.

"Hmm, and Maya could just be the key," the chief added.

The men parted company and agreed to meet at 1 in the doorway nearest to the outdoor pool.

25

Sitting in her AP Foreign Language meeting was the last thing Maya was in the mood to do, but it was a possible link to information about what had happened to Dana. While Maya's body may have been in the room, her mind most certainly was not. Her head was filled with thoughts of Dana. There were images of shopping excursions, concerts the pair had attended, and trips to Tuscany where Maya enjoyed opportunities to use her Italian. Had anyone noticed the expression on Maya's face, they would have been convinced she was suffering from a massive case of acid reflux, but her digestive tract was not the cause of her look of consternation. She could only imagine what the reaction at the high school was at that moment. She had called her principal at his home right after she spoke with Nya. Dana had been a very popular teacher and colleague. It was going to take time for everyone to deal with this.

In allowing her mind to run through her experiences with Dana, Maya recalled the immense amount of time they'd spent together at the high school. She remembered many of the wonderful students they had shared, the students they had joined forces to help, the conversations with their principal that led to decisive action being taken to help student after student. Her mind fixated on the one student Dana and Maya had vowed never to discuss again, and what the two women had labeled "The Incident."

***

In general, Lori Dark was an above average student. Tall, plain looking, and busty, she was popular with the right kids, belonged to a few after-school groups, and seemed to be as well adjusted as any high school girl. Dana first met Lori when the latter was a student in her junior year earth science class. The two had shared a fascination with the Twin Peaks program that appeared on television during the 1990's. Lori and Dana didn't bond right away, but Dana could tell there was some trouble in Lori's home life.

Maya didn't meet Lori until the latter was a student in Italian IV, during Lori's senior year. Initially, Maya did not pay particular attention to Lori, as she was not a particularly good Italian student. Lori constantly confused verb tenses and had terrible command of Italian grammar. Her one skill was in presenting orally in front of the class. Lori nearly drove Maya to distraction by constantly confusing the proper form for the phrase, "I knew you when." Instead of using the correct form *ti conoscevo quando,* she constantly offered, *ti sapero quando.* No matter how many times Signora Lassiter told her that *conoscevo* means "to know a person," while *sapero* means "to know a fact," Lori never seemed to get it. As a result, Lori went largely unnoticed by one of her favorite teachers. All that changed when Lori was elected treasurer of the Italian Club. Lori used her club office to get closer to Maya. She would arrive early in the morning and eat her breakfast in Maya's classroom. Still, there had been nothing out of the ordinary about the girl in Maya's mind until several weeks before Thanksgiving, when a tearful Lori began to drop hints to both Dana and Maya about some type of illness she was experiencing. During a conversation in the lunch room with a part-time teacher, the two women learned Lori had contracted colon cancer during her sophomore year at the high school. The teacher confided to Dana and Maya that Lori had undergone an operation to remove a tumor. Following that conversation, Maya began to notice that Lori was looking pale and was asking to go the girl's room quite a bit. Finally, the two women met with Lori after school to inquire about her health. Lori's response stunned the two women. She told them she had colon cancer surgery pending. This was shocking news in and of itself. When Lori told them she would be driving herself to the hospital because her mother would not come with her, Dana and Maya knew that they needed to help this young girl. They would have been on the telephone to the girl's mother that very evening, but Lori swore them to secrecy. After months had passed and the girl had undergone numerous treatments, Lori informed Dana and Maya that she wasn't going to do anything else about her disease since her mother didn't care whether she lived or died. In a tearful moment, Lori told the two women they were the only adults who cared about her. Then one day, Maya found Lori collapsed on the floor in pain. After that incident, Lori began to isolate herself from her classmates, meeting only with Dana and Maya during after-school hours.

Dana felt so bad about the girl that she spent time with Lori rather than her own daughter, who was home from college over Christmas break. The women began to be surrogate mothers to the girl, buying her presents, taking her shopping, inviting her to dinners she didn't eat, and even bringing her to their homes to sit and watch television. Ultimately, Lori's situation began to affect the teachers' health. They spent many sleepless nights wondering whether Lori would live to see graduation and were furious that Lori's mother seemed not to care. Only because of the girl's insistence had they not confronted this woman. Finally, Lori told Dana and Maya she was not going to do anything about her cancer until after high school graduation. This made both women cry, especially after their efforts to convince Lori to get treatment right away failed.

A couple of weeks passed and Lori missed a day of school. When she returned the next day, Lori told the two teachers she had missed school because she was having tests, as the cancer was spreading. As the two teachers continued to lose sleep, their husbands became extremely concerned for their wives' welfare. Finally, out of desperation, the women scheduled a confidential meeting with the principal. Charles informed them the student was now eighteen and making an informed decision, so there was nothing anyone could do about it. The two women were barely consolable because they were certain Lori would never live to graduate from college.

All at once, Maya snapped back to the present. Sitting in her AP meeting in the surroundings of the resort, she shuddered at the thought of their final days with Lori Dark. Lori had lived through the summer and was brave enough to begin her first year as a student at little Portsmouth College. She emailed the women to report that she was hiding an oxygen bottle under her bed so her roommates wouldn't know about the cancer. The teachers told Lori to talk with her dean about moving into a single room on the first floor. A few days later, Lori reported to them that the dean said there were no rooms available on the first floor. The two teachers kept in touch with Lori, even buying her a beautiful watch for what would be her nineteenth... and last... birthday. However, as time passed, Lori appeared to be flourishing at college. During her second semester, word reached Dana and Maya that Lori was playing intramural volleyball. At about the same time, since she no longer needed them, Lori gradually began backing

away from her two former high school teachers, even refus-
ing to answer emails from them. It wasn't long before the two
women realized they had been duped. They felt ashamed, violated, foolish, and, in time, angry. One night, over a glass of
wine, they vowed not to mention her name in one another's
presence, ever again.

For whatever reason, Lori had been needy, so she'd in-
vented a story certain to gain Dana and Maya's attention. It
was well known around the high school that Dana and Maya
couldn't resist helping needy students. Lori simply made herself into one. By designing a story to command their full attention, she could finally have the kind of consideration from
mother figures she had never received at home. Lori loved
her mother. Her mother was too busy with her own life to
give her daughter what Lori craved. Lori had researched Dana
and Maya very carefully. She knew that both teachers could
be trusted not to discuss her situation with others. With this
certainty, her plan could not fail.

PART III
INVESTIGATION

26

Kary was anxious to find Maya to bring her up to speed on the latest developments and to hear whether she had discovered anything during her meeting. The lobby was crowded with people from the three conferences. Along with Maya's Advanced Placement teachers group, the widely publicized Regional Economics Summit and the Indigenous Artifacts Repatriation League meeting were all holding coffee breaks at the same time. The result was chaotic and Candy McLee, the group booking coordinator, Len Banker, the banquets manager, and Barbara Rubstone, the ice carver, were at one another's throats. Unfortunately, their exchange spilled out into the lobby where they were calling attention to themselves.

"Poor form," Kary muttered as things continued to escalate. "They will have hell to pay when Tom Capstone gets wind of this. That's not my problem." He resumed his search for Maya.

It should not have been difficult to find Maya who, at nearly five foot nine inches, normally didn't blend into a crowd primarily comprised of women. When Maya appeared from behind one of the pillars in the lobby, she looked like someone who was carrying a burden.

"Maya, over here!"

"Oh, there you are, Kary," she replied without much enthusiasm in her tone.

"Are you all right?"

"I'm fine; I've just been doing some mental reminiscing."

"I know this ordeal isn't easy on you."

"No, it's okay Kary," she said while squeezing his hand for effect. "I just remembered one of the few unpleasant memories Dana and I had at the high school."

"Care to share?"

"No, it really isn't relevant. But thanks for asking. Did you have any luck with the general manager?"

"Yeah. Let's go sit somewhere and I'll explain."

They made their way through the crowd over to one of the many doors leading to the enormous porch that wraps around much of the hotel building. They took a left turn and walked along until they came to a pair of comfortable looking red rocking chairs. As they sat, Kary told Maya about the odd things he'd discovered, including the missing candidate and the AWOL employee.

"Do you think there is a relationship to Dana's death?" she asked.

"Could be. I have to wait for the Carroll Police to get back to Chief Brown. We need to examine the area near the pool and get a look at Dana's belongings. That will give us a much better idea if there is an investigation to conduct or not."

"What do you want me to do in the meantime?" Maya asked.

"Just talk to people. See if anyone remembers seeing Dana last night. As her dearest friend, you can do that without arousing any suspicion."

"There was something someone said as we walked into the meeting room this morning. I can follow up on that."

"What did you hear?"

"I think some guy from Portsmouth took an interest in Dana. But that's all I know."

"That's a good place to start." Then standing, Kary put his hand on his sister-in-law's and looked her in the eyes. "Be careful, Maya." With that, he strode away to meet Chief Brown.

27

Kary met Chief Brown in the comparative quiet of the lobby, standing between the registration desk and the main elevator. The chief was grabbing a quick look at a sports page from one of the copies of the Boston Globe that were laid out on a large mahogany table, when Kary approached.

"So what's first, Kary?"

"First, I need to know what the Carroll Police had to say," he replied. "We can't do anything further about Dana Cerone's death without their clearance."

"Funny you should mention that. I just talked with Sergeant Joe Crandall from the PD."

"Well, don't keep me in suspense, Chief. What did Sergeant Crandall have to say?"

"Before he approves anything, he wants to talk to you at the police station."

This news didn't make Kary happy. Time was being wasted on too many meetings of too little consequence. "Is that really necessary, Chief?"

"Afraid so. Until he appraises you up close and personal, he doesn't want us doing anything to upset the applecart."

"What applecart? Crandall said it was an accident, didn't he?" Kary's tone betrayed his aggravation.

"Sorry, Kary. Don't shoot the messenger, okay."

"I didn't mean to jump down your throat, Chief. We need to get a look at the scene of Dana's death, and the longer we wait the better the chance it's going to be tampered with."

"Well, let's see." The chief stroked his large chin. "We aren't due over there until two. It's 12:15 now and the ride won't take us more than ten minutes."

"That gives us about a half hour to look things over together. Are you okay with doing that before we talk with Sergeant Crandall?" Kary asked.

"You gotta promise not to move anything," the chief replied.

"You have my word as a criminology professor," Kary smiled.

"Then what are we hangin' around here for? Let's get downstairs and take a look."

Before the two men arrived at the scene, the chief reached into his pocket and removed a shiny object. "Here," he said, "better pin this on."

"What's this?"

"It's a badge. But don't look too closely. It's a replica of the badge Bat Masterson wore in Dodge City. I collect Old West lawmen's badges."

"So I see. But why am I putting this on?"

"So you'll look official. I don't want anyone else to get the idea that they can just duck under the police tape and snoop around."

"That's brilliant, Chief. I'll have to remember to share this one with my criminology class."

So the two lawmen ducked under the tape and began to look around. There was a triangular-shape collection of smoothed river rocks ranging in size from four to eight inches in length, placed both for ornamental purposes and to protect the ground from being trampled by hotel guests. On either side of the walkway was a granite boulder, each roughly the size of a Volkswagen Beetle. These were set back from the walkway about fifteen feet. In front of each rock were two large, dense cinnamon fern plants, each approximately five feet high and at least as wide. The gate to the pool consisted of a pair of swinging doors—wood with cedar lattice work—stained brown and with a criss-cross pair of slats to protect the fragile lattice work. Inside the fence were lounge chairs and a series of bright red square canvas umbrellas. The chief showed Kary the boulder where Dana Cerone's body had been found. When the chief pulled back two of the fern fronds Kary spotted the basketball-size splash of Dana's blood on the side of the boulder facing the hotel.

"Wow! She must have hit that with a hell of a lot of force. You wouldn't think a mere backward fall would do something like that."

"That was my reaction, too. And I said so to Joe Crandall."

"But the police are convinced it was an accident. Why?"

"I think it would be better if you heard that from the sergeant, Kary."

Next, the two men traced the distance from the boulder to the path that lead to the pool. Then they walked along the path back toward the hotel. Kary saw that the tops of several fronds of a shorter fern closer to the hotel had been bent back. Two of them were damaged irreparably and would need to be trimmed. A shorter plant that was closest to the hotel was noticeably undamaged.

"Wait a minute. Let me take a quick look at something," Kary said. Walking back to the area between the shorter damaged fern and the large one that had contained Dana's body, he asked the chief to carefully pull back several fronds so he could have a look at the ground. He noticed two marks that appeared to have been made by the heels of shoes, but one was deep and about the size of a quarter while the other was crescent shape and approximately two and a half inches long.

"That's strange," Kary said just loud enough that the chief could hear him.

"What are you thinking, Kary?"

"These marks appear to have been made by two different types of shoe, unless—".

Before the chief could inquire any further, Kary asked him to search the area between each of the shrubs more carefully. With the time to leave for Carroll's police department fast approaching, Kary felt a growing sense of urgency. Besides, a small group of onlookers had gathered just outside the police tape on the lower patio.

"Damn, and I was so sure—"

"Darn it all, Kary, what are we looking for?" the chief asked.

28

Maya returned to the AP meeting just in time to see one of the women she'd heard talking about Dana earlier. "Excuse me, my name is Maya Lassiter. I wonder if you would mind answering a question for me."

"I recognize you from your announcement about Dana Cerone, Ms. Lassiter. I'm Patti Stone. I guess you were pretty close friends, huh?"

"The closest," Maya replied. "I'm having a great deal of trouble with this. Maybe if I knew more about what she did last night, I could finally begin to let go." Maya was not about to tell Patti the entire truth of why she was really asking questions. Besides, what she had just told the young teacher was true, and she wondered if she would ever be able to shake the image of Dana's body lying in the bushes.

"I'll help you any way I can," Patti replied. "Dana showed up for dinner last night by herself." Maya felt a rush of guilt rush over her. If only Maya hadn't been involved with her board meeting. Damn that Priscilla O'Neal anyway, she muttered under her breath. Patti continued, "We invited Dana to join us at our table and she did."

Maya knew she would have to be careful how she asked Patti about the evening, so as not to arouse suspicion. "Did Dana seem okay to you?"

"She was terrific. There were five of us at the table, four of us women from Portsmouth High and a male teacher from Coastal Tech. We ordered a bottle of wine and ate like there was no tomorrow." Patti immediately realized she had made an unfortunate choice of words and apologized. "I'm so sorry; and they actually allow me to teach English."

The last thing Maya needed was to lose the woman's input, so forced herself to smile as she took Patti's hand and said, "That's just the kind of thing Dana would have said if she were here." Then she quickly added to her inquiry, "Did you stay at the table very late?"

"Three of us did. Dana was the first to leave. Then Benton, the guy from Coastal, left." Patti intimated to Maya that the three women, who had been meeting Benton at AP conferences for several years, were questioning whether he had followed Dana upstairs to her room.

The hair on Maya's neck was standing on end, but she continued to play it cool. "Oh," she said, "do you think this guy is the kind who would force himself on a woman?"

Patti eyed Maya with suspicion and took a deep breath before she answered. "Ms. Lassiter, if I were in your place I would want to know how my friend died, too. Benton Horn is a middle-aged man who chases after women because it makes him feel younger. At one time or another he's probably hit on half the women at this meeting, including me. When he did, I just smiled and said 'no thanks' and that was that."

At that point, Patti excused herself so she could head off to an afternoon session. She offered Maya her hand. She again expressed her sincere regrets while making direct eye contact. Maya had no doubt about the woman's sincerity and she dearly wanted to be able to dismiss Horn from suspicion. She also knew how aggressive her dear friend Dana could be. What if Dana had been offended by Benton Horn's advances and had tried to slug him. Suppose he had retaliated out of rejection and humiliation.

29

Before Kary could tell the chief what he had been searching for, a familiar female voice called to them. "Is this what you're looking for, gentlemen?" It was Maya. She had wanted to share what she learned during her AP meeting with Kary. By coincidence, she spotted him working the crime scene with Chief Brown, so had joined the small group of curiosity seekers. When she overheard Kary say he was looking for something, she scoured the nearby area outside of the police tape looking for anything out of the ordinary. That's when she saw what looked like a black, three inch heel lying in a crevice next to the base of the hotel. Rather than pick it up, Maya stood over the heel and pointed to it.

"Good work, Maya. That's precisely what I was looking for, or something like it." When he arrived by Maya's side, he looked back toward the boulder and whistled. "Do you two see what I'm seeing?" he asked.

The chief was the first to respond. "If that belongs to Ms. Cerone's shoe, why is it more than thirty feet from where her body was found?"

Kary couldn't help but notice that his sister-in-law had a thoughtful expression on her face. "What's up, Maya?"

"When they took me out here yesterday, I saw a small hole in the ground over there. It looked to be about the size that a heel like this would make," she said while pointing at the spot.

"And the bottom of this heel appears like it will fit into that depression," Kary observed.

"But there's something else," Maya replied. "Dana owned a pair of shoes just like that. I was with her when she bought them."

"Then it looks as though we have some matching to do," the chief said. "The PD confiscated Ms. Cerone's belongings."

"And if the police have a similar pair of shoes with one missing a heel...," Kary added.

"Then you gentlemen may have a mystery to solve," Maya concluded the thought.

30

While Maya once again returned to her conference, Kary rode with the chief in the latter's car during the six mile trip to Carroll. As they rode along, the two agreed not to discuss the disappearances of either Laureli Hopkins or Paul Grandhomme unless the chief brought up those topics.

"Why muddy the waters?" The chief had articulated exactly what was in Kary's mind. For all anyone knew, Paul could be hiding, and the candidate could have left the resort temporarily to go campaigning in a neighboring village.

The police station was a small, white clapboard building situated near the intersections of routes 3 and 302. The station easily could have been mistaken for a mom and pop restaurant were it not for the small wooden Town of Carroll Police Department sign hanging on the side of the structure facing Route 3. There was no lighting of any kind on the sign. Kary presumed that any after-hours business was conducted by telephone. Once inside the structure, Kary found himself in a long hallway. To the right was a door with a hand painted sign that read Dispatcher. A second door, this one unmarked, was situated another ten feet down the hallway on the same side. Across the hall from the dispatcher's office was a door with a sign painted in larger block lettering, Sergeant Joseph Crandall. Kary presumed that a fourth door, this one situated perpendicular to the hallway, led to the jail cells.

Chief Brown knocked softly on the sergeant's door.

"Come in," was heard from the other side. As the two men entered, Sergeant Crandall appeared to be in a better mood than expected under the circumstances. "Hey, Browny, good to see you. It's been what, seven whole hours?" Before Chief Brown could respond, the sergeant switched his gaze and attention to Kary. "And you must be the professor that Browny's been telling me about. Actually," he corrected himself, "I should say Browny and Mr. Capstone."

Kary wasn't terribly surprised to learn that the general manager had spoken directly to the sergeant. After all, Kary's presence and the circumstances of his arrival at the resort certainly were out of the ordinary.

"Call me Kary, Sergeant. That professor stuff is strictly for my undergraduate students." Kary hoped his comment didn't sound stilted. He needed this man's consent if the chief and he were going to continue looking into the circumstances surrounding Dana's death.

"Browny, why don't you get yourself a cup of coffee across the hall while I talk with Professor, er, Kary, for a little while." It was an apparent directive not a request, which caught both Kary and Chief Brown briefly off-guard. They complied without displaying even a hint of misgiving to their host.

31

Crandall wasn't accustomed to mincing words. "Kary, step over by the window with me will you?" Kary did as he was asked. "Now take a quick look outside and tell me what you see."

Kary wasn't sure where all of this was going. The sergeant was waiting for an answer. Scanning the landscape before him for several seconds, he pointed out several things that were obvious to him. "Well, first of all I can see a bunch of school children walking by. The traffic is moving very fast. The other thing that stands out is that banner about the Native American Festival."

Crandall beamed. "That's pretty good. In fact, you've just identified most of the problems I face whether or not anything is happening at the resort. The reason you don't see a police chief in here is this town has a force of four, plus a dispatcher. When our last chief left, the selectmen decided to wait awhile before replacing him. I've been in charge since January. As I think you can see, we have all we can do just to keep up with day-to-day problems around here. My number one priority is those school kids you just mentioned. And, of course, that necessitates that my men and I try to slow down the traffic. People seem to confuse small towns like this with the Indy 500. And things are even more complicated right now because we have that Native American Festival starting tomorrow. Then there are the larcenies and thefts that have increased since the Bretton Woods Ski Area increased to 300 condos. All I can tell you, Kary, is thank goodness we are rarely needed at the resort. Chief Brown and his security force are usually able to handle almost anything that happens up there." He paused to reflect for a moment, then added with a wry smile, "Now, what can I do to help?"

Kary could almost feel the clock ticking. He didn't need the sergeant to tell him they had one day—actually fewer than 24 hours—to get some real evidence that Dana's death was the result of foul play.

"What I need right now is to have a look at Dana's effects. Those will go a long way toward telling me whether she had an accident or someone contributed to her demise."

"I'll be happy to show you her things, Kary. Is there something in particular you're looking for?"

"As a matter of fact there is, Sergeant. I'd like to look over everything, but I'm particularly interested in Dana's shoes."

"I've gone over her things with a fine tooth comb and I think I know what you are expecting to find. Let's get Chief Brown in here and I'll have Corporal Stanton bring in Ms. Cerone's things."

While Kary went out to look for the chief, Crandall used his office intercom to request the evidence. Five minutes after the three men were back together in Crandall's office, there was a loud knock on the door. A tall, muscular man with blond hair and a trimmed mustache to match entered the room carrying a box that was twelve inches long, wide, and tall. Kary could tell this was Corporal Stanton by the double chevron on the man's sleeves. Crandall briefly introduced the corporal to Kary. The two nodded at one another and Stanton promptly left the room.

The sergeant brought the box over to an empty table and

set it down. When Kary and the chief had joined him there, Crandall removed a seal from the box. Then, lifting the lid, he invited the men to look at its contents. A majority of the space was taken up by the small cocktail dress Dana had been wearing. A clear plastic zipper bag contained her rings, earrings, and a gold necklace Kary was fairly certain Maya had given her. The remaining items consisted of a small evening bag, undergarments, and a pair of evening shoes. Kary asked to take a closer look at the shoes. His suspicions were immediately verified when he saw that one shoe was missing its heel. Reaching into his pocket, he removed a paper cocktail napkin containing the heel Maya had found at the resort. The match was unmistakable.

"I had a feeling this was what you'd come to see. Once I had seen her effects, I sent a man back to the resort to find the heel, but he came back empty-handed. Where in the world did you find this?"

"It isn't surprising your man couldn't find this heel," Kary replied.

Now it was Chief Brown's turn to speak. "It was the damndest thing I've ever seen, Joe. We found the heel a good 30 feet from where the body was."

Sergeant Crandall thought about this before he spoke. "So, what does this tell us gentlemen? Do you think someone moved the heel? I sure as heck haven't seen any evidence to indicate anyone besides my men was wandering through that part of the garden."

"I don't think the heel was moved either, Sergeant. My best guess is Dana was moving backwards at such a rapid rate that the heel snapped off and traveled to the position where we found it."

"Which suggests she was hit by a vehicle or a very large, strong man. Since the Green Bay Packers weren't staying with us, this limits the number of suspects greatly," Chief Brown said.

Crandall asked Chief Brown, "Do you recall seeing anyone who might have been strong enough to do this, Browny?"

The chief stood silently for two minutes before he answered. "I can think of a couple people, one is a guest and the other an employee."

"Let me guess, the employee is Paul Grandhomme," Crandall said.

"Yep."

Crandall reflected for a moment on this. "Grandhomme isn't all that big, but he is strong. And we know he has a temper. But what about the guest; who is that, Browny?"

"I don't know his name but he stands out like a sore thumb. He has to be the biggest freaking Indian I've ever seen in my life. This guy must be six foot eight and has shoulders like a shot-putter. No wonder Little Bighorn turned out the way it did."

Kary was feeling uncomfortable and the chief was cognizant of that. "I apologize for the offensive remark, Kary. I was over the line. No disrespect was intended, I can assure you. When you see this guy, you'll understand what I mean about his size."

"Just because this gentleman may have a lot of size doesn't make him a suspect, but it gives us something to go on."

It was Sergeant Crandall's turn to speak. "I've seen enough to indicate there may be some validity to your suspicions about how Ms. Cerone died, gentleman. I'm going to give you exactly twenty-four hours to see what you can find out. After that, we need to either declare the lady's death an accident or bring in some outside help. So, I suggest you return to the resort without delay. I don't need to remind you to be damned careful of what you do and touch."

Before Kary and the chief could leave the room, Crandall called them back. "One other item, gentlemen. It has come to my attention that our congressional candidate is AWOL. Since she's been missing for only a few hours, I'm not going to involve my men, yet. If she's still missing at breakfast tomorrow, I'll need to get involved in an official capacity. You two are under no such constraints, so please keep an eye out for her, will you? And, one more thing, there is the matter of our friend Paul who remains missing. While there may be no connection, I suggest you look into both of these events while you're doing your hunting."

32

Back at the resort, Maya was nearly beside herself. Never the most patient person in the world, she was experiencing something that left her feeling disconcerted. The more she thought about it, she began to realize she was worrying about her brother-in-law. This was something unusual for Maya. During the last decade when Kary had been largely ignoring her sister, Maya gradually developed disdain for him. Those old feelings had begun to change during the last several hours. With no word from him, she had growing concerned for his welfare. Besides, she was anxious to hear what he'd learned about Dana's shoe. She also had news of her own to share. After Kary, the chief, and she had parted company, Maya decided to see what else she could learn about the man named Benton Horn. It hadn't taken her long to make a connection. During a coffee break, she was hailed by Patti Stone. Patti, with Benton in tow, had been looking for Maya. She introduced the two by saying, "I think you two should talk." And with that Patti disappeared into the crowd. At first, Maya was taken aback by this circumstance. After all, what if Benton had murdered Dana? How could Patti have been so clueless as to introduce the two like that?

Benton invited Maya to walk with him along the porch. Maya was reluctant to accept his invitation but saw no way out. So she accompanied this total stranger while remaining a safe distance from the railing. It didn't take Benton long to dispel Maya's fear, as well as any concern she may have had that he was Dana's murderer. She recognized his type immediately. Clearly this was a man who would never do anything that would displease, much less hurt, a woman. He was more of a dilettante than a demented beast. Furthermore, had he physically accosted Dana, short in stature though she was, Benton would have been no match for her.

Thus satisfied, Maya couldn't wait to share her information with Kary. "Where is he anyway?" She smiled in spite of herself at the realization that she actually cared about her brother-in-law's welfare.

33

Kary and the chief had barely returned to the resort when they were met by Denny Dupont. The ubiquitous Denny knew everything that was going on at the Mount Washington. The chief introduced Kary to Denny. As he did, the chief told Kary no one knew more about the inner workings of the resort than the man they called The Cowboy.

"That's a good thing to know. I'm sure I'll need to talk with you again, Denny."

"It'll be my pleasure, Pard. I'm not hard to find. Oh, and by the way gentlemen, Mister Capstone is looking for both of you. I think it has something to do with the sighting on the roof."

"What sighting?!" the two men exclaimed in unison.

"I'd better let Mr. Capstone tell you himself. He's not very pleased, I can tell you that."

While Kary wanted nothing more than to find out how his sister-in-law was doing, he knew Capstone would be anxious to talk with them. So Kary and the chief headed directly to the general manager's office. Entering the reception area, they were immediately ushered in to see Capstone but he was on the telephone. Looking up from the pad he was scribbling on, he held up one finger to indicate he would be right with them. Then, using his hand, he indicated they should take a seat.

Several minutes later he returned the telephone receiver to its cradle and asked, "Are you just getting back from Sergeant Crandall's office?" The two men nodded. "Did you learn anything of significance there?"

After being brought up to date, Capstone sat facing the two men. "We've had an incident," was all he said.

"What kind of incident, Mr. Capstone?"

"Apparently some crazy has been spotted climbing along the roof."

"Which part of the roof? The top of the hotel?"

"Actually there have been several sightings and the person—if it is one person—has been seen on at least two fire escapes, on the top roof, and on the roof adjacent to the kitchen. All I can tell you is our climber has been described as being dressed in kitchen whites. Oh, and he's wearing some type of cap that's either gray or silver."

"Sounds like Pothead to me, Mr. Capstone."

Kary looked confused, so the chief explained to him how Paul Grandhomme had been given his nickname of Pothead.

"So you figure that Mr. Grandhomme and the room climber are one and the same?"

"It would appear that way," the chief replied.

"Then we better find this guy before he hurts himself or scares the hell out of someone else."

***

As the two men departed the general manager's office, they made their way toward the Main Dining Room where Kary hoped to find Maya. He was feeling anxious knowing his sister-in-law might have been looking into the relationship between the Benton Horn and Dana. He dearly hoped she hadn't bitten off more than she could chew. As the two men entered the corridor leading to the dining room, Kary had a strange feeling. Nearing the Ammonoosuc Room, he had the sense they were being followed. He turned around. There was no one behind them in the hallway. Just then, he spotted something moving in the rectangular window above their heads, looking up just in time to see a head and shoulders quickly duck out of sight.

"Did you see that, Chief?"

"See what, Kary?"

"Up there, in that window above the hallway."

"I didn't see anything; what was up there?"

"I can't be a hundred percent certain because it all happened very fast, but I'd swear I just saw a person wearing a white jacket and a gray cap of some sort."

"I wonder if it was our old friend Pothead."

"Holy mackerel! You mean he may have been watching us all this time?"

"It's possible," the chief replied. "There are lots of places where someone who knows this old hotel can spy on us without us seeing them."

"I'd like to check this one out right now; can you show me how to get up there?"

"Sure, that's a piece of cake." The two men turned around and walked past the elevator, around the corner, and continued toward the Conservatory. There was a doorway on the left just before the entry to the small lounge known as the Rosemont Room. The chief opened the door and Kary saw a steep set of stairs that looked as though they hadn't been painted in several decades. The chief indicated that Kary should go first. As Kary mounted the stairs the chief closed the door behind them and turned on a single light bulb by means of a wall switch Kary hadn't seen. At the top of the stairs, the two men found themselves in a room tucked under the eaves that was roughly eight feet wide and twelve feet long. There was a desk covered with old logbooks and a number of items ranging from a baby stroller to gardening tools lying about. Kary pushed his way past some of the equipment and placed his face against the window. He looked down and had a perfect view of the comings and goings from both the Main Dining Room and the Ammonoosuc Room.

"This is definitely where that guy was when I saw him looking at us," Kary said.

"Unfortunately this doesn't narrow the list of suspects very much," the chief said. "Just about anyone who has worked at this place for any length of time knows about this room. It's one of many places where our employees can sneak a quick break without much risk of discovery by management."

"Unless they keep popping their heads up," Kary replied. "Well, at least I know about it now, too. Maybe we can use this to our advantage eventually."

But the chief's attention was focused elsewhere.

"Uh, oh."

"What's wrong?"

"This window over here is open."

"So I see. But where does it lead?"

"Oh, just about anywhere. Someone could easily hide up here for a while then use this window to have access to the various fire escapes. Our mystery person could go almost anywhere on the resort grounds without anyone stopping him. Someone who is smart—"

"Or desperate enough," Kary interjected.

The chief nodded his agreement, then continued. "Like I was saying, someone who is smart could find enough places to spy on people and hide to keep us going for a month. If it's Paul or someone else who works at the resort, and now I'd bet it is, it's going to take a lot of luck to catch this guy within the time frame Crandall's given us."

Kary absorbed what he just heard. "Then I suggest we get cracking, Chief."

34

The two men agreed to meet near the outdoor swimming pool in a half-hour. Kary was anxious to touch bases with Maya, while the chief needed to check in at the security office. So they parted company and Kary once again walked up the hallway toward the Main Dining Room where he hoped he'd find Maya. As he walked along the hallway, he could feel the hair standing up on the back of his neck. Feeling somewhat embarrassed, Kary stopped and quickly turned to his right while glancing up at the window where he'd glimpsed the person spying on them earlier. He didn't know whether he was more disappointed or relieved to find no one was up there. He turned and continued walking toward the Main Dining Room.

Upon arriving at the entry to the dining room, he noticed there were numerous tables occupied by small groups of people. It was going to take a while to find Maya under these conditions. He also had another problem with which to contend. Because he was not a registered guest at the resort, Kary didn't have a credential to enter the dining room. The maitre d' requested his dining card and didn't appear terribly supportive when Kary told him he was not staying at the resort.

That's just great, he thought to himself. *I can see the*

headline: state university professor removed from plush resort. Fortunately for Kerry, the man they called The Cowboy chose exactly that moment to take his shift at the maître d's podium. As soon as Denny explained that Kary was at the resort to work on a project for Mr. Capstone, he was admitted without further scrutiny.

"Now, don't you be sneaking any food while you're in here, Professor," The Cowboy wise cracked.

"You have my word of honor as a gentleman," he said while smiling back over his shoulder.

Within seconds Kary heard his name being called. Turning, he saw Maya moving toward him as fast as proper etiquette would allow. To Kary's surprise, Maya threw her arms around him. As she did, she quietly said, "Where have you been. I've been worried sick, besides I have information to share with you."

At first Kary was taken aback by his sister-in-law's gesture. Getting hold of himself, he said, "I'm not supposed to be in here because I'm not registered at the hotel. Let's take a walk and discuss what each of us has learned." So the two walked out onto the porch to a spot facing the Presidentials which stood out against the clear, blue sky. The view was spectacular, but they hardly noticed as they were completely immersed in what one another was saying. Just as Kary finished telling Maya about the person spying on them, Chief Brown approached.

"How's it going, Maya? Are you holding up all right? I'm sorry Kary and I have been running around so much."

"That's very kind of you, Chief. Kary and I have been bringing one another up to date on all we've learned. The sightings of your mystery person send chills up my spine just to think about it."

"Well you better get ready for some more chills."

"Why?" both Kary and Maya asked.

"Because there have been more sightings, and one guest reported hearing a commotion behind the hotel at about a quarter to ten last night."

"This could be a big break, Chief! We should go talk to this person."

"I completely agree. But didn't you want to take another look at the site of Dana's demise first?"

"Yes, I'd like to see it one more time before all the police tape is removed. Besides, this will give us an opportunity to see which parts of the hotel offer a view of the scene."

Once again Kary and the chief headed outside while Maya returned to her meeting. As they were parting company Maya turned to Kary and said, "My meeting will be over in about an hour. Dana and I were going to spend the last part of today and most of tomorrow relaxing and using the resort's facilities, but that can't happen now. So, I'll be available in about sixty minutes to help in any way I can." And then she added with a tear, "I certainly don't feel like sitting at the pool all by myself. Please let me help."

35

As Kary and Chief Brown made their way downstairs to the lower level, Kary turned and asked, "What is all of this about other sightings of people on the roof?"

"It's true, Kary. We've had at least three guests now who've said they've seen a person dressed in kitchen whites, wearing a type of gray hat, making his way from one part of the hotel to another using the rooftops as a passageway."

"I notice you keep saying *he*, Chief. Has anyone provided a description or are they all simply assuming that only a man would be up on the roof?"

"I'm really not sure, Kary. We've been so busy with this that I haven't been able to interview any of the witnesses face to face."

"Then that should be our next step, right after we look around the pool."

"Roger. And then we need to interview our one potential eyewitness to the crime."

"Tell me about this so called eyewitness," Kary said.

"Supposedly this woman was in her room last night and heard a noise. Apparently she got a brief glimpse of some-one. She may be able to shed a good deal of light on whoever it is we're looking for."

"Let's hope so. I don't know about you, Chief, but this

seems to be getting more convoluted the more we delve into things."

The two men made their way along the lower terrace until they reached the yellow tape the police had strung around the area where Dana's body was found. They walked along the path leading to the outdoor pool and peered beneath the bushes with the aid of a nine iron the chief brought along to move the branches without stepping between them.

"As I look at this landscape, here's what I think took place," Kary said. "Dana was confronted by a person or persons where the pool path adjoins the edge of the lower terrace. At that point she either was pushed, pulled, or dragged approximately fifteen feet to the boulder over there. What's your take on this, Chief?"

"I'm pretty sure we can rule out any dragging."

"I feel the same way. But just to talk our way through this, tell me why you feel that way."

"If Mrs. Cerone was dragged we would have seen more evidence of footprints, bent and broken shrubbery, not to mention fibers from the participants' clothing."

"I couldn't agree more. Dana wasn't dragged to the spot where Paul Grandhomme found her. If anything she was tossed over there like a sack of fertilizer."

"Of course, there's one possibility we haven't discussed," offered the chief.

"And what's that?"

"She may have been standing on that big rock and slipped and fallen."

Kary pondered this for a minute. "I hadn't considered that possibility and there's an easy way to eliminate it from further consideration. Indulge me for a minute, if you will. Let's take a look at the area right around the boulder. If she was standing on the boulder and simply fell, what would we expect to see here?"

"We'd see some skid marks on the rock and we'd definitely see evidence that both of her feet landed hard within a foot or so from the bottom of the boulder." Then with the aid of the nine iron, the two men peered near the base of the boulder. "I don't see anything like that here."

"Neither do I, Chief."

Having ruled out a slip from atop the boulder as a contributing factor, the two men returned to the front edge of the path.

"For the same reasons we don't believe Dana was dragged to her death, I think we can eliminate pulling as the cause of death, too. Again we would see footprints in the shrubbery other than the one heel print Dana herself left."

"Not to mention a bunch of messed up shrubbery. So that leaves us with a death caused by pushing the victim."

"And once again we're back to the thought that the perpetrator or perpetrators were very strong."

"I think we need to keep that particular image in the forefront of our minds while considering the possibility that the culprit wasn't built like a Green Bay Packer," Kary said.

"But who else could have done something like this?" the chief asked.

"I'm not certain," Kary replied, "but there's something about this that's all too familiar."

"Do you mean you've seen a case like this before?"

"No, that's not my meaning at all. I'm thinking about something else, but I'm going to keep it to myself for the time being because I don't want to divide our attention too much at this juncture."

The chief pondered this for a moment. He decided to trust his colleague's judgment. Besides, there were several other leads that required their immediate attention.

"Before we go back inside, I'd like you to stand next to me for a minute."

Kary obliged. "What are we looking for?"

"Look up at the resort. What do you see?"

Kary scanned from left to right, from the lowest level to the roof line, carefully pondering the landscape before he replied.

"For one thing, there are a number of public rooms, plus the porch and lower terrace, that face the area where we're standing. However, there may be only a handful of guest rooms that offer a clear view of this site."

"We're on the same wavelength here. By nine o'clock at night, most of our guests would have returned to their rooms, with the exception of Cave patrons and a few souls who might have been out walking along the terrace."

"I doubt anyone was walking on this part of the terrace at the time of the incident," Kary added, pointing to the area immediately above their heads.

"I suppose you're right. If they'd seen something, they would have come forward by now."

"Absolutely. While people generally don't like to get involved, I have to believe that anyone witnessing such a violent act would have let someone know. The grapevine in a resort is amazing at most big hotels like this. In the same way we've heard about people seeing someone on the roof and a woman who claims she heard something last night, we would know if someone had witnessed what happened here."

"Yes, unless... "

"Unless what, Chief?"

"Unless the person, or persons, who witnessed what happened wanted to protect the perpetrator."

Kary appeared skeptical about this. "Do you really think that's likely?"

"Think about it. We have a number of people who are here attending a conference or another type of meeting, and then there is our entire staff. A number of these people are longtime friends while others are related by blood or marriage. A lot of those people would avoid coming forward. Besides, any witness to what happened might believe it was innocent rough housing and that Dana was simply dazed. Of course, then the question is: wouldn't they come forward after the police were out here investigating?"

"Not necessarily; not if it meant ratting on your best friend or husband," Kary responded.

"Holy shit, then how are we ever going to solve this?"

"By considering all of the possibilities and leaving no stone unturned, if you'll pardon the play on words." Kary could see that the chief was becoming discouraged, so he added, "These cases sometimes solve themselves when you least expect it, Chief. A piece of evidence often presents itself out of the clear blue. That's precisely how The Balsams case played out. I was this close to throwing in the towel when the one item I needed became apparent. My guess is there's plenty of information out there waiting for us. All we need to do is find it."

"When this is over, I hope you'll share the details of The Balsams case with me."

"It's a promise, Chief. Now, here's how I think we should proceed. Can you get a list of the occupants of the rooms that have a clear view of this apex of the lower terrace and the pool path?"

"It will be a short list, but I'll take care of that right away." Pointing up along the hotel, Chief Brown ruled out most of the windows they could see from where they were standing. "See those windows on the North Tower? Those rooms have been empty for years. The same is true of the five rooms above the Conservatory's roof. We use 'em for storage now. That pretty much limits us to the two windows you can see at the north end of the building—Rooms 263 and 363. With such a limited number of candidates, you'll have your list within the half hour. So what do you plan to do in the mean-time?"

"Let's go pick up Maya and see if we can locate the people who saw our roof climber. Then we should pay a visit to that woman who may have witnessed something," Kary replied.

"Sounds like a plan, Stan."

"That's Kary to you, Chief," he said with a smile.

36

While Kary went to find Maya, the chief headed to the security office. Inside, sitting at the front desk, was Officer Sandy Thurston. Officer Thurston had been working security at the resort for nearly thirty years. A tall man with a graying red beard, he looked like he'd be more at home at the helm of a sailing ship than manning the security desk at a grand resort."

"Aftanoon, Chief," he said as Chief Brown walked into the room.

"Hi, Sandy, how's things going? Are there any pressing messages?"

"Well that depends, Chief. We had those three people who saw someone wandering along on the roof. And that lady called again to talk to someone about the commotion she heard last night. I wrote up slips with their names and room numbers. Figured you'd want to handle it."

"You were right, Sandy. This is something I'd best deal with myself. Now where's the new guy?" The new guy had, in actuality, been working as a security officer at the resort for more than three years. However, as the last person hired, Lonny Goss was doomed to be regarded as the new guy until someone replaced either Chief Brown or Officer Thurston. Chief Brown no sooner asked about his whereabouts when Officer Goss entered the room.

"Where ya' been, Gossy? The chief here was just asking about ya'," Sandy Thurston asked.

"Oh, I was up on the third floor. One of the guests reported someone had been through her personal belongings."

"What?!" Chief Brown responded.

"Someone's been in one of the rooms. It doesn't appear that anything has been taken, but the guest was pretty upset."

"Not as upset as I am!" exclaimed the chief. "This is terrible. How on earth could someone have gained entry into another guest's room?"

"Musta' had a key, I guess," replied Officer Goss.

"No shit, Sherlock!" Officer Thurston replied.

"Belay that kind of talk, Thurston," Chief Brown scolded.

"Sorry, Chief, I was just having some fun with the new guy here."

"I ain't a new guy; I've been here more than three years! When are you going to get that through your thick skull?" Thurston just laughed at Goss's outburst.

But Chief Brown was in no mood to appreciate these shenanigans. "Okay, you guys, this is a serious breach of security. Officer Goss, what is the name of the guest and what's the room number? I'm going to need to check on this myself," he sighed. In the back of his mind, Brown felt sure the break-in may have something to do with the Dana Cerone case.

"Let's see," Goss replied, "it's room 317 and the guest's name is—"

Brown didn't need Goss to say another word. He finished the officer's sentence for him "—Maya Lassiter." The chief knew where he was going to find Kary. He started out the door on his way to room 317. Then he remembered why he had stopped at the security office in the first place. Reversing his steps, he returned to the office and said to Officer Goss, "I need you to do a little field reconnaissance for me. I want you to walk outside and stand where the lower terrace and the path leading to the outdoor pool meet. Then I want you to turn and face the hotel. Look up and determine which rooms would have a view of the spot that you're standing on. I want you to get me a list of those room numbers and the guests who are occupying them. Can you do that for me right away, Lonnie?"

"I'm on my way, Chief."

The chief didn't hear his colleague's response. He was already on his way to room 317. As he walked briskly up the stairs he thought, poor Maya. She's already gone through so much during the last 24 hours. She certainly didn't need this.

***

Chief Brown was so upset by the news of the break-in that neither of his officers remembered to tell him about the telephone message from Mrs. Helen Grandhomme, Paul "Pothead" Grandhomme's mother. Mrs. Grandhomme had called to talk with the chief—or anyone at the hotel—about her son. She was frantic with worry, not to mention angry, because Paul failed to come home the previous night and had not called her. This was unlike her son and she was concerned some type of foul play might have befallen him. Since he had just returned to work from his one-month punishment, Mary was more concerned that Paul was a victim of revenge than the perpetrator of some horrible act. Had she known about the incident at the pool, she might have felt differently. But for now, Helen Grandhomme had a great deal in common with Chief Brown and the others at the resort: she was looking for answers from Paul and finding none.

37

By the time he reached Room 317, Chief Brown was fit to be tied. His knock on the door was too loud and way too persistent. Kary opened the door and, having taken one look at his fellow investigator's face, knew all was not well.

"What's going on, Chief? You look worse than we feel."

"Oh, it's just that damned pop up," he said.

"Was the pop up you're talking about Laureli Hopkins' announcement for congress?" Kary asked.

"Roger. All hell broke loose downstairs yesterday and, unfortunately, it spilled over into today's work schedule. One of the most difficult things about working in the hospitality biz is dealing with the personalities. If that isn't tough enough, the person who was affected most by the pop up is in no mood to compromise. She's requested that the Gold Room be set up and taken down at least three times. I'm sure you can imagine how cranky that makes the set-up staff. They're ready to hang her by her manicure. Two of the staff had to carry a 12-top up and down the stairs twice because it wouldn't fit into the elevator, and Ms. Sadler couldn't make up her doggone mind."

"The ramifications of Laureli Hopkins' decision to announce here are spreading, eh, Chief?"

The chief immediately apologized for his insensitivity to Maya's plight. Kary explained that Maya was taking a hot shower in an effort to gather her wits after the ordeal of being victimized by the break-in. He suspected there was something else behind his colleague's anguish. "Is there something you're not telling me, Chief?"

"You bet there is. Ms. Sadler just happens to be the very same person you and I need to interview, and she just told me to stay out of her way until after this evening's reception is over."

"And do we have to honor that request?" Kary asked.

"You may not, but I do. She's a guest here, a guest who has brought us thousands of dollars worth of business. If I try to push her on this, she'll complain to Mr. Capstone. And if that happens, you'll need to find me a job at the university because I sure as hell won't have one here."

"Ouch!" Kary replied. Then he smiled and placed his hand on the chief's shoulder, "We still have plenty to do. We need to interview the three people who saw someone on the roof. And, once Maya is finished pulling herself together, you're going to find what she has to say very interesting."

As if on cue, Maya emerged from the bathroom. She was dressed in a pair of jeans and a short sleeve blouse that buttoned down the front. Kary smiled at his sister-in-law as she emerged, appraising how her body, like Nya's, had remained surprisingly nubile. Kary silently thanked the twins' parents for their excellent genes.

Maya was surprised to see Chief Brown standing in the room.

"Oh Chief, I didn't hear you come in. Pardon me for not combing my hair yet. Kary suggested I take a hot shower while he did a little snooping to see if anything is missing."

"And what's the verdict, Kary?" the chief asked.

"As best I can tell, nothing has been taken. Maya's only valuables are her jewelry and her wallet. Since she had both with her at the conference all day, there was little of value to steal," Kary offered.

"Now isn't that just like a man," Maya snorted. "Those blue shoes over there are Ferragamo and this cocktail dress is Sophie of Saks Fifth Avenue. It's obvious to me the person who came into this room knows as much about fashion as you do, Kary."

Kary smiled wanly and shrugged while the chief's expression was one of concern.

"I can't apologize enough about this, Maya," he said. "This kind of thing just doesn't happen at the Mount Washington."

"It looks like your GM needs to convert to an electronic key system like The Balsams has," Kary offered.

"It's being considered. We're trying to maintain the tradition of brass keys. However this incident may cause the management to rethink that."

"The great benefit of having the electronic key system is we would already know the name of the individuals who had entered this room, not to mention the day and time they'd entered."

"Yes, sadly, brass keys can't talk. So we may never know who has entered this room. However, I have a meeting in about ten minutes with the head of housekeeping and the personnel responsible for cleaning this room."

"Hopefully, that will tell us something," Kary said. "In the meantime, let's consider who may have done this and why."

"Do you have any ideas, Kary?" Maya asked.

"I'd be very surprised if it was anyone on the housekeeping staff. They'd be the first ones we would suspect in the event of a break in. Clearly the person who was in here is someone with both a motive and the means to enter."

"How will we ever determine who that is?" Maya replied.

"I think we can make some suppositions about motive, but we'll leave the means up to Chief Brown here. I think we have to presume this break-in has something to do with Dana's death."

"But why? I'm not even in the same guest room anymore."

"Precisely. My best guess—and it's only a guess at this juncture—is that someone followed the transfer of your luggage from your other room to this one. Since nothing appears to have been taken, that person may simply have wanted to know who you are. He or she has been snooping and knows the three of us have been asking questions. I can't be easily traced because I'm staying at the place across the street and it's pretty obvious who the chief is. You're the obvious target because you are still a guest here. Our culprit can't simply go to the desk to find out who you are, thus the motive for the break-in."

"That makes a good deal of sense to me, Kary" the chief said. "Now let me see if I can do my part to narrow down the list of suspects."

"Great. I'll stay here with Maya. Why don't you come back as soon as you're through talking to the housekeeping folks."

"I'll come right back. Only, there is something else you need to do while I'm gone."

"What's that?"

"You need to go down and talk with Milly Spaulding, our director of public relations."

"Okay, but why?"

"Because she is the resort's first line of communication in the event this thing turns out to be a murder investigation."

"But why talk to me. Wouldn't it make more sense to talk with Joe Crandall, or to you?"

"She did ask to speak with me, but I can't do it right now. I'd really be grateful if you can cover for me."

Kary looked at Maya who nodded as if to say, I'm fine. So Kary told the chief he was on his way.

38

While Chief Brown made his way to the far reaches of the hotel where he was to meet with the housekeeping staff, Kary walked into the Sun Dining Room where Milly Spaulding, director of resort communications, was waiting for him. Milly was one of those women whose age was indeterminable. Her slim figure, long brown tresses, tanned lovely face, and sparse character lines gave her the appearance of a woman in her mid-30s. However, Kary suspected a person in her position had to be as much as a decade older.

"Come in, Professor Turnell, I heard you were here today."

"Do you know something about me, Ms. Spaulding?"

"Please, call me Milly."

"Only if you'll call me Kary."

"That's fair enough, Kary. This resort is a small community. Information travels fast. I know you're up here because your sister-in-law's friend died under strange circumstances yesterday."

"What else do you know?"

"I know you're working with our own Chief Brown, which is a good thing."

"And why is that, if I may ask?"

"Don't take what I'm about to say incorrectly. Chief

Brown is a hard-working security guy. He does his job by the book and never lets his ego get in the way, which is precisely why he is overjoyed you're willing to work with him. Chief Brown, for all of his good traits, is no investigator, which is why the management was more than happy to allow you to get involved. Besides, my understanding is that you're both working under the watchful eye of Carroll's finest, Sergeant Joseph Crandall."

"You are certainly very well-informed, Milly."

"I do try," she said with a smile.

"What is it I can do for you?"

"That's really very simple. I would like to be informed of any developments. Please try to understand. I'm not trying to impede your investigation. What I am determined to do is limit any misinformation from leaking to the press as well as our guest population."

"I can well understand your need for caution. The last thing anyone needs is for this resort to be placed in a bad light. Believe me, I understand it can take years to overcome a bad reputation, and let me assure you I'll do my best to assist you. But, please understand this is a very complex situation." Then pausing to consider his next words, Kary asked, "Can I trust you, Milly?"

"Completely."

"I suspect Tom Capstone has informed you we have a potential murderer on our hands." Milly nodded. "There is also the matter of two missing persons, one or both of whom could be the perpetrator, or even another victim."

"I presume you're talking about Paul Grandhomme."

"Yes, and Laureli Hopkins."

"The congressional candidate? She's missing?!

"She hasn't been seen since early evening yesterday."

"Why in hell didn't someone tell me about this? This is

terrible. The death of a congressional candidate on property could close this place down, Kary."

"Let's not jump the gun. No one said anything about any harm having come to Ms. Hopkins. She simply hasn't been seen for some time. It's entirely possible she's off campaigning somewhere."

"That will be easy to verify if it's the case," Milly said.

"You can do that?"

"Certainly. Her campaign manager's cell phone number is in my Rolodex. I'll tell you what. Since you're such a nice guy, I'll go downstairs right now and call her myself."

"That's very kind of you, but we'd better discuss what you're going to say," Kary said.

"I'm not sure I follow you."

"You don't want to let on that Ms. Hopkins may be a missing person."

"Oh, I get it," Mandy said. "Then I'll just ask what Ms. Hopkins' campaign schedule looks like for the next twenty-four hours."

Kary smiled. "Perhaps you're in the wrong business, Milly. Have you ever considered making private investigation your new career? You're a natural."

Milly smiled at Kary's flattery. She was feeling very proud of herself. For his part, Kary felt confident he could trust Milly Spaulding's actions.

39

Chief Brown knocked on the office door of Erma Hearns, head of housekeeping at the Mount Washington Resort. Erma, a sixtyish gray-haired lady, had the body of a marathoner and the muscle tone of an arm wrestler. Years of mopping floors at an Atlantic City ballroom had toned her shoulders, arms, and lower body. Twenty years before, Chief Brown had seen Erma wearing a two piece bathing suit. In an era when women were much less into body sculpting, Erma sported eight-pack abs, not merely six. Because Erma had "walked her talk" over the years, she was highly respected by the entire staff—even the general manager and the CEO—and feared by her housekeepers. More than a decade earlier, a surly Russian housekeeper had made the mistake of shoving Erma Hearns after the former was confronted about stealing from a guest's room. Erma grabbed the much larger and seemingly stronger woman's arm in a vice-like grip nearly pulling it out of the socket. It took several of the male wait staff to convince Erma to loosen her grip, but not before the Russian woman admitted to the theft and confessed exactly where the authorities could find everything. The legend of that confrontation grew over the years, and no housekeeper was anxious to face a similar treatment, despite Erma's advancing age.

"Erma," Chief Brown nodded as he entered the room.

"Browny," she responded. "So there's been a theft. Tch, tch, tch," she said with a shake of her head.

"Thanks to you, we haven't seen one of those in quite a number of years."

"Oh, come on, Browny, yer givin' me too much credit."

"Now, don't be modest with me, Erma Hearns. After what you did to that woman, Ludmilla, I wouldn't steal from one of your rooms, even if I was starving."

"Wal, 'parently someone 'round here's braver than you, Browny," she replied with a big smile.

"Crazier or more desperate is more like it," he replied.

"So, how do you want to handle this?" she asked.

"Well, normally I'd say we should play good cop-bad cop, with me as the bad cop. But, in this case, your housekeeper may be happier to talk to me. Why don't we reverse the roles? This way you can just be yourself," he said with a smile. Erma just looked at the chief with a twinkle in her eye.

In old hotels like the Mount Washington, each housekeeper had her own master key that opened every guest room door. A houseman, as a general rule, was not issued a master key. As a result, a houseman could only enter a guest room with a housekeeper present. This was because housemen have had a greater propensity to steal whatever might be loose and unprotected, including guests' cash and jewelry, or any tips left for the housekeeper.

Because each houseman was assigned a block of rooms twice in number as that assigned to a housekeeper, anything missing generally could not be automatically attributed to any one individual. Housekeepers only had their own rooms to tend and no one was permitted to enter one of these without the assigned housekeeper being there to watch their behavior. Unfortunately, with the passage of time, the number of dishonest housekeepers had begun to increase, thereby necessitating the adoption of the electronic key system. Erma Hearns' presence had eliminated the need for this change at the Mount Washington—at least until now.

****

Raluca Moldeeva had the appearance of a condemned woman as she entered the office of the chief housekeeper. Like so many of her Eastern European compatriots, she had a system-honed fear of authority figures in general, and Erma Hearns in particular. After all, if Erma had throttled a larger Russian woman, what would she do to a five-feet tall, hundred-pound waif like her? While she was waiting in the hallway to see Erma, Raluca was shocked to see the resort's chief of security was also going to be questioning her. Raluca remembered the stories her parents and grandparents had told her about Ceaușescu's men coming for people, most of whom were never seen again. Terrible images swirled through the nineteen-year-old's head as she waited to be called into the room.

"Come in and sit down, Raluca," Erma said. "The chief of security and I have much to talk with you about." By the look on her face, it appeared the young woman might wet herself at any moment. This only added to the impression she was guilty of something.

"The chief and I are wondering if you've been a bad girl, Raluca," Erma immediately said as she stared the young woman in the face. If Raluca were an American-born worker, Erma would have been in hot water with the authorities on two fronts: taking an accusatory tone and referring to her as a girl. But Raluca knew nothing of these issues, so Erma's tone would go unchallenged.

To the surprise of both the chief and head housekeeper, Raluca began to wail, and she immediately confessed.

"Yas, I have been veddy bad, veddy veddy bad, Mizern. I stole something from one of the rooms I clean."

"That's what we suspected, Raluca, which is precisely why you are here right now. It would be best for you if you tell us all about it," the chief said.

But Raluca arose without warning and bolted from the room. As she ran down the hallway, they heard her say, "Raluca be right back." By the time Raluca returned, the chief and Erma were doing all they could to maintain their stern demeanor. At first, both wondered if it was her partial confession or the act of emptying her bladder that had produced the look of relief on Raluca's face. Once she was reseated, the young Romanian woman told her story.

"Raluca has had cold. So while cleaning in Room 328, Raluca saw a—" she paused while she searched her limited vocabulary for the phrase she wanted—"sooking cundy."

The chief and Erma looked at one another as each mouthed the words in an effort to understand what Raluca had just confessed to stealing. "Sooking cundy, sooking cundy? I'm afraid we don't understand what you mean, Raluca."

"Raluca took a sooking cundy, a lemon sooking cundy from the dresser," she replied.

"Lemon sucking candy!" the two interrogators said in unison. "Oh," said Erma. Then fixing the girl with her hardest stare, Erma asked her, "What else have you taken from the guest rooms while you've worked here, Raluca?"

"Oh, nussing, Raluca hasn't taken nussing. I swear on my mother's life, Mizern."

Now the chief chimed in, "Are you sure that you haven't taken anything from Room 317, Raluca?"

"Oh, no sir. Raluca don't ever steal. Raluca left quarter on bureau where sooking cundy was."

The two looked at Raluca and then at each other, fighting the urge to smile. The chief somehow found his voice. "All right, Raluca. But, there is one thing before you go. Can you be certain that the houseman who works with you hasn't taken anything from any of the guest rooms you clean?"

"Oh, yes, sir," she answered with complete conviction. "Houseman is David. He is Raluca's boyfriend. He more afraid of Raluca than Raluca is afraid of Mizern."

Erma placed her hand on the young Romanian woman's shoulder, squeezing lightly but enough to command her full attention. "You may go now, Raluca," she said.

Raluca was fighting back tears as she rose to leave the room. "Does this mean Raluca is fired?" she asked.

"No, Raluca," Erma replied with a look that ineffectively disguised the compassion she was feeling. "You are not fired but no more taking candy or anything from guests' rooms. Do you understand?"

"Yes, Mizern," she replied, then left the room with all the speed her thin legs could muster.

"Well, that was a good news-bad news situation if there ever was one," the chief said.

"Bad news?" Erma asked. "How was this bad news?"

"We still have a guest whose room has been violated, and we haven't the foggiest idea who could have done it," he replied.

40

Room 317 was not a joyous place after Kary and the chief returned from their respective meetings. Maya was still feeling violated by the unknown person who had burglarized her room. While nothing of value was missing, she did find evidence, by happenstance, that supported Kary's theory about the intruder's motivation. While going through her conference papers to eliminate those which were not completely necessary, she noticed her registration form and receipts had been removed from the conference folder. A brief search led to their discovery on the bureau nearest the room's entryway. Maya was a hundred percent certain she had not left the two documents in that part of the room.

Maya's confirmation that Kary had been correct did nothing to lift his spirits. Ten minutes earlier, Kary had remained in the Sun Dining Room while Milly Spaulding went to her office to call Laureli Hopkins' campaign headquarters. As a longtime educator, Kary was an excellent reader of faces. When Milly returned, she didn't have to say a thing. Everything he needed to know was written across her tanned face.

"Let me guess," he said preemptively, "they don't have any idea where Laureli Hopkins is, do they?"

"Not a clue. As far as Laureli's husband and his witchy campaign manager know, Laureli is still participating in the economic summit here at the resort until later today. Then she's going to get a ride to Littleton to do some campaigning."

Kary could sense that something else was on Milly's mind. "What's the problem; is there more you haven't told me?"

"No, I'm just mortified with the lack of professionalism I just exhibited," she said. "I've been in public relations for more than fifteen years." Some quick math told Kary that Milly was nearly forty, just as he suspected. She continued, "I had no business calling that woman 'witchy' in front of a total stranger."

"Stranger? And here I thought you and I were old friends," he smiled.

Milly was becoming flustered. "Oh, we are. But I really don't know you that well and frankly, I don't know Mandy Tomkins well enough to be calling her names out loud. I'm sorry, Kary."

"Consider it forgotten. When you get to be my age, forgetting is easier done than said," he smiled.

"So what does this news mean to your investigation?"

"What you've just told me has added days to an investigation that has to be concluded by early afternoon tomorrow. I need to get some kind of handle on Laureli Hopkins' disappearance. But I keep asking myself what, if anything, it has to do with Dana Cerone's death."

"I can tell you one thing, if it will help."

"It certainly can't hurt," Kary replied.

"While I was careful not mention Laureli's disappearance, I had the distinct impression that neither Bob Hopkins nor Mandy Tomkins particularly missed her."

"What makes you say that?"

"Bob made some typical husband-like comment about having more peace and quiet around the condo. And then Mandy made a rather stupid comment."

"Really, how stupid?"

"Very stupid, actually. She made reference to Bob and her having some 'down time' together while Laureli is away."

"That's pretty innocent in and of itself," Kary offered.

"I don't know, Kary. It's the way she said it. Down time is what she said."

"Interesting. Of course you may be on to something, or you may have just added two plus two and come up with six."

41

The chief and Maya were divided about the meaning of Milly's story. While Maya uttered something that sounded like "that hussy," the chief said there wasn't enough information to arouse his suspicions. Kary had to admit his suspicions were aroused. School was still out, he said.

When the chief reported his story of the housekeeper's interrogation, Kary whistled. "That Erma sounds like a piece of work. I sure wouldn't want to meet her in a dark alley."

"That's for sure," Maya laughed. "I've seen you in a bathing suit."

That comment was the only source of levity for the three. The rest of Chief Brown's story contributed no suspects and did nothing to lift their spirits.

"Let's go interview our other witnesses," said Kary. "Maybe we'll get the break we need."

"I'm coming with you gentlemen," Maya said.

"Actually I was hoping you would conduct one of the interviews," Kary said.

"Really? Are you teasing your favorite sister-in-law?"

The chief was looking at Kary, wondering the same thing himself.

"No, I'm not teasing you. Time is money right now, guys. We need to cover as much ground as possible in a hurry."

Then looking at Chief Brown he asked, "Who are the three people who saw someone on the roof and where can we find them?"

"I've arranged for each of them to meet with us," then looking at his watch he added, "right about now."

"Then give us our assignments, Chief."

"Fine. Kary, why don't you take the guest in Room 211? His name is Mr. Bird. He was playing tennis when he noticed someone on the roof."

"Done."

"Maya, you should go to the dining room and ask to speak with Bud Bland. He's a waiter here who can tell you his story. Bud's a good guy and you can interview him in a public area."

"Oh, Chief, you're concerned about my safety. That' so chivalrous of you," she said while patting his forearm.

"Just looking out for my star interviewer. While you two are doing that, I'll speak to Miss Johnstone in Room 302."

"Saving a lovely lady for yourself, Chief?" Maya said.

"Believe me, Maya, I'm not doing myself any favors. Miss Johnstone has been staying with us for more than thirty years and her disposition hasn't improved a bit during that time."

Kary looked at Maya. "It would appear our Chief here is taking one for the team."

"You have no idea, Kary."

42

Kary knocked on the door of Room 211. Silence. He knocked again, this time a little louder.

"Keep your shirt on, I'm coming; I'm coming!"

Great, Kary thought to himself. This isn't off to a very good start.

The door opened and a frail octogenarian with an acute case of rosacea stood in the doorway. Hoping to verbally disarm the man before he incurred the former's wrath, Kary said, "Hello, Mr. Bird. My name is Kary Turnell. Please allow me to apologize for knocking so hard. The doors in this old hotel always leave me wondering whether I've knocked too loudly, or too softly. Obviously it was the former this time."

Kary's little speech had worked. "Oh, that's all right, young fella'. Don't mind me. I'm just cranky 'cause my arthritis is kickin' up somethin' fierce today." With that, the older man extended a gnarled right hand and introduced himself. "Bill Bird."

Kary took the man's hand in his own and squeezed it ever so gently so as to impart sincerity without causing pain. "Kary Turnell," he replied.

Bill Bird didn't believe in mincing words. "So you're here to ask me about the person I saw on the roof this morning."

"Yes, I understand you were playing tennis this morning when you spotted him."

This made Bill Bird laugh. "Take a look at these hands, young man. My tennis days are over. I was out there walkin' on the courts, but I sure as hell wasn't playin'."

"Was anyone with you at the time?"

"No. You're missin' the point. At one time, I played tennis every minute I could, morning, noon, and night. I played so much it cost me two marriages. But I can't do it anymore."

"So?"

"So, this is as close as I can get. I like to go out on the court and walk around. It kinda' helps me remember some of the better matches I've had. One of the reasons I still come up here to the Mount is because the courts are clay."

"I don't follow."

"Clay's easier on an old man's feet. My bunions don't hurt anywhere near as much walking on that wonderful red clay out there."

Kary was curious. "Doesn't the management frown on taking up court time?"

"You aren't a tennis player are you?" Kary shook his head to indicate he wasn't. "I can tell. Otherwise you'd know that tennis's popularity in this country has tanked. Next time you're driving by a tennis court, take a gander to see if anyone's playin'. I'll bet you dollars to donuts the courts will be empty. It's sad, really. Tennis is such a beautiful game. But it hasn't caught the imagination of the last coupla' generations."

Kary thought for a moment. He realized this must be a sad state of affairs for an aficionado like Mr. Bird, but he needed to find out what the older man had seen that morning.

"While you were walking on the court this morning, what did you see?"

"It was about 8:15 and the sun was up, so his white outfit was glowing in the sunshine. Of course, I almost didn't see him because he blended in with the white walls of the hotel."

Kary tried to visualize this for a moment. "It really is quite amazing that you were able to see him at all, wasn't it? After all, the courts aren't that close to the hotel."

"That's true. But, I'll tell you what, if my hands and feet worked as well as these eyes, I'd still be playing tennis. I have twenty-forty vision and I'm eighty-five years old."

"That's amazing," Kary said. He meant it. He had long ago given up on his bifocals and had been wearing trifocals full time for more than twenty years. "Tell me, Mr. Bird, you keep referring to the person you saw as 'he.' Are you certain it wasn't a woman out there on the roof?"

"To be honest, I can't be completely certain. He—or she—looked to be fairly tall and I'd say fairly young. Of course most folks are young compared to me."

Kary smiled. "How can you be certain the person you saw was young?"

"I'm an old tennis player. I know a younger person's movements when I see them. This person wasn't real young, you understand. We're not talkin' about someone in their teens or even early twenties. I'd say the person I saw was somewhere between twenty-five and thirty-five."

Kary thanked Bill Bird for his time and insight. As he walked back toward Room 317 to meet Maya and the chief, he wondered how old Paul Grandhomme was. As he would soon learn, Paul was thirty-three years old.

43

Miss Lena Rae Johnstone was sitting and reading a novel in a high back chair with her feet resting on an Ottoman when Chief Brown knocked on her door. She didn't hesitate to open the door because she was expecting room service.

"Oh, it's you," she said with little effort to disguise the disdain in her voice.

"Yes, it's me, Lena. I know you're as thrilled to see me as I am to be here."

"Why are you here then?"

"You were one of the three people who reported seeing someone walking around on the roof. Each of us is visiting with one of the witnesses. We drew straws. I lost," he lied.

"We lost, you mean."

"Yes. Whatever."

"Come and sit down with your little pad and I'll tell you what I saw so you can leave me alone."

"That suits me fine. I'll sit over here," the chief said as he pointed to the Victorian couch that adorned Lena Rae Johnstone's room.

"An excellent choice. It's the one chair in here that will accommodate your large arse," she laughed.

"Well, good for you, Lena—that's one area where you have me. While you're at it," he said as he removed his security officer cap, "you might as well take a shot at my bald head, too."

"That's too easy of a target. Besides that, you were already balding when we were—"

"Lovers?" Brown interjected. "Look, Lena, after all of this time, do you think we could just call a truce? We had something nice together a long time ago. You decided to try out some other stock. I found another woman who would be happy loving me for who I am. You've been holding a grudge against me for more than thirty years because I had the gall to fall in love and be happy."

"While I—"

"Didn't," Brown interrupted. "But that's not my fault, Lena. Besides, from where I sit, it was just bad luck. Despite your one lapse in judgment," he said with a wan smile, "you're a nice person to everyone but me. And you were, and still are, a beautiful woman. So please, let's finally have peace between us and let old memories lie."

Lena Rae Johnstone looked at the man for whom she had been carrying so much venom all these years. She felt foolish for not having had this same discussion years ago. Perhaps her life would have been different if she had. When Lena finally spoke, it was as if she were being interviewed by a security chief with whom she didn't share a past.

"He was on the fire escape near the Main Dining Room," she said.

"You're sure it was a *he*?" the chief asked, relieved that Lena had decided to be cooperative.

"Yes. No. I think so. I was out for my morning constitutional when I saw him."

Chief Brown was more than a little familiar with Lena Johnstone's morning constitutional. Years before, he had taken the walk around the entire hotel, including the kitchen building and the employees' quarters, on a daily basis with her.

Lena continued, "The person I saw moved on that fire escape with great confidence, the kind of movement I would normally associate with a man. I suppose that makes me a sexist." It was a statement more than a query. "Whether he was a she or she was a he, the person I saw had been out there on that fire escape before. There must be a number of places where one could easily slip and fall. Yet, this person moved with great assurance."

"Could you see what he, or she, was wearing?" he asked.

"Oh, yes, clearly. He was wearing a white chef's outfit. You know, a pair of white pants and a white jacket."

"Could you see his face or can you tell me anything about his hair color?"

"No, I'm afraid not, on account of the cap he was wearing."

"Can you describe it?"

"Not very well. It appeared to be some type of gray stocking cap. For all I know, it could have been a small helmet or a pot," she said while shrugging her shoulders for effect.

"A pot, did you say?"

"Really, Boyd, I was being facetious."

"But could the person actually have been wearing a pot."

"From what I could see of him, he could have been wearing a kettle or a colander for that matter."

Chief Brown sensed that the productive part of his interview with Lena had ended. As he rose to leave, Lena spoke in a tone that was so soft he was uncertain whether she was talking to him or herself.

"I hope I'm smarter next time," she said, without meeting his surprised gape. Lena retrieved her novel and began reading. Their conversation was over.

44

Maya couldn't mask the excitement she felt as she entered the Main Dining Room in search of Bud Black. Before she could ask one of the wait staff to point Bud out to her, a young woman shrieked, "Signora, is that you?"

Maya blanched. She didn't have the foggiest idea who the young waitress approaching her was. Obviously, seeing Maya meant a great deal to her or she wouldn't have called out and come running across the huge dining room, a distance akin to half a football field. As the young woman drew closer, Maya still was searching her memory for a name. Her stomach was beginning to churn. No teacher wants to hurt the feelings of her former favorite student and all of Maya's former students were certain they'd been Signora's favorite. When the young woman was ten feet away, arms wide apart in preparation of bestowing a giant hug, Maya had the presence of mind to read her name tag.

"Julie! It's wonderful to see you."

"I'm so surprised to see you here, Signora. I haven't seen you since graduation day," she gushed.

"Wow. How long has that been, Julie? Time is just flying by."

"Would you believe it's been twelve years?"

"You're making me feel old, Julie," Maya said without the slightest memory of who this girl was.

"You made my senior year the best," she said. "I used to come to see you every morning with Lori Dark."

Now it was all coming together. Julie Woods had been Lori Dark's best friend. Only back then, Julie had long dark hair and weighed more than two hundred pounds. The young woman who was embracing her was blond and wearing no larger than a size 6 waitress uniform. At the mention of Lori Dark's name, Maya began to feel a little nauseated. She prayed Julie wouldn't start talking about Lori. Lori was the last person Maya wanted to hear anything—good or bad—about.

"Lori just loved you and Mrs. Cerone." Maya's head began to spin at the mere mention of Dana Cerone's name. How she wished Dana could be here right then to help her make some sense out of all that had happened since their arrival at the Mount Washington. But Dana wasn't here, which is precisely why Maya was in the dining room waiting to interview some waiter she had never set eyes upon.

Julie continued, "Me and Lori started working here together in high school. Her dad got us these jobs at the same time."

"And does Lori work here, too?" Maya prayed that she wouldn't run into Lori Dark here, or anywhere, ever again. After all of the time, effort and love, yes, love, Maya and Dana had poured into Lori, it hurt like hell to find out they were being used. Lori had been an average Italian student at best. Yet Maya had manipulated things for her to become Italian club treasurer and, worst of all, Maya had betrayed her principles by boosting Lori's grade a bit, not wanting to give the poor girl a D. Of course, Maya did this at a time when she thought Lori Dark was dying of cancer. Maya had told herself, "What difference does it make if she hasn't earned everything she's getting? Lori won't live to see twenty."

"Work here?" Julie repeated. "Don't you know about Lori? She's going to—"

"Excuse me," a young man's voice interrupted, are you Mrs. Lassiter?"

Relieved to be changing the subject, Maya answered, "I am. Are you Bud Black?"

When the young man nodded in the affirmative, Maya turned to Julie and said, "I'm sorry Julie, but I need to speak with Mr. Black for a few minutes. I'll have to catch up with you again later."

"Oh, no problem, Signora. I need to get back to work anyway. It was good seeing you."

"You, too," Maya said. As Julie girl retreated toward the kitchen, Maya found it interesting that she hadn't asked Maya why she was interviewing Bud Black and she hadn't hugged Maya goodbye.

***

Maya really didn't learn much from Bud Black, who also referred to the person he saw on top of the hotel as being of the male gender. The person Bud saw was wearing kitchen whites and some type of hat on his head. Bud had been on the roof himself when he said he, "Seen the other guy flash by." It had all happened very fast but Bud was convinced the person he saw was running away from something—not toward any place in particular. This led Maya to believe that someone else may have seen the climber right before Bud had. The one thing in Bud's description which was different from Bill Bird and Lena Rae Johnstone's was the red pants cuff. Bud felt seventy-five percent certain the person he saw was wearing pants with red cuffs under his kitchen garb. Maya was anxious to share this information with Kary and the chief. So she quickly left the dining room to do just that.

45

Kary was the first to arrive back at Room 317. He knocked on the door and, when no one answered, he decided to see if he could get a different view of the site where Dana Cerone had died. He headed for the elevator and rode to the top floor. The elevator operator that day was a gentle octogenarian named Elton. Elton made easy conversation for the brief time it took to ascend. When the elevator stopped, Kary asked him if there was a good place to get a view of the small rock garden by the entrance to the outdoor pool. Elton said there was and he'd be happy to show Kary how to get there. Elton pulled the stop lever and instructed Kary to follow him. The two men wended their way through a short corridor, opened a door to enter an area behind the elevator shaft. Elton showed Kary a bare wooden staircase.

"Climb up there. Be careful, young feller. When you get to the top you'll be in the South Tower. At one time, these were highly sought after rooms. But it was too tough to maintain them. So they let some of the younger staff sleep up here for a number of years."

It was the second time in an hour that Kary had been referred to as young. He rather enjoyed it. He climbed the stairs carefully, making a mental note of which steps appeared to be rotting to avoid them on them on the way down. "And now?" he asked.

"They pretty much use the place for storing mattresses and such."

"Doesn't appear anyone uses these stairs much," he called to Elton as he neared the last step.

Elton, whose hearing was remarkably good replied, "Just some of the young staff and they aren't supposed to."

"What do they do up here?" Kary asked as he was finishing his careful ascent.

"Hell, you were young once weren't you? Things haven't changed that much since you and I were youngsters."

Kary felt a bit embarrassed by his naiveté. As he searched his mind for a clever retort, he heard a noise coming from the tower above him. A second sound was like the thud of a closing door. Kary heard all he cared to. He would make a point of returning to the tower. Next time he'd have Chief Brown or one of his men accompany him.

***

When Kary returned to Room 317, he heard voices emanating from inside. Knocking, he was admitted to the room by Maya, who was brewing with excitement. Before Chief Brown or Maya said a word, Kary announced, "I'm sure we have much to share with one another and I hate to be a party pooper, but I'm starving. If I don't eat something in a few minutes, I'm going to go into energy deficit."

Maya had heard Nya mention that Kary could become ill whenever his stomach was empty. She suggested they discuss what they'd learned over dinner in the Main Dining Room. When Kary demurred, Maya asked, "What's wrong, Kary. I know you need to fill that stomach. So why not go first class?"

"Did you forget, my favorite sister-in-law, I'm staying across the street and am not allowed into the inner sanctum as you are?"

"Not true," Chief Brown interjected.

"Pardon me?" Kary replied.

"While we were waiting for you, Maya had a suspicion that you'd need to eat. I arranged for you to have your meals here at the resort until tomorrow evening."

"That's very kind of you, Chief. I'll have to thank Tom Capstone when I talk with him."

"Only if you want to get me fired; it was our friend The Cowboy who approved your meals. He figures your time is worth money for everyone who works here."

"Great! Let's stop talking and start eating," Kary said with a big smile. With that, the three of them headed for the Main Dining Room. Fortunately for Kary, he was still wearing the sport jacket he'd worn to campus that morning because a sign at the entry advised men they would not be permitted to attend the evening repast without proper attire.

46

The three entered the main dining room to be met by the ubiquitous Cowboy, who assigned them a table in the middle of the cavernous room. Kary sat facing the entryway with Maya to his left and the chief to his right. Kary took a moment to admire the ambiance of his surroundings. Located on the lobby level at a distance of nearly 50 yards from the registration desk, the dining room was designed as a great octagon. The ceiling featured one great and four smaller crystal chandeliers. The great chandelier had large amber glass balls and crystal tear drops; the chandeliers hanging in each of the four corners were smaller versions of the main one. A set of doors at the rear of the dining room provided entry into the newer Sun Dining Room. These surroundings made Kary lonesome for Nya. She would love the way the tables were graciously set for dining and doubtlessly would have dragged him out to the small wooden floor where dancing to a live musical ensemble was a nightly event.

"Next time we'll make it a foursome," Maya said with a smile. It warmed Kary's insides to hear his sister-in-law talk about spending time with Nya and him in the future. It had been years since they had done anything like that.

Kary couldn't begin to count the number of tables in the room. He took note of the fact that the tables nearest the windows were square and seated only couples and a few people dining alone. The other tables in the room were round and had been set as 4, 6, or 8-tops. While Kary didn't particularly find his chair comfortable, he appreciated the fact that they were all uniform. He wondered about the upkeep on hundreds of upholstered, dark mahogany chairs. He noted that their talble was set with a white table cloth, water glass, stainless steel flatware, napkins folded to represent a lily, a candle in a glass fixture, and a clear glass vase containing water and flowers of the season. What a delightful place.

They were handed leather-bound menus by a uniformed member of their three-person wait staff. Chief Brown quickly decided on a simple meat and potatoes meal of Black Angus steak with garlic-laced mashed potatoes. Kary and Maya were eager for a wonderful full-course dinner. Kary ordered an appetizer of Maine peekey toe crab with a cucumber dressing and a salad of spring greens and pea shoots with a walnut vinaigrette dressing. His entree would be a selected roasted rack of lamb in a tarragon jus. He also was salivating at the thought of the chocolate hazelnut cake ala Parisian. Maya decided on the cold smoked salmon with condiments as her appetizer. She selected a salad of Romaine lettuce with a poppy seed tuile and an entrée of sautéed medallions of veal, braised vegetables, and morel mushrooms.

Kary continued to peruse his surroundings. On the main level, there were large plate glass windows that afforded beautiful views of the surrounding countryside during daylight hours. The curtains were mauve. The chief commented that they were pulled back for the first time in twenty-four hours, as the general manager had ordered them closed immediately following the discovery of Dana Cerone's body. Looking up, Kary noticed there were sets of translucent Tiffany glass windows, each bearing the resort's crest, surrounding the dining room at the second story level. He was just about to comment about the Tiffany glass when something captured his attention.

"What the hell?"

"What is it, Kary?" Maya asked.

"Hey, what's wrong, buddy?" the chief said.

"What's up there?" Kary asked while pointing at the Tiffany glass windows.

"Windows, Tiffany glass windows," the chief replied.

"I realize that. What's behind the windows?"

Realizing that Kary was drawing the attention of the people at surrounding tables, Maya quietly told him to lower his voice. Kary modulated his voice but not his animation level.

"Chief, I believe we're being watched again. Is there a way to get up there behind those windows."

"Yes, but—"

"Please take me up there now."

"Kary, we're about to order dinner!" Maya exclaimed, though she knew there was no way to convince her brother-in-law to hang around until the waiter took their orders.

"Maya, please make an excuse for us. We'll be back in a few minutes." Leading the way, Chief Brown knew exactly where he was going. Like every employee who had ever worked at the resort, he was well aware of how to access the area behind the Tiffany glass windows. The two men walked quickly and as inconspicuously as possible toward the north wall of the dining room that served as the backdrop to the small stage where the band was playing. Behind the wall was a doorway that led to the pantry and ultimately into the main kitchen for the dining room. A second door led to a long, narrow room filled with old round tables that had been collapsed and stacked sideways. Dodging many folded round tables, the chief opened a door leading to a staircase that no guest would ever suspect was there. This stairway was littered with old fixtures and plastic crates for glasses. Moving swiftly up the stairs right behind the chief, Kary noticed there was handwriting everywhere on the walls. He was curious what this was all about but it would have to wait for now. The stairway led to a room above the Main Dining Room. The two men reached the top of the stairs and Kary noticed a doorway and more walls with writing on them. The chief found a light switch and Kary realized exactly where they were. They were in an area above the entrance to the Main Dining Room. The ceiling was low and much of the room was taken up with duct work for the resort's climate control system. It was also precisely the same place where, minutes before, Kary had seen the shadow of someone spying on the dining room. Kary moved closer to the Tiffany glass windows where he spotted several small clear patches. Whomever had been watching them was long gone.

"What a great place to spy on someone; someone's made clear patches in the glass," Kary remarked. "But, who is doing this?"

"Those patches have been there for a long time, Kary. But, if we can find out who's been spying on the dining room, I'll wager we'll have our killer," the chief replied. "My question is: who is this guy spying on?"

"I think I can answer that one for you, Chief."

"You can? Who?"

"Based on everything that's happened today, especially the break-in to her room, I think our spy's target is Maya?"

"Maya, but why?"

"Just a hunch. I think you'd better post one of your men outside her room tonight."

"I'm not sure I follow you Kary, but consider it done. Now can we please go and eat? I'm starving."

As they retraced their steps, Kary stopped for a moment to examine some of the handwriting he'd seen.

"What are all of these names? Look, each one has a town name and a date under it."

"Those are the signatures, hometowns, and the years employed of almost everyone who's ever worked here."

By coincidence, the chief happened upon one name he recognized. "Lori Dark, Bretton Woods, 1997," he read aloud. "She's a local girl and probably had Maya in school."

If Kary had any intention of telling Maya he'd seen the Dark girl's name, he soon forgot all about it when he approached the door at the top of the stairs.

"Where does this lead?" he asked.

The chief stepped forward and opened the door. It was too dark for Kary to see where the door led. "This leads out onto the roof. Those lights you see are coming from the kitchen. From here, someone could climb the fire escape and make way to almost anywhere—to the parking lot, the top floors of the resort, or even to the top of the roof. All it takes is knowing how."

"I'd like to take another look at this tomorrow morning," Kary said. "But every new place we look has me more convinced we're searching for someone who has worked here."

"Like Paul Grandhomme," the chief said.

"Yes, he or someone else," Kary replied.

47

When Kary and Chief Brown returned to the dining room it was already 8:30.

"I was becoming frantic," Maya told them. Then looking at her brother-in-law's expression she asked, "What's wrong, Kary? I can see something's bothering you."

"I'm just angry that we missed whoever was up there." He wasn't sure he sounded convincing. Fortunately, Maya did not choose to question him.

"What did you see up there?"

"It's a very interesting place. We can't tell from down here in the dining room, but there are several places where some-one can spy on us while we're eating."

"Brr, that sends chills up my spine," Maya said.

"Mine, too," Kary said. He didn't want to alarm his sister-in-law needlessly, but he knew neither of them was going to be able to rest until this investigation was resolved.

"While we're waiting for dinner, let's review what each of us learned from our three eyewitnesses."

"Eyewitnesses! Oh damn, I nearly forgot," Chief Brown blurted.

"What is it, Chief?" Maya asked.

"Our fourth witness has finally deemed herself ready to talk with us, but she said not to arrive any later than 9:30 or she won't talk with us until tomorrow morning."

"What's this all about, Chief," Maya asked with a look of concern on her face.

It was Kary who answered her. "In all the commotion, I forgot to tell you that the woman who says she may have overheard something last night wouldn't talk with us unless and until her meeting came to a satisfactory resolution."

"Wow! I figured you guys would have talked to her by now."

"Don't we wish. Well, we had better not keep the lady waiting. Let's eat our meals and keep the chit chat down to a minimum. Then we'd better hustle right on up to see Ms.— what was her name again, Chief?"

"Sadler, Carolina Sadler."

"Is she staying in one of the rooms that overlooks the area where Dana died?" Maya asked.

"Yes, and she appears to be quite a character. However, Mr. Capstone knows her very well and says she is an unimpeachable witness with an eye for detail."

"This could be a real break. I'll even pass on my chocolate hazelnut cake so we can go see her."

Maya had to smile at this. She knew this was a real sacrifice for her sister's man.

48

The Indigenous Artifacts Repatriation League meeting had not gone off without a hitch. Quite the contrary, nearly everything that could go wrong in setting up for a meeting, had gone wrong. As the man affectionately known as The Cowboy liked to say, "Damned pop ups." The staff—which included everyone from the activities manager, conference manager, sales manager, food and beverage director, set-up manager, and security—never liked it when a last minute meeting, conference, or event suddenly appeared on the Delphi, the mechanism resort supervisors used to recheck the list of a day's events. Generally, a daily schedule was built and then times were put into the computer system for each part of the day. Any space or time conflicts were immediately detected by Delphi. The information from the spreadsheet was then entered into the Banquet Event Order, or BEO. But if a pop up was added to the mix, all hell could break loose. And when Laureli Hopkins decided to make her announcement at the resort, carefully set plans had fallen like dominos. However, with a father who was a longtime employee at the resort, no one was going to say no to Laureli's people, particularly since she might become their next congresswoman.

As the smallest meeting of the day, the Indigenous Artifacts Repatriation League session somehow had taken the brunt of the changes forced by Laureli's announcement. No one at the resort could have predicted what a buzz-saw Carolina Sadler turned out to be. When Carolina arrived at the Ammonoosuc Room only to find the economic development meeting already set up in there, she immediately went on the offensive. A visit to her old friend Tom Capstone produced immediate results, however, the integrity of the Delphi had been breached. As a result, there was a shortage of chairs, not enough linens for Carolina's tables, food was late and it was cold. The final straw occurred when the wrong salad was brought to the luncheon in the Gold Room. Each time a mistake was made, Tom Capstone heard about it. Each time the GM received a call, so did each of the department heads, starting with The Cowboy.

It wasn't surprising that Carolina Sadler was less than co-operative when the chief of security called to interview her about what she reported having seen and heard on the night Dana Cerone died.

"When I'm satisfied that my meeting has been completed satisfactorily then, and only then, will I sit down with you for an interview. Do I make myself clear, Chief Brown?"

The chief had little choice but to agree to Ms. Sadler's demands. After all, she was a guest—not to mention a dear friend of his boss.

With some trepidation Chief Brown knocked on the door of Room 363.

**

"Please come in, gentlemen." It didn't seem possible the attractive and genial woman who welcomed them could be the same person who had singed Chief Brown's ears earlier that day. "Please take a seat. My name is Carolina Sadler." With a flourish of her hand she identified a gentleman seated in an upright, stuffed chair by the window. "And this is my associate, Jon Growscorn."

Kary and the chief did a double take, for sitting in the room was the large Native American they had discussed earlier in the day. It didn't take long to assuage any concerns the chief had about this man.

Chief Brown sought to break the tension. "Please allow me to apologize for all of the problems you had with your meeting, Ms. Sadler. I understand you were shorted several chairs, several linens weren't delivered on time, and there were problems with the food."

"You forgot to mention the AC not working, and no one was available to correct it for about half an hour." Chief Brown cringed despite the fact she was actually smiling as she said this.

"I know it doesn't help you to know this, but we're usually pretty efficient around here. Unfortunately, we had a political candidate drop by with very little notice."

"It's all right, Chief Brown. Besides, the end justifies the means."

"I'm afraid I don't follow you."

"We had a very successful meeting at this facility, didn't we Jon?" The large fellow looked up and smiled broadly at Chief Brown and Kary.

"That we did," he said.

Relieved to hear Carolina was no longer peeved at the resort, Chief Brown suddenly realized he hadn't introduced Kary. Once the formalities were taken care of, Kary took the lead.

"Perhaps it would be helpful if you can give us some background. Will that be okay, Ms. Sadler?"

"Please, call me Carolina. Most of my friends do. And will it be all right if I call you Kary?" Kary smiled and nodded. Kary could always tell when he'd been away from Nya for too long by the way he reacted to the women he was interviewing. He would have found Carolina Sadler attractive under any circumstances. Carolina was about five feet four and would be judged as a few pounds overweight by modern media's exacting standards. Her stylishly cut brown hair, hazel eyes, and curvaceous figure would be attractive to most men Kary's age. The way she conducted herself, however, was most appealing. Clearly here was a woman equally at home talking to business leaders in her native Philadelphia or congressmen in Washington. While Kary appreciated strong, intelligent women, he didn't have to remind himself that Nya was the only one he ever wanted in his life. He'd made the mistake of keeping her at arm's length for too long, and he never intended to jeopardize their relationship again.

"Just to help me put things into their proper context, what does the Indigenous Artifacts Repatriation League do?" Kary asked.

"Our charge is to find artifacts that have been stolen by a group of oppressors and return them to their rightful owners," Carolina responded.

Kary was as impressed with this idea as he had been with its leading female proponent. "Do you have many members?"

"No, the league is small but we are influential. We've been able to restore artifacts stolen by the Nazis to their rightful Jewish owners. A number of early Chinese immigrants who came to this country to build the railroads were forcefully relieved of numerous possessions that had religious or personal significance to them. Our own U.S. cavalry and the civilians they protected, including a number of so-called scientists, removed numerous artifacts from Native American tribes and placed them in museums and vaults. In truth, they stole them."

Looking at Jon Growscorn, Kary couldn't imagine anyone having the temerity to take anything from him.

"What is your tribe, Jon?" he asked.

"I'm a Lakota, Kary."

Refocusing his attention on Carolina, he asked, "What form does repatriation take?"

"Form? Do you mean how do we accomplish it? Not by stealing, I can assure you, Kary," Carolina said with a gracious smile. "We have experts who identify artifacts. Then we try to reason with their present owners to return them. In a few cases that has been successful. Where it hasn't, we use the law to help us. In a few cases, we've raised money from benefactors and simply bought them back."

"Wow!" Kary didn't hide his respect for what he had just learned.

Chief Brown found all of this interesting. The day had been long and stressful for him, and tomorrow promised to be the same.

"Carolina, please tell us where you were and what you saw or heard last night. First of all, what time was it?"

"Jon and I returned to the room at about 9:45."

"So, you are both staying in this room," Chief Brown stated rather than asked.

"No," Carolina and Jon replied simultaneously. Then, Jon continued in a soft tone, "I can't afford to stay in this place. I have a room in the motel across the street."

"So do I, Jon. I couldn't swing the rent here either," Kary added with a smile. Jon smiled at him in return. Kary was beginning to like this large man.

Carolina continued, "Jon and I function as the executive officers of the League. We came up here to go over what needed to accomplished today. That's when I heard a woman's voice."

"A voice?" Kary repeated. "Can you be certain it was a woman's voice?"

"Yes, I'm sure. It was more of a shout actually. Otherwise, we couldn't have heard it from this distance." Jon nodded his agreement.

"Could you hear what was being said?"

"No, but the tone was unmistakable. Anger."

"So, what did you do next?"

"Being a curious sort, I ran right over to the window to see where the racket was coming from."

"And did you see anything?"

"I saw a woman standing on the edge of the terrace." Then, beckoning Chief Brown and Kary to come and stand next to her by the window, Carolina pointed and said, "Right over there where the path to the outdoor pool adjoins the lower terrace."

"You saw a woman standing on the terrace. Was she alone?" Kary asked.

"As best I could tell."

"And did you see any of this too, Jon?"

"Yes, the woman was still standing there when I got to the window. She seemed to be staring into the distance, as if she was looking for something."

"And you're both certain it was a woman."

"As sure as you can be these days," Jon said with a wry smile.

"And why is that?"

"The person we saw was wearing a bright red pants suit. From this angle, I couldn't tell whether it was well made or not," Carolina added.

"Is there anything else you can tell us?"

"I'd say her hair was shoulder length, certainly no longer. It was either light brown or honey blond. The lighting outside was fair but not terrific, so I can't be sure which it was." Jon nodded his agreement. "And I'm pretty sure I saw an earring dangling from her left ear. Whether it was gold or silver I couldn't tell you. That's all I know."

"Can either of you think of anything else?" Kary asked.

Hearing no response, Chief Brown stood and offered his outstretched hand to both Carolina Sadler and to Jon Growscorn. "Thank you both so much for your time. This has been enormously helpful," he said.

As Kary rose to leave he added, "And I'm very interested in learning more about your repatriation league. Can you send me some information?" With that he exchanged business cards with Carolina Sadler and left the room.

Once they reached the hallway, the chief said to Kary, "That was very helpful. I wish I had the energy to stay up and talk with you about all we've learned today; but I'm bushed."

"Same here, Chief. I'm going to make certain Maya's okay then head back across the street and get some rest."

The two men shook hands and Kary stopped briefly at Maya's room. He was relieved to see that Lonnie Goss was sitting in the hallway about thirty feet from Maya's room. Satisfied his sister-in-law was in good hands, he turned and walked down the several flights of stairs to the lobby. Exiting the stairwell, Kary noticed there was a copy of that day's newspaper sitting on the table in front of the registration desk. He picked it up. Nodding toward the registration desk clerk, he said, "This will help me sleep." Nothing could have been farther from the truth.

49

Kary couldn't possibly have known that an innocent act like picking up a newspaper would engender a night of insomnia. He had already read the sports and the front page sections of the paper, grumbling all the while about the conservative bias of the editorials and the amount of space devoted to the NASCAR circuit.

"Jesus, and people think the South is conservative. I feel like I'm living in Alabama," While Kary was liberal in his political thinking, like the majority of academics, he dearly loved the state he'd adopted as his home more than two decades earlier. When people asked him what it was like to live in the Granite State, he would give them a description that rivaled anything the state's tourism office could produce. What he liked most was the slow pace of life north of Concord. To Kary, grand resort hotels like the Balsams and the Mount Washington were two little slices of heaven. That was Kary's frame of mind until he saw the lead story in the State section of the newspaper.

Hopkins Declares for 2nd District, the headline read. There was nothing earth-shattering in that announcement. He scanned several photographs. One showed the candidate with Ray Burton, the governor's councilor from northern New Hampshire; another was of Laureli with Tom Capstone, general manager of the Mount Washington. A third was taken

with some of the well wishers who attended the announcement. None of these photographs told him much other than
the fact the candidate was a tall, average looking woman with
a rather large bust, who had succumbed to the temptation to
put blond highlights in what appeared to be light-to-medium
brown hair. The dress she was wearing looked to be Dodger
blue with a neck line that Kary found to be tastelessly low for
a congressional candidate. He was about to fold the paper
and call it a night when he noticed a fourth picture on the
second page of the section. It was a candid shot taken as the
candidate was leaving the room. There was Laureli Hopkins,
her gaze locked on a shorter woman whose back was to the
camera.

"Hmm, what an interesting expression," he said to himself. "I wonder what that was about." There was something
about the photograph that bothered him. Realizing it was
nearly midnight, Kary set down the paper, removed his clothing, and headed toward the shower. Something made him
turn back. He returned to the paper on the coffee table. He
opened the paper to the fourth picture. Staring at the image
of the woman who soon could be representing New Hampshire in Washington, he said, "I wonder what she seems so
upset about." He suspected it had something to do with her
having gone AWOL

50

The first light of day provided relief for a man who had been awake much of the night. While Kary showered before retiring as was his custom, he knew he'd be unable to function unless he took another shower and had a couple cups of strong coffee, preferably as soon as possible. He showered, shaved, brushed his teeth, and put on a clean white dress shirt. Reaching into his travel kit, he was amused to find he'd packed the tie given to him by his good friend, Warn Barson. Warn, longtime general manager of The Balsams, had given Kary a maroon silk tie that bore numerous pineapples, universal symbol for hospitality. This is perfect, he thought. He had worn the tie when he cracked The Balsams case.

"Hopefully, you can be lucky for me twice," he said aloud to his image in the mirror as he put the finishing touches on the four-in-hand knot, which he preferred to the more formal Windsor knot.

Finished dressing, he drove over to the Mount Washington. Kary didn't bother to call either Maya or the chief. He preferred to drink his first cup of coffee alone. It was barely six a.m. when he locked his car, then started walking up the long drive leading to the resort's main entrance. Like so many guests before him, Kary stared up at the twin towers dominating the roof line of the beautiful resort building. Suddenly he caught a fleeting glimpse of a hooded figure running along the eastern-most edge of the roof. The person appeared for less than five seconds, long enough for Kary's well trained eye to see the phantom he was chasing was dressed in white pants and a white jacket. Unlike the person who had been reported by several other guests, this intruder also wore a long gray sweatshirt with a hood. As the phantom disappeared atop the resort's roof, Kary was determined these forays were about to come to an end.

With his mental set thus affected, Kary entered the resort, went right to the house phone and dialed Chief Brown's number. When the chief answered, Kary said, "Good morning, Chief. Kary Turnell here. I'm about to have a cup of coffee. Why don't you come up and let me tell you about the interesting things I've seen since last night."

***

Maya made an early appearance shortly after the chief joined Kary. The three shared whatever information was left to disclose, including Kary's sighting of the phantom, then spent another half hour reviewing all they had learned to date.

"We know," Kary said, "that Dana was walking down by the pool the night before last, probably sometime between 9:30 and 10. What happened next is pure conjecture, but it appears Dana got into an argument with someone wearing a red dress or pantsuit. There might have been a second party."

Maya spoke up. "Didn't you say that your two witnesses saw only a lone person standing there?"

"True. But I find it hard to believe that a woman, acting on her own, could have pushed Dana hard enough to cause the heel of her shoe to break like that, and for Dana herself to be launched far enough to hit her head against the boulder near the pool."

"My, but aren't we being sexist!" Maya chided.

"Hell, Maya, I know I couldn't push anyone that hard," he said in his own defense, then added, "Could you, Chief?"

"Not me! 'Course when I was younger—"

"Yeah, sure, Chief, but to get back to reality," Kary added with a grin, "we also know that three people, make that four, including yours truly, have seen someone wearing what appears to be kitchen whites climbing on various parts of the resort."

"And let's not forget the two times someone was spying on us," the chief added.

"And the person breaking into my room," Maya exclaimed.

"I haven't forgotten. In fact, that concerns me most of all."

"What do you mean, Kary?"

"Listen, Maya, I really think it would be a good idea if you took my car and got the heck out of here."

"But, I don't want to leave. Besides, I'm finally getting to actually like you."

"Me, too," Kary said, "and so does my wife. Which is why I think this would be a good time to pay her a visit."

"Do you think I'm in danger?" She fixed him with her large brown eyes.

"Maya, I don't have a clue what's going on here. The chief and I probably aren't going to find out who this person is in time to satisfy the police anyway. Whoever he is, he's like chasing a ghost; we never know where he's going to turn up or what his motives are. So, yes I think we may all be in danger."

"That's very sweet, Kary, but I've decided I'm not leaving here until you do. Hell, someone has to watch out for you boys," she added with a smile.

Kary sighed. "Suit yourself, but please don't leave the public areas for any reason."

"And what are you going to be doing?"

"First, we're going to get high," he replied with a smile, which drew a raised eyebrow from Chief Brown. "We're going to pay a visit to the South Tower, where I thought I heard some scurrying yesterday."

"Couldn't it have been mice or squirrels?"

"Not unless the vermin in this part of New Hampshire have footfalls as heavy as pachyderms."

***

The meeting broke up, but not before Kary extracted yet another promise from his sister-in-law to remain in the public areas of the hotel, and to return to her room only if absolutely necessary. The chief alleviated some of Kary's concern by promising that Sandy Thurston would stand outside Maya's room anytime she'd let him know when she needed to go up there.

Chief Brown said to Kary, "You two seem to be very close."

Kary smiled. "The truth is we've hardly talked to one another in years. It's that Maya is my wife's favorite sister, not to mention being her twin. If anything happened to Maya on my watch, there'd be hell to pay." The truth was Kary felt protective of Maya because the last two days had broken down their old animosities. Now, for the first time in years, Kary loved Maya like a sister and Maya clearly returned the sentiment.

51

The chief and Kary made their way up to the top floor of the resort. From there, the two men walked up the rickety stairs leading to the South Tower. They were careful to stagger their climb, keeping five stairs between them. Once they reached the tower, Chief Brown remarked how he always hated that climb.

"It's not as though climbing a few stairs is gonna' kill me," he said.

"No," Kary interjected, "but falling through a few stairs might."

"No kidding. Tell me, Kary, what do you expect to find up here?"

"I'm not sure, Chief. I thought I heard footsteps coming from up here yesterday. Seeing our phantom on the roof a half hour ago suggests this could be his lair."

"Makes sense. Maybe I should have brought my pistol."

For the first time, Kary realized that the chief was unarmed except for a can of pepper spray. "Too late now. Hopefully, he won't decide to throw us off the roof."

The thought gave Chief Brown a chill. "Don't even think about that."

The two men entered the hallway and made their way in a counterclockwise direction. Along the outside wall were doorways leading to small quarters that Kary surmised were occupied at one time by employees of the resort. To their left, most of the doorways were open to what once were probably bathrooms and a small kitchen. In most of the former quarters, old bedroom furniture and mattresses that had been soiled by time and, in all likelihood, the activities of young men and women, were stashed. Each of the rooms looked to have been long since abandoned, except for one. In the far southeast corner of the tower, the chief and Kary spotted a blanket and a pillow that were too fresh to have been in the tower for very long.

"Someone's been sleeping up here recently," Chief Brown said. "Damn! I knew I should have sealed that doorway off a long time ago."

"Why hasn't it been sealed, Chief?"

"I'll show you. Follow me."

The two men turned the corner to the last part of the eight-sided hallway. There Kary saw the doorway he knew must exist. "So, there it is. I heard this door bang shut yesterday. Where does it lead?"

"Out to the top of the roof and over to the North Tower or to any of several fire escapes that can get you to the top floors of the resort, or to one of the lower roofs, and from there—"

"Anywhere," Kary completed Chief Brown's sentence.

"Exactly."

In the room where they'd found the blanket and pillowcase, they looked for any clues as to who the phantom of the roof tops might be. The room offered no other information.

"This makes me wonder whether your friend Pothead really is our phantom," Kary said.

"Why is that?"

"Because our friend has been fastidious about removing any trace of evidence—too careful for most men I know. There isn't so much as a single strand of hair on the pillow."

"I'm afraid we still can't rule out Pothead," the chief replied.

"Why is that?"

"Because Pothead has Alopecia."

"Alopecia? You mean he's bald."

"As a billiard ball, from the top of his head to his toes. It's one of the reasons he wears the pot on his head."

"Makes sense. I'd probably do the same thing," Kary said, "although I think I'd wear a beret. That pot must hurt like hell if he bangs his head on anything, or when some of the yahoos in the kitchen pound on it with a stirring spoon." The visualization made Kary wince.

"The question now is do we remove this bedding and close this area up or—"

"I wouldn't recommend that," Kary interrupted.

The chief thought about this for a minute. "I follow you, Kary. Our phantom would be able to find his way up here anyway, and we'd be the ones who were locked out."

"Precisely. However, there is something we can do with this new found evidence of ours."

"And that is?"

"Can you check with housekeeping? Ask them to find out which rooms are missing a spare pillow and a blanket. We may be able to find out who's doing the roof walking."

"Or not," the chief replied.

"Why not?"

"Remember. Someone found a way to gain access to Maya's room. If that's the case, this person probably has access to others. And maybe, just maybe, he's filched a blanket and pillow from someone."

"Damn, that's a good point, Chief. Boy, do I wish you had those electronic keys right now." The chief shared the same thought at that moment.

Kary and the chief parted company with the promise to meet up in fifteen minutes. Kary headed downstairs to check up on Maya, while the chief wanted to see if there were any messages waiting for him.

52

Kary found Maya sitting on the veranda sipping a glass of ice tea. While he was relieved his sister-in-law was alive and well, Kary felt frustrated and more than a little anxious by what was transpiring at the resort. The strange circumstances surrounding Dana Cerone's death aside, Kary was having difficulty getting a handle on the disappearances of Paul 'Pothead' Grandhomme, long-time employee at the resort, and Laureli Hopkins, whose political star was rising. Under normal circumstances, Kary would not be concerned about Pothead's failure to report to either work or home. After all, the young man had exhibited problems as of late and, given the instability of his emotional compass, his coworkers had become increasingly spooked by him. From the first he'd learned about Paul, Kary wondered why the resort kept him in its employ for so many years. Then, Tom Capstone explained to him Paul actually performed well at the resort until the incident that led to his one month suspension. Of course, there was the small matter that Paul was the great grand-nephew of none other than Joseph Stickney, founding owner of the Mount Washington Hotel. While firing Paul was not completely out of the question, it was going to take a very serious offense for that to happen. Of course, Paul appeared to be working on one.

Laureli Hopkins' disappearance had Kary, as well as Tom

Capstone, Chief Brown, Joe Crandall and all the king's horses and all the king's men more concerned. Here was a woman with everything to gain by remaining visible, and remaining visible meant attending her economic development summit and shaking every hand and kissing every baby at the resort, and in communities from Pittsburg to Plaistow. Instead, she'd simply vanished. Still more troubling, neither her husband nor her campaign manager seemed to have any idea of her whereabouts. Then there was Milly Spaulding's reaction to her conversations with those two. While Milly was no detective, she was convinced neither Bob Hopkins nor Mandy Tomkins cared a whit where Laureli was, just as long as she wasn't in their way.

Kary considered all of this. Could those two be having an affair and has Laureli gone off to consider her next move? As he thought about this a bit more, he considered the possibility that Bob and Mandy had arranged for Laureli Hopkins to be kidnapped and possibly even murdered. There must be some logical explanation. "What am I missing here?"

***

"Excuse me. Are you Professor Turnell?" It was the voice of a young bellman. Kary was wandering through the cavernous lobby of the resort when the young man had approached him.

"Yes, I am. What can I do for you?"

"I was told by the front desk to give you this." The young man removed an envelope from the inside breast pocket of his vest and handed it to Kary. Kary thanked him as he tore open the envelope and began to read a note in long hand on a piece of resort stationery. The young man had moved five feet away but remained nearby.

Kary scrutinized him. The bellman said, "I was told to remain here for a response."

Kary found the letter difficult to read. The author's long hand was nearly illegible. *Please meet me at the Maitre d'Hotel's desk ASAP. Chief Brown.*

"Please tell Chief Brown that I will meet him there in five minutes."

Kary headed down the main floor hallway in the north wing of the building. He needed to relieve himself. The elegant wood paneling and marble counter tops of the main public restroom were on Kary's top ten list, right there with the men's room at the Madonna Inn in San Luis Obispo. Two minutes later, Kary headed up the hallway leading to the Maitre d'Hotel's desk at the entry to the Main Dining Room.

53

Chief Brown looked anxious as he waited for Kary to arrive at the dining room.

"There you are. I was hoping the bellman would be able to find you. I told him to start in the lobby, then make his way down to the ballroom and so on, until he found you."

"But how did he know what I look like? Did you tell him to look for someone tall, with a build like a professional athlete, and a face like a movie star?"

"Something like that."

Kary figured it was best that he didn't know what the chief told the bellman because, whatever he had said, the young man had no trouble finding him.

"Why are we here, Chief?"

"To talk with Armand Desmoreau."

"And who is Armand Desmoreau?"

"Laureli Hopkins' father. I can't believe that fact escaped me. He must have three daughters. I thought there were just two. At any rate, Mr. Capstone's secretary Betty Binder was looking at yesterday's paper when I walked into the GM's office a while ago. Betty's the one who told me about their relationship."

"This is great news, but I wish we knew about this yesterday," Kary replied.

"It wouldn't have done us any good. Armand took the afternoon off after Laureli's announcement and was gone all day yesterday, too."

"That's interesting. Do think it's just a coincidence?"

"That's just something we'll have to ask Armand."

As if on cue, Armand Desmoreau entered the dining room from behind the barrier along the north wall of the main Dining Room.

"Bonjour, mes amis," he offered with a smile. While Armand generally said his hellos and goodbyes in French, the language of his Quebecois immigrant family, he spoke English passably, although heavily spiced with an accent.

"Hello, Armand. It's good to see you," the chief replied.

"And how is my fav'rite policeman, today?"

"Not a policeman, Armand, merely a security officer."

"But the chief security officer, mon ami."

"Armand, I'd like you to meet Kary Turnell. He's a professor at the university. He'd like to ask you a few questions." about the woman we found dead in the shrubbery."

"C'est un pleasure', Monsieur Desmoreau," Kary offered the best French he could muster.

"Hon, hon! Vous parlez Francais, Monsieur Turnell, non?"

"Un peu, and only un peu I'm afraid," Kary replied quickly. He could feel his face getting warm as it always did when he tried to use another language.

"That is fine. I'm grateful for the effort," Desmoreau replied.

Seeking to quickly change the subject, Kary told the maitre d'hotel he must be very proud his daughter was a candidate for congress.

"Oui, I am very proud of her."

Kary could see no reason to delay asking the man when he had last seen his daughter.

"Why do you ask me this; did my Laureli do something wrong?"

"No, not at all. No one has seen Laureli since she walked out of her meeting unexpectedly late yesterday afternoon."

"Mon dieu," he exclaimed. "I left here right after the announcement. I had no idea she was not still here."

"So you didn't see her between the time of the announcement and right now?" Kary asked.

"No. I did not see my daughter. But that is not particularly surprising."

"It's not?" the chief asked.

"No."

"May I ask why?"

"If you must know, my daughter and I are not very close. You see, my daughter's mother Lucy and I separated more than twenty years ago. Lucy was a difficult woman to live with and, like most men, I had needs which she no longer served. We argued about this for two years before I decided I'd had enough. One day when Lucy and the girls were away shopping, I moved out."

"How did the girls handle that?"

"Worse than I ever would have imagined," Armand replied sadly. "My daughters and I had been very close. They were their daddy's little girls, but all that changed after I left their mother."

"What do you mean?"

"My daughters took their mother's side. They didn't understand that Lucy had a large part in pushing me away. As far as they were concerned, I had abandoned them. They wanted nothing to do with me. In fact, when Lucy took her maiden name—Dutton—Sara, my older daughter did the same. Matthew, my son, kept my name. He's the only one I remained close to, that is until Laureli married Bob Hopkins."

"That changed things between you?" Kary asked.

"Somewhat. We're still not close. But at least Laureli will call me now and then. To Sara, I'm dead."

"I'm very sorry, Armand," the chief said. "However, I must also congratulate you."

"Congratulate me? But why?"

"Because you've managed to keep all of this to yourself. In most cases, everyone here knows one another's business. All it takes is for one person to learn about you and it spreads all over the resort." Looking at Kary he said, "It doesn't matter if it's an affair, a bad medical report, or a case of constipation. Everyone knows everyone else's business around here." Returning his gaze to Armand, he added, "I wish I knew how you kept all of this to yourself all of these years."

"I'm a very private person, Chief. My father was the same way. Perhaps it's one of the reasons my wife withdrew from me." Armand shrugged.

"Do you have any idea if your daughter likes to go off on her own unannounced? Do you have any idea where she could be?" asked Kary

"No, I'm afraid I don't know anything that can help you. Perhaps her mother or sister can help you, but I suspect not."

"Why do you say that?"

"Because Laureli was very much like me. As a little girl, it was easier to get water out of a stone than to get her to tell us anything. Hopefully she's better with her husband than I was with my wife," he said thoughtfully. "I doubt it will help, but here is Sara's telephone number. Would you believe Laureli's campaign manager gave that to me yesterday? I had to learn from a total stranger how to reach a member of my own family."

***

Kary and Chief Brown walked out of the Main Dining Room and headed toward the lobby. Out of curiosity, Kary looked up toward the window where he had first seen the phantom spying on them the day before. There he was. "I don't believe it," Kary cried out. As he started to sprint toward the entryway, the chief yelled after him.

"Kary, stop!"

"It's him, Chief. He was spying on us again."

"I saw him, but he'll be long gone before you can get there. All you're going to accomplish is getting yourself winded."

"Damn!"

At that moment, Lonnie Goss came around the corner as fast as he could move at a walk.

"There you are, Chief. I have something to tell you."

The two men huddled together near the entrance to the Princess Room for thirty seconds. When the chief turned around to face Kary, he was smiling broadly.

"Finally, a break!"

"What did Officer Goss tell you, Chief?"

"They just found Pothead Grandhomme."

54

As Kary had told Chief Brown, the first major break in a case often comes when you least expect it. Such was the circumstance now. Ironically, Laureli Hopkins' announcement affected Paul Grandhomme being taken into custody. Several days earlier, when Mandy Tomkins called the resort requesting a large hall for Laureli's announced candidacy, a chain reaction occurred at the Mount Washington. While the most apparent impact was fostered upon Carolina Sadler's Repatriation League meeting, one other event was forced off site completely. A planned memorial service honoring World War II hero Major David Schmidly could not be accommodated at the resort. It was feared the Schmidly service would have to be moved to a venue in Littleton or North Conway. That was before a member of the New Hampshire Preservation Alliance discovered that Major Schmidly had been an Episcopalian. Once this fact was made known to the Bishop of New Hampshire, the Episcopal Church of the Transfiguration—otherwise known as Stickney's Memorial Chapel—was made available for the ceremony honoring Major Schmidly. The Memorial Chapel had been built in 1907 by Carolyn Stickney. Mrs. Stickney had the church built as a memorial to her late husband Joseph, who was the creator and original owner of the Mount Washington Hotel.

Stickney had built the hotel for optimal luxury and comfort with the intention of attracting the wealthy and elite away from resort communities situated along the New England coast. Accomplishing this necessitated making the kinds of services available that catered to this class. As a result, Stickney's new hotel made bathrooms available in every room, a novelty in July of 1902, and the hotel boasted the first indoor swimming pool. When Stickney died within a year after the hotel opened to the raves of his wealthy clientele, his widow sought to erect a suitable memorial for her husband. The beautiful stone English Tudor chapel which she commissioned has a veranda on its south side providing spectacular scenery as the backdrop for outdoor ceremonies. It was here that the ceremony for Major Schmidly would be held.

In order to ascertain that all was in readiness for Major Schmidly's memorial service, Officer Sandy Thurston was dispatched to open the building and to determine whether the maintenance and housekeeping staffs could be of service in readying the structure for the event. As he was about to make the short drive along Route 302 to the church, Officer Thurston noticed the "check engine" light was blinking. Not wanting to risk burning out his engine, he pulled over and notified a local garage. Officer Thurston approached the church on foot, which turned out to be one of those small quirks of fate that sometimes changes the course of history. In this case, it was to have a substantial impact upon the Dana Cerone investigation. By walking up to the front door of the church, Officer Thurston surprised Paul Grandhomme before he could run away.

"Don't you go anywhere, Paul! I'm going to call your momma." For reasons only he could understand, Officer Thurston called Mrs. Grandhomme first, then called his own boss, Chief Brown, to say that he had apprehended the missing kitchen worker. When Chief Brown and Kary arrived at the church, they found Officer Thurston waiting outside the church. When asked why, Thurston told Chief Brown that Mrs. Grandhomme had asked him to do so.

Not bothering to ask how Mrs. Grandhomme had arrived at the scene before Kary and he had, the two men entered the building in time to see Paul, his buttocks bared, about to bend over his mother's knee. Mrs. Grandhomme had ordered her son to remove the belt from his pants and was about to brandish it on his bare behind.

"Hold it right there, Helen! Paul, stand up and pull up your pants right now," Chief Brown called out. Paul stood up, his lower body exposed for all to see. He looked at his mother then at Chief Brown and Kary, not knowing what to do next.

"Mrs. Grandhomme, you can't beat your son," Kary said.

"To hell I can't, stranger. He's my son and he deserves to be punished. I'm his mother and it's my job to do 'er."

"Not like that, Helen," the chief quickly interjected. "There are laws against corporal punishment in this state. If you beat that boy's behind, Joe Crandall is going to arrest you and put you in jail for a long time."

"Whatterya talkin' about, Browny. I've been beaten this here boy's behind since he was two years old and I ain't gonna stop now. He's gone an' disobeyed me. He got to be punished."

Kary was quick to follow up. "Do you want to spend the next ten years in jail, Mrs. Grandhomme? Because that's exactly what will happen if you're arrested for beating him."

"And we mean you can't beat him now or any other time, Helen," the chief added. "Now you go back home and we'll talk to your son."

Reluctantly, Helen Grandhomme handed the still naked Paul back his belt and instructed him to "put yer breeches back on." As she stood up, she fixed a concerned look on Chief Brown and asked, "You goin' have him back home tonight, ain't ya?"

"We need to question the boy, Helen. Depending on what he tells us, I'll either bring him home myself or he may need to be turned over to Joe Crandall. I promise I'll let you know either way."

"Sounds fair," she replied. Then she looked at her son and said, "You behave yerself Paulie. Ya' hear?"

"Yes ma'm," Paul replied.

With that, Helen Grandhomme strode purposefully from the church.

As they waited for her to depart, Kary wondered what it would take for people to perceive Paul Grandhomme as a man—a thirty-three-year-old man—not as a boy. Chief Brown was wondering what had possessed Officer Thurston to call Mrs. Grandhomme, then compound the problem by leaving her alone with her son.

55

The two men didn't waste any time trying to interrogate Paul Grandhomme once his mother left the room; however, if they expected him to be contrite, they were in for a surprise. Finally freed from the threat of one of his mother's beatings, Paul Grandhomme exhibited passive-aggressive behavior.

"Listen to me, Paul," the chief began.

"My name's Pothead," he retorted.

"It will be better for you if you answer our questions. We're trying to keep you out of trouble, young man."

"I don't have to answer nothing."

Chief Brown looked over to Kary, a help-me-out-here look on his face. Kary could only imagine the young man's humiliation at being seen with his pants down, a grown man about to be spanked by his mother. Experience told Kary he had better not waste time. The longer Paul Grandhomme had to mull over his humiliation, the less likely he was going to cooperate with them.

"Hello, Pothead. My name is Kary Turnell." Kary offered his hand to the young man. After looking at it for what seemed like an eternity to Kary, Paul grasped his hand. His grip was insubstantial. "Chief Brown and I are not here to harm you and we would like to help you if we can."

"I don't need no help," was his reply.

"Well, actually, Pothead, yes, you do. You know that woman who you found dead in the bushes by the swimming pool the other night? Some people think you may have hurt her."

At the mention of the dead body, Pothead wrapped himself in a fetal position and began to rock. He mumbled something that was indiscernible to both men.

"I'm afraid I didn't understand you, Pothead. What did you just say?"

"I didn't do anything to that lady. I told the police where she was, was all."

"But then you ran away. That makes people wonder why you would do that."

"I ran because I was scared."

Chief Brown put his hand on the boy's shoulder. His grip was firm but warm and supportive. "Pothead, a bunch of folks saw someone walking on the roof and the fire escapes. Was that you?"

"Not me... lady in red."

"What did you just say, Pothead."

"I wasn't on the roof. I get dizzy up high. It was the lady in red."

Kary knew from experience this could be a key point in the investigation of Dana's death. He also knew if they pushed Pothead too hard he might refuse to tell them anything else. So Kary made eye contact with the chief, and then, placing a hand on his own chest, he signaled for his colleague to allow him to ask the questions. The chief blinked once to let him know that he understood. All of this went unobserved by Paul Grandhomme.

"Let's talk about what you saw two nights ago."

"You mean down by the outdoor pool?"

"Yes. Why were you down there?" Kary asked.

"Sometimes when it gets tough I go down there to be alone."

"Do you mean it gets tough at work?"

"Yeah. Sometimes the other guys pick on me. And they laugh at me, too."

"That isn't very nice, Pothead. I don't like it when people laugh at me either."

"You mean people laugh at you, too?"

"Yes. Everyone gets laughed at sometime, Pothead. I know this may be hard for you to understand, but people who laugh at other people are usually afraid about something."

"Afraid. You mean Tommy and Willie and those guys are afraid? Are they afraid of me?" he asked.

"No, not you necessarily. They may be afraid that they're not doing their jobs well or that someone they care about— maybe a girlfriend—doesn't like them. There are all kinds of reasons people are afraid. So you should never feel you're the only one who is."

"Gee," Paul said without much energy.

Kary hoped he had earned enough of Paul's trust so he could resume asking questions which would help the young man to remember the episode from two nights before he sought to escape.

"Pothead."

"Yeah." While not making eye contact with Kary, it was apparent the young man was still engaged in listening to him.

"I want you to tell me why you were at the pool two nights ago."

"I told you, I go there to be alone and to get away from the mean boys in the kitchen."

"Do you remember what the boys were bothering you about before you went down to the pool?"

"They were talking about girls and how real' soft they are, and how they kiss, and how no girl was ever going to be interested in me."

"And that kind of talk bothers you, doesn't it, Pothead?"

"Yeah, I— I—"

"You'd like a girl friend too, wouldn't you?"

Paul Grandhomme didn't answer at first. The topic of girls was new to him, and it was embarrassing for him to talk about them. "Yeah, I suppose so."

"You could find a nice girl someday. You know that, don't you?"

"No, I can't! That's what the other boys in the kitchen said anyway."

"That's just the fear we were discussing, Pothead. I know you find this hard to believe, but those boys are unsure of themselves around girls and so they're just voicing that by making fun of you."

"I don't understand," Paul replied.

"Look at it this way, Pothead. If I were afraid to do something, like climb up to the top of the roof, I would say that you're afraid, instead of admitting that it's me who has the fear. Those boys are unsure of their ability to attract girls, so they say that you can't get a girl." Kary knew he wasn't going to get Paul to understand the concept, but he hoped he'd been able to relax the young man enough to make him comfortable enough to keep talking.

Whatever amount of Kary's dialogue Paul was able to understand, it was having the desired effect. "I was sitting in the bushes on the opposite side from where the lady was laying. I think I was sleeping when I heard a noise in the bushes across the sidewalk."

"What happened next?" Kary asked.

"I stuck my head up in the air just a little. Sometimes when the boys in the kitchen know where I'm hiding they throw water balloons at me, the ones that look like white hot dogs."

Assholes, Kary muttered under his breath.

"I was afraid they knew where I was hiding."

"When you looked up, what did you see?"

"The bushes across from me were still moving. But when I saw the woman in red standing there I was scared, so I got down like this and closed my eyes so she couldn't see me." Paul showed Kary and Chief Brown the fetal position similar to the one he had been in ten minutes before.

"Can you describe what the woman in red looked like?" Kary asked.

Paul sat there rocking for what seemed like an eternity before he answered. "She was in a red jacket and pants," was all he said.

"Could you see her face or her hair?"

"Face. No. No face. Her hair was the color of a bee's honey."

"That's good. You're doing a great job, Pothead. How about jewelry, was she wearing a necklace or maybe some earrings?"

"Her neck was naked but her ears were sparkling."

"Could you see the color of her earrings, Pothead?"

"They were the same color as my mother's knives and forks."

"You mean they were silver?"

"Yeah, like the knives and forks."

Kary was about to ask Paul if he could remember anything else when he saw that the young man was holding his feet and rocking slowly back and forth. So he put his hand on Paul's shoulder and said, "You've done very well, Pothead. Thank you. Would you like Chief Brown to take you home now? Your mother will be worried."

"No home. Not home. No!"

At this point, Chief Brown came over and spoke quietly to Paul Grandhomme. "Pothead, it's okay. You can go back home now. Your mother knows she can never hit you again. Besides, when I tell her what a good boy you've been she'll probably make you a great big dessert. You'd like that wouldn't you, Pothead?"

"A big dessert. That's nice," he said.

Then come with me and I'll bring you to your mom. The chief helped Paul to his feet and started him walking along the path. Then he turned to Kary and said, "Just in case, I'm going to give Helen Grandhomme a quick primer on mothering in the twenty-first century. I'll see you in about an hour."

Kary smiled and waved to the chief, then went to find Officer Thurston who was waiting to take him back to the resort. It was time to check up on Maya again.

56

As they were returning to the hotel, Kary didn't know what to say to Officer Thurston. The officer knew he had really screwed up and was going to be reprimanded when the chief had time. He only hoped Mr. Capstone wasn't going to be notified. A meeting with the general manger would surely mean a letter in his file, and might even result in his suspension without pay. That was the last thing he needed. Thurston and his wife had recently taken over care of their grandson, Luke. The Thurston's son and daughter-in-law were going through a tough spell and had asked his parents to look after the boy for a while. With an extra mouth to feed and a growing stack of bills to pay, the last thing the officer could afford was an extended period without pay.

Kary looked over at the officer. He was in his mid to late fifties. The expression on his face showed he was extremely upset. Kary wondered whether he should say something to the officer, then thought the better of it. As the car approached the entry to the golf course, Officer Thurston's radio squawked. The officer grabbed his radio and spoke quietly into the mouthpiece. He listened for less than a half minute, then returned the radio to its holster. Turning slightly toward Kary he said, "GM wants to see you right away."

Kary almost asked the officer if he, too, was to be included in the meeting, but Thurston beat him to the punch.

"Not me, though, thank goodness," he said with a wry smile. "But this day is going to suck."

Kary figured the worst the officer would receive was a stern verbal lecture from Chief Brown, which he deserved. Hopefully the anguish he was feeling would affect Sandy's judgment in the future.

***

Kary received a subdued greeting from Tom Capstone. He was invited to sit down in one of the two wooden captain's chairs that had been strategically placed a substantial distance from his desk. Capstone used this office for his meetings with the resort's staff, whereas he met with hotel guests and VIPs in his small conference room. In the latter chamber, plush leather chairs and a small mahogany table created a more intimate environment. The formality of the setting where Kary and the GM were meeting was designed to create the perception of physical and professional distance between the general manager and those who had been called on the proverbial carpet. Most arguments or concerns were resolved in favor of the general manager within moments after a staff member entered that room; however, if Kary felt intimidated by this venue, he didn't let on.

"So, Kary, where are we with these matters you and Chief Brown have been pursuing?"

Drawing upon a baseball analogy Kary replied, "We're one for three, Tom."

"Please bring me up to date."

Kary told Tom Capstone they had found Paul Grandhomme and, based upon the information he had added to that of the other eye witnesses, it appeared the person who attacked Dana Cerone and the phantom, as he'd begun calling his adversary, were one and the same.

"Interesting. Are you any closer to identifying who this person is?"

"Yes. Based upon the eyewitness account of Ms. Sadler and Mr. Growscorn, plus the account of Paul Grandhomme, the person who attacked Dana was a woman wearing a red pants suit."

"But can we trust those accounts, particularly Mr. Grandhomme's."

"I believe so, yes, Tom."

"And what about all of this roof-walking business; what's up with that?"

"I think our phantom is spying on us, particularly Maya."

"Spying? Why would someone be spying on Mrs. Lassiter?"

"For the time being that eludes me; however, the spying began right after your security staff moved Maya from the room she had been sharing with Dana Cerone. It also occurred in conjunction to a break-in to Maya's room."

"A break-in? Why wasn't I told of this?"

"Look Tom, with all due respect, Chief Brown and I are doing the investigative work of a team of six or more. Chief Brown would be the one handling a break-in anyway wouldn't he?"

Tom Capstone nodded.

"And he's handled it quite well, I can assure you."

"A possible murder, spying, a man lurking on the roof tops, a break-in! Where does this all lead?"

"Unless my powers of deduction have gone haywire, everything that has been occurring, including the now solved disappearance of Paul Grandhomme, relates to the death of Dana Cerone."

"And what, if anything, have you learned about Laureli Hopkins?"

Kary related what they had learned from Armand Desmoreau, then added, "That's about all we know. It's still possible she's visiting with friends or out campaigning somewhere." Kary chose not to divulge Milly Spaulding's contention that the Hopkins marriage was on the rocks. "I'll have to put the Hopkins disappearance on hold until the chief and I find all we can about Dana Cerone's death."

Tom Capstone thought about what he'd just heard for several minutes. As he did, he stared alternately at Kary and at a large oil painting of Joseph Stickney that hung behind his desk. When he finally spoke, it was with a tone of concern and respect for Kary Turnell.

"What you've turned up in such a short time is phenomenal, a true testimony to your intelligence and perseverance."

Kary thanked Capstone. He assured him he had been receiving a lot of help from both Chief Brown and Maya Lassiter.

"Yes, Mrs. Lassiter has acted with amazing grace under the circumstances," he agreed.

"It's a family trait."

Capstone interjected, "Wouldn't you agree it's time to call in the proper authorities?"

The buzzer on Tom Capstone's intercom system went off. Capstone excused himself. He picked up his telephone receiver.

"He is. That's terrific timing. We were just beginning to talk about him. Yes, please send him right in."

The door to the GM's office opened. Sergeant Joe Crandall walked in with purpose.

Tom Capstone stood and extended his hand to the sergeant. His demeanor was substantially warmer and less formal than that with which he had received Kary ten minutes earlier.

"We were just discussing whether it was time to bring in the Carroll police when my intercom buzzed."

"Funny how those things work," Crandall said without smiling. "I was just talking to Browny. He told me how Paul Grandhomme was apprehended and questioned." Then looking at Kary he added, "Browny's going to be tied up for another fifteen minutes or so. He asked me to let you know if I saw you, Kary. Seems Mrs. Grandhomme required a bit more convincing than he'd assumed."

Before Kary could say anything, Capstone fixed his gaze on Crandall and said, "I'm thinking it's time for you and your men to get involved in this, Joe."

"I figured you might have reached that conclusion, Tom. That's exactly why I've driven over here."

"So you're in agreement?"

"Not exactly, and let me explain before you say anything." Tom Capstone didn't look happy but he nodded.

"Based upon what I'm hearing from Browny, Professor Turnell here is better at making tactful inquiries into a matter like this than anyone I can offer you, Tom. We're just a small town police force that is in over our heads with this Native American Festival in Twin Mountain. And I have to tell you, my so called detectives spend as much time directing traffic as collecting evidence. While Kary isn't a licensed professional investigator, I trust what he's doing. Besides, if you go to the next step and call in the Staties or the Feds, you're going to spook a hell of a lot of guests, not to mention the person who whacked Mrs. Cerone. The first uniform he sees walking around here with a purpose and he's gone. Am I right about that, Kary?"

Kary nodded.

Crandall wasn't finished. "Look, Tom, unless I miss my guess, this guy is hanging around here for a reason. Otherwise he would have been out of here long ago. The best thing about having Kary look into this is he doesn't look threatening." Crandall smiled at Kary as he said this.

Kary considered puffing out his chest and asking Crandall what he'd meant by that remark, but discretion was still his middle name.

"You look like a geek who's snooping around with his sister-in-law. On the surface, you don't appear to be any threat at all. And that's to our advantage."

Tom Capstone listened intently to what Sergeant Crandall had said. "All right, Joe, you've made a convincing argument. Kary, I apologize if it sounded like I didn't trust you. Nothing could—"

Kary cut him off, "I understand, Tom. You're trying to do the best you can for your resort."

"I appreciate your understanding, Kary. Do you agree with Sergeant Crandall's assertion that having you continue is the best course of action?"

"I agree with everything the sergeant has just said, except for one thing."

"What's that?" Sergeant Crandall asked.

"Our suspect isn't a he. We're looking for a she."

57

The message Chief Brown sent to Kary indicated he would be returning to the resort by noon. He had asked Kary to meet him in the Main Dining Room. As Kary sat with Maya waiting for the chief to arrive, he brought her up to date on what had been learned.

"So, Sergeant Crandall is going to let you continue to lead the investigation? I'm so proud of you, Kary."

"I'm not certain there is any reason for you to be proud. Besides, I don't have unlimited time to stay up here. I've cancelled one Monday-Wednesday-Friday class and one Tuesday-Thursday one. Tomorrow's a university holiday, but I really need to get back to my students after that."

"I can relate," Maya replied. "After I called my principal and told him about Dana he told me to take as much time as I need. I have a ton of sick days to use, but it's hard to reestablish continuity with my students once I'm out a few days. Fortunately my sub is a native speaker, so my students will actually be learning some Italian while I'm away."

"To be honest, my students can probably do just fine without me right now. They have projects to work on. To tell you the truth, I'm just glad Nya is away right now."

A couple of days earlier the latter statement would have made Maya bristle. But she had been convinced Kary was a changed man. His next words confirmed her trust. "Because, if she were at home right now, I couldn't stand being away from her. This way, we're both away at the same time. That's been pretty fortuitous, I'd say."

Hearing this, Maya felt a sense of joy. The new Kary Nya had been bragging to her about was the real deal. At that moment, Maya felt closer to the man sitting across from her than she had for years.

Changing the subject, Maya asked Kary if he had any news about Laureli Hopkins' whereabouts.

"Not much, I'm afraid. We're beginning to agree with Milly Spauldings' suspicion that all is not well with Ms. Hopkins' marriage. It seems Mr. Hopkins and their campaign manager, Mandy Tomkins, are not terribly concerned where Laureli is, as long as it's not near them."

"You think they're having an affair?"

"I don't have any evidence that that's the case. Circumstantially, it's beginning to make sense. Our candidate came here alone, gave her speech, and arranged to stay for a two-day conference. The husband opted not to stay with her in this beautiful resort, but left in the company of a more attractive woman. Meanwhile, the candidate remained in her meeting only until the press left. The next thing you know, the candidate vanished into thin air. Her father isn't very close to her, so he's not surprised she left without saying goodbye. Telephone calls to her mother and sister, thus far, have revealed nothing that can help us."

"Wow!"

"Wow, indeed. Frankly, we can't rule out the possibility Laureli Hopkins may have taken her own life."

Do you think it's possible she's the second victim of Dana's killer?"

"At this point, anything's possible. What's more likely

is she's found some little out-of-the-way motel where she's passed out drunk."

"Kary Turnell! Honestly, you men can be so insensitive sometimes."

"Not insensitive, my dear sister-in-law, just preoccupied."

Laureli Hopkins' situation aside, Maya was as surprised as Tom Capstone and Joe Crandall to learn that Kary now suspected a woman to be the principal suspect. "Do you have anyone in particular in mind?" she asked.

"Not right now. I think we need to consider whether Dana had any enemies in your teachers' organization."

"The NHTAP? I don't think that's very likely."

"Why not?"

"Because we attend these things to learn how to prepare our students to take their AP tests. We sit, listen to people tell us about techniques, drink coffee, and eat dinner together in small groups. That kind of activity doesn't make a person a whole lot of enemies. Now, being a member of the board is another ball of wax. In fact, if I could kill our chairperson and get away with it—"

"Did Dana have any dealings with the board?"

"None, except for having to listen to me whine about it. It's a miracle Dana didn't strangle me before now."

"Sweet little Dana; I can't imagine her doing anything like that."

"Sweet little Dana! That's pretty funny, Kary."

"What do you mean?"

"Don't get me wrong, Dana was wonderful—my best friend." Maya hesitated for a moment to stifle the tears that were brimming in her eyes. "But, Dana was feisty and physical, too. She wasn't reluctant to get right in someone's face if they said the wrong thing. Hell, one time she made Mr. Denton, the gym teacher, back down after he made a stupid comment about women's place in the workforce." The thought of little Dana Cerone confronting the jockish Sal Denton actually made Maya smile. "You'd think he had waltzed into a nest of hornets; that's how fast he ran out of the teacher's room."

Kary pondered what he'd just heard. "This creates a whole new set of possibilities."

"Such as?"

"What if Dana got into an argument with another teacher, not that guy Benton, but a woman. And maybe this was a woman with a temperament like Dana's, except bigger and stronger?"

"Do you think that's what happened?"

"I'm just saying it's a possibility. There is, though, one problem with that theory."

"Which is?".

"Whoever did this appears to be the same person who is crawling all over the resort."

"So?"

"So, this person has to be someone who really knows the ins and outs of this hotel."

"And that's the kind of information someone would only have if she'd worked at the resort?"

"Exactly."

***

Chief Brown looked exasperated when he sat down with Kary and Maya.

"Tough day, Chief?"

"You wouldn't believe it. I've just spent most of the last two hours convincing Helen Grandhomme she has to stop beating her son. I think I finally was able to scare her into stopping."

"How, by threatening her with jail time?"

"No. That wasn't working. She was convinced the whippings were part of her responsibility as a parent."

"Even assuming that were true, isn't her son in his thirties?" Maya asked.

"He is. But you won't believe what actually worked. I told Helen Paul was a fully grown man who was undergoing changes. I also told her he was feeling his oats, and if she kept this up she might be the one being stripped and whipped, not Paul."

Kary had to laugh at this preposterous suggestion. "And that worked?!"

The Chief leaned back in his chair and smiled. "Time will tell, but I'd put even money on it. Helen Grandhomme is a religious woman. The thought of finding herself in that predicament scared the living hell out of her."

Putting the discussion of Helen Grandhomme aside, Kary brought Chief Brown up to date on his meeting with the GM and Sergeant Crandall. When he heard that Joe Crandall was allowing Kary and him to continue their own investigation unimpeded, the chief whistled.

"I thought for sure they were going to tell us to go back to our day jobs," he said.

"Me, too, Chief. But no such luck."

As the three of them continued to rehash the case, Maya said to the chief, "Kary thinks we're looking for a woman." Kary explained his rationale yet again. When Kary concluded, the chief simply said, "Then you'd better listen to what else Paul Grandhomme had to tell me."

As Kary and Maya drew nearer, Chief Brown looked at Kary and asked, "Do you remember when we first started talking to Paul in the church?" Kary nodded. "And do you remember how he said the lady in red was climbing on the fire escapes?"

"I do."

"After I freaked out at Helen Grandhomme, she left us alone for a while. So I asked Pothead if he knew who the lady in red is."

"What did he say, Chief?" Maya asked.

"He didn't know her name, but said we should talk with Julie Woods. Paul thinks she knows the lady in red."

With the mention of Julie Woods' name, Maya felt a sudden surge of nausea. Concerned about the sudden change in his sister-in-law's complexion, Kary asked her what was wrong.

"Nothing...actually everything," she said. "I know Julie Woods, in fact, I talked with her yesterday just before Bud Black came out from the kitchen." Maya put her head in her hands and muttered, "I can't believe this."

"Believe what, Maya?" Kary asked.

"Do you remember the story I told you about a student who pretended she had cancer? It was more than ten years ago."

Kary had to admit the story didn't sound familiar to him.

"You've got to be kidding! That's all I talked about back then. First Dana and I thought this girl was dying. Then it turned out she was using the two of us to get ahead in school. I've never been able to share the same level of trust with a student again, Kary, and neither could Dana."

Kary muttered something about how he wasn't particularly with it ten or so years ago. Maya realized she was opening up old wounds with her brother-in-law. Back then, Kary was in the beginning throes of his writer's block. It had been about this time that he distanced himself from everyone.

"I'm sorry, Kary. Of course, you didn't know—"

Kary held up his hand to signal it was okay. He wanted to hear the crux of Maya's story.

"So this Julie Woods was the girl who pretended to have cancer?" he asked.

"No. Julie was the girl's best friend. Her name was Lori Dark."

"Lori Dark, Lori Dark," Kary repeated. "There's something familiar about that name. Chief, wasn't that one of the names we saw scrawled on the former employees wall upstairs?"

Chief Brown indicated it was and reminded Kary he had said at the time that Lori Dark may have been one of Maya's students.

"Was she ever!" Maya interjected. "Oh, Kary, if Lori Dark is here, I don't want to see her."

"I understand. But all of this is beginning to make sense. This Lori Dark is the link between Dana and you. You told me that Dana was aggressive. Do you think she might have had a fight with this Lori Dark?"

"I don't think Dana would want to have anything to do with Lori, not any more than I would."

"But what if they accidentally ran into one another on the lower terrace?"

Maya sobbed at the thought. "I don't know, Kary. I honestly don't know."

"Well, one thing is for certain—we need to talk with this Julie Woods and we need to do it sooner than later."

"Consider it done." Chief Brown said. "Let's set it up in my office. I'll have Officer Goss bring Julie to us."

"Not Officer Thurston?" Kary asked with a smile on his face.

"Let's not go there," the chief replied.

As they walked toward the security office, Kary was already beginning to plan his interrogation of Julie Woods. He knew full well the next half hour could provide the key to unraveling the circumstances surrounding Dana Cerone's death.

PART IV
INTERROGATION

58

For months, Maya and Dana had looked forward to their third day together at the Mount Washington Resort. This was to be the day the pair was going to sit by the outdoor swimming pool, relax, and laugh together. When Dana saw the picture of the facility on the resort's web site she had referred to it as a killer pool. Little did she know she would take her last breath within several yards of its azure waters. Maya made no attempt to block out thoughts of her friend. As tears streamed down her face, she remembered all of the good times the two had shared. There were so many hearty laughs, tears of joy, and moments of anguish. It was been uncanny how the same students who gravitated toward Maya also adored Dana, and vice versa. There were so many good kids. Why did she find herself focusing on Lori Dark?

Maya couldn't shake the image of Lori sitting in her Italian classroom and telling the two compassionate teachers about the battle with cancer she was waging. The girl's words had saddened, sickened, and ultimately aged the two women because it hit so close to home for both of them. Both Dana and Maya lost their mothers to cancer. As Maya sat there by the pool, the memories of caring for her dying mother all of those months were vivid; it was as though Nya and she were back by their mom's bedside. The prone figure of Maya's mother was an image she would never be able to erase.

Her mother, who had been so vibrant—still shopping, eating lunch out, and even playing golf as an eighty year-old—until the disease ultimately sentenced her to a few terrible months in bed. Per her mother's wishes, Maya and Nya cared for their mother at home so she could drink in the sights and sounds of her children and grandchildren until she would breathe her last. Dana's mother had fought—and lost—a similar battle. To think that a student who was so special to both of them would feign the very disease that had curtailed the lives of the women who were so very dear to them. How could she?!

There would be no escape from these memories as long as Maya remained in her chaise lounge by the outdoor pool. What could have been such a peaceful place to sit with Dana and stare at the majestic Presidentials, instead was a launching ground for disturbing thoughts. Maya suddenly stood up and sought refuge in another part of the resort. It was an action that was being watched carefully.

59

Julie Woods arrived at the security office in the company of Officer Goss. She walked in with a scowl on her face.

"I really can't stay here long, Chief Brown. Cap has an attitude." Chief Brown took that to mean that Ken Kizer, the captain of Julie's serving team, was not pleased to have her leave the dining room this close to dinner.

"Please sit down, Julie," Chief Brown pointed toward a gray Steelcase office chair. "If you're cooperative, you'll be back at work in several minutes."

"Cooperative? What's this about?"

While Kary had never set eyes on Julie Woods before, he participated in enough interrogations to know this young woman had a pretty good idea why she was being questioned. The look in her eyes told him that Julie was nervous. What was she so nervous about?

Chief Brown decided to pull out all of the stops, so he introduced Kary as a special investigator.

"But what does a special investigator want with me?" Julie looked at Kary through brown eyes that were as big as saucers. She began to twirl her hair nervously between her right thumb and index finger. Clearly there was something on this woman's mind.

"I'm here to look into the death of a woman who may

have been killed here several nights ago," he began.

"Killed! But I don't know—"

Kary held up his hand and said, "To save time, young lady, I recommend you allow me to ask the questions and you just answer them. Do you understand?"

Julie nodded.

"Let's begin by having you tell me a little about yourself. Where are you from?"

Julie seemed impatient. Why was this guy asking about where she lives? Why didn't he just get to the point so she could get the hell out of there? "I'm from Carroll, just up the road."

"So that means you attended Crawford Notch High, is that correct?"

Julie slouched in her chair. "Yeah, I went to Crawford Notch High. I graduated in '95."

"Did you know Mrs. Cerone while you were there?"

"Yeah, she was my junior year science teacher."

"Did you get along well with Mrs. Cerone?"

"Yeah, she and Mrs. Lassiter were my two favorite teachers. Wait a minute! You don't think I had anything to do with—" Julie began to sob. Her voice grew weak, "hurting her, do you?"

Chief Brown broke in, "No one is accusing you of anything, Julie. Please answer Dr. Turnell's questions."

"I'm not accusing you of anything, young lady, but we will need to hear anything you know about Mrs. Cerone's death."

"But I already told you, I—" Kary silenced her by placing his right index finger to his lips.

"What was your relationship with Mrs. Cerone like?"

"I loved Mrs. Cerone. She was so good to Lori and me. She and Mrs. Lassiter were like our moms, only they never yelled at us."

"And Lori is?"

"Lori Dark. She was, is, my best friend."

Kary absorbed this information for a moment then asked how long Julie had been working at the resort.

"I started here my junior year of high school right after I turned sixteen. Let's see, that's about fourteen years now."

"Was it difficult to get a job here at such a young age?"

"No, they always need people to bus tables, clean the kitchen, that sort of thing."

"Still and all," Chief Brown interjected, "there are a lot of applicants for the jobs here."

"Really?" Kary replied. Fixing his gaze at Julie, he asked, "What gave you an advantage?"

Sensing Kary might be willing to go easier on her than Chief Brown, Julie's expression changed from a frown to a slight smile. "I had an in," she said.

"And what was your in?"

"Lori's father worked here, still does," she replied.

At that moment, the door to the security office swung open and an angry Ken Kizer stormed in, followed by a red faced Officer Goss.

"I thought I told you we didn't want to be disturbed," the chief said while glaring at both men.

"Sorry, Chief, he just bulled past me."

"Look, Chief Brown, I don't know what the hell you want with my waitress, but we have a job to do up in the dining room, you know."

"I apologize, Ken. We need to ask Julie some questions about an investigation we're conducting."

"Did Julie do something wrong?" Kizer asked while fixing both the chief and his waitress with an angry stare.

"No, Ken, but she may have some information that's integral to this investigation."

"Is that true, Julie? Do you have information that's important to these gentlemen's investigation?"

Julie was relieved to be rescued. Thanks to Ken Kizer, Kary and Chief Brown were about to be pre-empted from finding out why. "No Cap; I've been trying to tell them that."

"Then you come upstairs with me young lady. I need you in the dining room. We have two hundred people who are going to want to be served in a little over an hour." Then turning to Chief Brown he said, "We have a resort to run here, Chief. I'll have Julie back down here right after dinner and dessert have been served. That's a promise. Of course, if you have a problem with that, then call Mr. Capstone. If he doesn't like it, he can have my job. Frankly I don't care. Good day gentlemen."

Before Chief Brown could respond, Ken and Julie had vanished and the door was closed firmly behind them.

"Wow! Was that guy ever in the Marines?" Kary asked.

"I don't know, but he should have been."

"I'm tempted to call Tom Capstone and get that young woman right back down here," Kary said. "I think there's much more to her story than we know. It apparently has something to do with this Lori Dark person. Does she still work here?"

"No, she hasn't worked here in years. You know, it's too bad Thurston pulled that nonsense today, because he's the one who's been around here the longest."

"How about the personnel files? Do you think they can tell us more about her?"

"I'll find out what I can."

"Meanwhile, I'm going to go and find Maya. She may be able to spread a little more light on this, even though Lori Dark is not exactly her favorite subject."

***

While Chief Brown placed a call to personnel, Kary went down to the outdoor swimming pool to talk with Maya. Not finding her there, he looked through the windows at the deck surrounding the indoor swimming pool, but there was no sign of Maya. Without a sense of urgency, Kary walked through the lower level of the resort peering into the shops, Stickney's Restaurant, the ice cream parlor, and even the real estate office, where a public computer was situated. No Maya. Now beginning to be concerned, Kary ignored the elevator and quickly climbed the stairs to the resort's main level. He searched the Main Dining Room and the Sun Dining Room then retraced his steps down the corridor leading to the registration desk. Reaching for a house phone, he dialed Room 317 and waited until the answering service picked up. Kary left a short message asking Maya to meet him at the security office as soon as possible. He hadn't wanted to alarm her, but Kary's concern for his sister-in-law had definitely colored the tone of his message.

"Damn, if only our cell phones worked up here, but there's no reception at all. I'll just have to keep searching." There was a rumor one could get cell phone reception by going out to the flag poles in front of the resort and facing west. It hadn't worked. Besides, even if it did, Maya would have to be standing right next to him with her cell phone on, too.

Thinking Maya may have gone to use the public restroom, he decided to wait by the women's room door in the north wing. When Maya didn't appear after several minutes, Kary walked, then ran, toward the Conservatory. There still was no sign of Maya. He pushed open the door to the east side porch and stepped outside. Looking left and right, then peering toward the tennis courts, golf course, and the outdoor swimming pool, his sister-in-law was nowhere to be seen.

With a momentary pang of guilt about the awful thoughts

he had about Maya over the past several years, Kary looked down at the shrubbery where Dana Cerone's body was found two days earlier. There was no body in the bushes to be seen, but remembering how Maya's and the chief's description of the way the ferns had wrapped their fronds around Dana's inert figure, Kary felt the urge to take a closer look. First, he bolted across the lobby to the west-facing porch and scanned both left and right, then ran down to the grounds below him. Kary was frantic with worry. He realized it wasn't concern over what Nya would think. The last forty-eight hours had brought Maya and Kary as close together as any brother and sister. Kary wasn't about to lose her now. Returning to the lobby, Kary searched the area near the front desk before heading quickly toward the ballroom. To his consternation, neither the ballroom nor any of the small meeting rooms contained a soul. He ran down the stairs and up the path toward the outdoor pool searching among the ferns on either side of the path as he went. Maya had simply disappeared.

60

When Kary returned to the security office, he looked nothing like the cool operator Chief Brown had become used to working beside. Kary's face was red, his hair was matted with sweat, his shirt was coming out of his pants, his tie was askew, and his breathing heavy.

"Holy shit, Kary. What does the other guy look like?"

"A lot better than me, I can assure you."

"Where have you been and where's Maya?"

"I've been running all over the place looking for her. She wasn't by the pool where I expected to find her. I looked in the shops, the dining areas, the internet room, I even called her room."

"She couldn't have just disappeared."

"You wouldn't think so. She promised me she'd stay in the public areas."

"Geez, I hope Thurston's implosion didn't leave her exposed to the person we're after."

Kary dearly hoped not, too. "I just hope she's all right. This just adds to the urgency to find whoever killed Dana."

"At least I have some good news on that front."

"You do. What did you find out?"

"Housekeeping came up big in the search for the missing pillow and blanket we found in the South Tower."

"Great! What do we know?"

"There are three rooms that were missing items and you're going to find this really interesting."

"Don't keep me in suspense, Chief!"

Chief Brown noticed Kary's color, breathing, and energy were returning to normal.

"Erma Hearns gave me this list."

"Isn't Erma the head of housekeeping, the tough old broad you've been telling me about?"

"She's the one. But let me give you a piece of advice. Don't ever let her hear you call her an old broad if you value your health."

"I'd never do anything to hurt a woman's feelings, at least not deliberately. But, come on Chief, is she really that tough?"

"Let's put it this way, if she ever went on that ultimate fighting show on TV, my money's on her."

"Come on. Didn't you tell me she was sixty years old?"

"Yeah, she's about that. She is also one tough broad."

Given the shape he had just found himself to be in, Kary winced at the idea of taking on Erma Hearns, or anyone else for that matter, in a fight on national television.

"So who's on our list?"

"Like I said, three rooms: Mr. Dale Hall in Room 232 was missing a pillow."

"But no blanket?"

"No, and Mr. Hall claims he took it to the golf course to pad the seat of his golf cart. It seems he's been having problems with hemorrhoids. Once the round was over he absent-mindedly left it in the cart."

"That eliminates him from further consideration."

"Yep. Person number two is Nan O'Toole. Nan says she spent most of last evening in the Cave, our resort watering hole. She thinks she saw the blanket before she left the Cave, but hasn't seen it since. Did I mention that Nan has a hangover of gargantuan proportions?"

"That's not much help. Was anyone missing both a pillow and blanket?"

"Yes and that's where this gets interesting."

"Don't just stand there smiling, damn it, whose room is it?"

"Room 317," the chief smiled.

"Maya's room? So the person who broke into Maya's room stole the blanket and pillow we found in the tower?"

"It would appear that way," the chief replied. "I'm not sure this helps us much, but it does narrow things down a bit."

"It does, but not quite the way I'd hoped. I'll tell you this, Chief, I'm more convinced than ever that the relationship between Julie Woods and Lori Dark will hold the key to a lot of this."

***

While the two men sat and tried to reconstruct a puzzle that was still missing too many pieces, Chief Brown's office telephone rang.

As Kary sat waiting intently, the chief was listening to the voice at the other end of the line. Occasionally he would interject, "She did?!" or "That's unbelievable." Kary thought he would leap out of his skin before Chief Brown enlightened him with the news he'd just received. Finally, the chief thanked his caller, hung up the telephone, then turned to Kary.

"You really aren't going to believe this."

"Believe what? Jeezus, Chief, don't keep me in suspense."

"That was Joe Crandall. Take a wild guess who he just heard from."

"How about Laureli Hopkins?"

Chief Brown's face dropped a foot. "How in hell did you know that?"

"Just a lucky guess," he smiled. In truth, Kary might have guessed from the chief's surprised expression that Laureli was the subject of the telephone call—he might have guessed had he not distinctly heard Crandall's gravelly voice through the telephone receiver Chief Brown was holding away from his ear.

"What did Crandall say?" Kary asked.

"You mean you're not going to tell me that, too?" Then consulting his notes, the chief said, "Laureli called Joe Crandall about an hour ago."

"Where's she been keeping herself?"

"She says she's been driving all over the north country campaigning, mostly in little places like Bartlett, Stark, Columbia, Groveton; also, says she'll be back at the hotel in time for dinner tonight."

"Hardly seems to be worth the effort to go all the way up there," Kary replied. "There aren't a lot of votes in the places where she's campaigning. Also, I wonder how she is getting around."

"What do you mean?" the chief asked.

"Remember how Milly Spaulding talked to her husband and campaign manager on the telephone?"

"Yeah."

"Well, according to what they told Milly, Laureli Hopkins didn't have a car up here. She flew up while Bob Hopkins and the campaign manager drove. Unless I'm mistaken, the husband and manager took the car back to Concord with them."

"That means Laureli didn't have a car," the chief said. "But she might have taken the resort shuttle to meet someone with a car."

"I suppose that's true. Find out if your shuttle operator recalls seeing Laureli anytime between two nights ago and this morning, will you?"

"I'm calling upstairs as we speak." A short while later, Chief Brown had his answer—no one answering Laureli Hopkins' description had boarded the shuttle within the last forty-eight hours."

"By the way, did Crandall say where Laureli was calling from?" Kary asked.

Chief Brown consulted his notes. "Yeah, she told him she borrowed a phone at the bookstore in Colebrook."

"I know that place, it's right on Route 3, just before the turn off to The Balsams. In fact, I know the owners. They're a couple of kids who graduated from the university where I teach. They've developed quite a nice store there. In fact, they carry my book. I'll just give them a call and ask how sales are going. And while I'm at it, I'll find out if Laureli did stop by to use the phone."

"Sounds like a plan. Use my phone."

Kary called and spoke to Jane at the bookstore in Colebrook. When he hung up the phone he was deep in thought.

"What is it, Kary?"

"They haven't seen hide nor hair of Laureli Hopkins. They did see a picture of her on the news and Jane said she would have recognized her if she had been there."

"Why go to all the trouble to call Joe Crandall and why tell him she was in Colebrook?"

"Probably to throw us all off the scent."

"But, why?"

"Something happened to Laureli Hopkins since her arrival up here and whatever it was she doesn't want it to be found until she can straighten matters out."

"Do you think she found out her husband and the campaign manager are having an affair?"

"It's possible," Kary replied. "Frankly, Laureli is on my back burner right now. I've got a murder investigation and a missing sister-in-law to worry about. After that's cleared up, I'll be happy to head back to Plymouth while you hunt for your candidate, wherever she's gone to lick her wounds."

***

At that moment, Kary couldn't have known Laureli Hopkins was fretting about the situation she found herself in.

"Damn my luck. I've worked so hard and everything was perfect. My campaign was off to a good start, and Bob and I make a terrific team." In her own mind, Laureli had always been such a creative problem solver, but not this time. Her life was in turmoil, and it appeared to her there was only one way to fix it.

"If she thinks she can get in the way of my life, she's messing with the wrong woman. I may not have handled things very well thus far, but all that is about to change."

61

In this day and age, one might not expect a newspaper to be such a valuable resource to a crime investigator. But that's exactly what a day old copy of the Manchester newspaper proved to be. Kary and Chief Brown were seated in a pair of plush chairs just outside of the ballroom when Kary remembered the section of the previous day's newspaper was folded and placed in the breast pocket of his sport jacket.

"Did you see yesterday's paper, Chief?"

"No, I seldom get the time to read a paper anymore."

"This one has pictures from the tenth's campaign speech," Kary said as he removed the folded New Hampshire section from his pocket.

The chief took a brief look and commented, "She's a tall, rather plain woman, but fills out that blue dress pretty well."

"I hadn't noticed," Kary replied, then added with a smile, "but I'm surprised she didn't wear red, white, and blue to make her campaign appearance."

"Maybe she brought three separate dresses to the resort—a red one, a white one, and a blue one."

"Holy cow! You've just given me an incredible idea, Chief."

"I have?"

"Yes, you have. Ms. Hopkins stuck around for the economic conference after her announcement, didn't she?"

"As far as we know, she was there, then bolted right after the press left," Chief Brown replied.

"Can you see if anyone has a copy of this morning's paper?"

"I can do better than that. Whenever there's a conference here, the newspaper distributors place copies of their papers on the table over near the registration desk. They're intended for people attending the conference, but guests pilfer them. I can tell you it drives the woman who runs our store downstairs nuts. For her, it's like stealing money right out of the cash register."

"Let's go see if there are any copies left." The two men walked briskly across the length of the lobby, Kary with an intent look on his face, while the chief bore the visage of a man who was a step behind in his thinking. When they arrived at the table, Kary's face fell.

"Damn, there are only copies of the Times here."

But Chief Brown was more persistent. Rummaging through the remaining papers he found the New Hampshire section of that morning's paper at the bottom of the stack. Removing it from the fan of papers he said, "Looks like someone wasn't interested in the news of our state." The chief handed the section to Kary who quickly scanned it. He knew precisely what he was looking for.

"Got it!" he exclaimed.

As the chief moved shoulder to shoulder with Kary, he instantly saw what they had been looking for: a picture of Laureli Hopkins with the Quebec delegate to the economic summit.

"Thank goodness for color photography," Kary said with a broad smile on his face. "So, you were right after all, Chief. Laureli was wearing a red pants suit."

The two men weren't able to spend much time congratulating one another. It was difficult to say how long it took before they realized the full meaning of what they had just learned, probably no more than several seconds. Kary reached inside the pocket of his sports jacket to retrieve the previous day's newspaper.

"It says here that Laureli's father is Armand Desmoreau."

Kary's mind was in overdrive. He was beginning to put the pieces together and they were all adding up to one thing: Maya Lassiter.

"Listen Chief, we need to talk to Mr. Desmoreau and Julie Woods right away."

Before Kary could blink, the chief was speaking to Officer Goss on his walkie talkie. He told Goss to round up the maitre d'hotel and the waitress and to tell Sergeant Crandall to come to the resort ASAP. Then he called Tom Capstone and informed him of what they were doing. Hanging up, he turned to Kary with a sardonic look on his face and said, "Let's see Ken Kizer interfere this time."

Still grinning from ear to ear, he said to Kary, "If Ken Kizer tries to protect Julie again, he's in for a little surprise."

Kary had been concentrating intently during Chief Brown's conversations. "I don't follow; what's the surprise?"

"The GM and Sergeant Crandall will be joining us during the interview."

Despite all that was weighing on Kary's mind, he smiled at the chief's cunning plan.

62

There is nothing like a change of scenery to soothe a restless soul. Maya was unable to control her thought process while sitting by the outdoor pool. Her close proximity to where Dana had been found did not help Maya's mental state. After all, in the past forty-eight hours she endured a succession of events that wouldn't be wished on one's worst enemy—the loss of her best friend, people spying on her, the burglary of her room, and then there was the appearance of her former student, Julie Woods, and the dredging up of horrible memories about Lori Dark. Having stirred up this cacophony of old and new memories, Maya was on massive negative sensory overload, and she was experiencing the mental equivalent to an acute case of heartburn.

Maya Lassiter was a strong willed woman. So, while she knew it would take some time to erase the pain, it was only a day or two before she needed to return to her family, friends, and her high school. The first step in her healing process was to get away from the swimming pool. Maya told herself she never again would set eyes on the site where Dana died. Maya fully intended to honor her promise to Kary to remain in the resort's public areas, but she needed to find a place which offered her sanctuary—a place where she could hide away in plain sight. She walked slowly along until she found the perfect place—the porch on the east end of the covered veranda. Situated just outside the large picture window behind the ballroom's large stage, it was a part of the hotel that was available to the public, but which offered quietude and almost total privacy when the stage curtain was drawn, as it was that day. Maya's chosen refuge had been built to replicate a piazza, with fluted Doric columns, connecting balustrades, and heavy entablatures. Between each pair of columns hung a white plastic basket containing a red geranium plant. From the white wicker chair Maya selected, she could look out toward the Mount Pleasant Golf Course, with the Ammonoosuc River and Crawford Notch beyond. Within minutes, Maya felt a sense of peace descending upon her. It was a feeling that would be short-lived.

***

Julie Woods was the first to arrive at the general manager's office but she did not appear alone. Chief Brown looked up as Julie knocked on the partially open door to the security office. At her left shoulder was Ken Kizer. Only the chief was fully visible to the pair as they stood in the doorway; Kary was partially obscured by the door. It did not take Kizer long to begin his bullying tactics anew.

"Listen to me, Chief Brown, because I'm only going to say this once. You think because you've got a badge on your chest you can interrupt my operations and bully my employees." Then eying Julie Woods he added, "I told you not to bother my waitress here until the evening meal was over. Did you listen? Did you even have the courtesy to call me first? No. Because of that, here's how this is going to play out. I'm not going to allow Julie to talk with you until tomorrow. And this isn't my doing. It's yours, Chief. You know the unwritten rules around here and you broke them. You crossed into my turf without your Go Card, and I just can't allow that to happen."

The chief appeared to be remarkably calm in the face of such an insulting tirade. If he was angry, Chief Brown was doing a remarkable job of camouflaging it. Perhaps he was simply tired. More likely it was because Chief Brown was holding better cards than he was showing to the irate Ken Kizer.

"Now Ken, be reasonable." The chief's voice was calm. He betrayed not a single ounce of rancor. "You know I wouldn't have bothered Ms. Woods or you if it weren't vitally important, don't you? So let's be reasonable. I don't want to—"

"Don't want to do what, Chief? Call Capstone? You know what? Why don't you call the GM. See if I care. I'm not budging on this."

Ken Kizer had just taken a gamble. He had been dreaming about getting into Julie Woods' pants for the past month. Now Chief Brown handed him the opportunity he needed on a silver platter. Ken would play the role of protector to the hilt and before he knew it, she'd be in his bed. Ken also knew Chief Brown didn't carry grudges. In a day or so, Ken would stop by with a tray of hors d'oeuvres and he'd explain what motivated his performance. Unfortunately for Ken, he drastically underestimated the importance of the Chief's summons of Julie.

The voice that emanated from behind the security office door was enough to make Ken Kizer's hair stand on end.

"Why don't you come in here where I can see you, Mr. Kizer." It was the unmistakable voice of Tom Capstone, the resort's general manager.

Ken Kizer peered behind the door at the expression of displeasure on his boss's face. Sitting beside the general manager was Sergeant Joseph Crandall from the Carroll Police Department.

"Mr. Capstone, I had no idea—"

"That is abundantly clear, young man. How dare you come in here and use that tone of voice with a colleague? More to the point, what gives you the balls to think you can impede an investigation?"

Ken looked as though he might cry. "Investigation? Mr. Capstone, I had no idea—"

"You had no idea the resort's chief of security might be conducting an investigation? Is it too much of a reach for your feeble brain, Mr. Kizer, to be able to understand this is precisely the kind of work Chief Brown does?"

"No, sir, it isn't."

"Well then next time you think about playing hero in front of one of the female staff be sure to first read the reprimand that will be in your file. You will do that, won't you Mr. Kizer?"

"Yes, sir. Sorry, sir! Sorry, Chief! I was way out of line."

Ken Kizer turned slowly and walked back toward the kitchen without making eye contact with Julie Woods. While he wasn't going to have the wonderful night of sex he'd envisioned. He clearly had screwed himself in more ways than one.

***

With her erstwhile protector out of the picture, Julie Woods entered the room to face the four men who were anxious to question her. As she headed toward the chair to which Kary directed her, Julie's knees were shaking and she was beginning to feel nauseated. Her afternoon wasn't going to get any better. A minute after she had seated herself, Armand Desmoreau entered the room.

63

Julie Woods placed her face in her hands and began to sob, "Oh what have I done, what have I done?"

Her face was still in the same position when she heard Tom Capstone reply, "That is precisely what we're here to learn, young lady." Julie did not look up at her boss but she could feel the stares of the five men. Had she looked over at Armand Desmoreau at that very moment, his look of disdain would have completely unnerved her.

Kary's voice was the next one she heard. As opposed to Tom Capstone's tone, Kary's voice was soothing. He was a strong believer in the "you can catch more flies with honey" proverb, so he used carefully contrived mannerisms designed to gain Julie's confidence. Before Julie could begin talking, however, Armand Desmoreau's spoke in a booming voice.

"Still in trouble, eh, Julie? Just like when you were a girl."

Julie was shaken by Armand's words. "What are you talking about, Mr. Desmoreau?"

"You know fully well. You were a terrible influence on my little girl. It's a miracle she's where she's at today, no thanks to you."

Tom Capstone started to interfere in an effort to get the conversation back on track. But Kary realized this and quickly put up his right palm thereby signaling the others in the room to let the discussion between Julie and Armand continue.

These two hold the key to this entire investigation, he told himself. Let's let them play it out.

"My little girl would never have done half the things she did if it weren't for you."

"If it weren't for me, what about you? You took off from your family. How easy do you think that was for Lori?"

Kary was nonplussed. Lori, did she say Lori? He stood up.

"Wait a minute here," he cried out. "I'm asking you about Armand's daughter Laureli and you just mentioned Lori. Are you talking about the same person?"

Julie bowed her head and, without looking up softly responded, "Yes."

Armand was next to speak. "Miss Woods always called my daughter Lori, but her name is Laureli."

"To you, maybe, Mr. Desmoreau, but not to any of her friends."

Ignoring Julie, Armand spoke slowly and softly to the four men in the room. "I wasn't the best husband—"

"That's for damned sure," Julie interrupted.

Tom Capstone fixed an icy stare at Julie. "Don't say another word until you're told to, young lady."

Julie looked down at her hands which she had grasped in her lap.

Armand continued, "I wasn't the best husband but I love my children. It wasn't easy for me to leave them behind with a mother who was so cold, cold to me and distant from all of my children except Sara. For whatever reason, Lucy thought Sara was special, while Laureli and my son were not so fortunate.

"What does this have to do with Kary's question?" Chief Brown asked.

"Please, sir, allow me to continue. When I finally decided I'd had enough, I wanted to leave without a confrontation. I arranged to come home at lunch time when Lucy and the children were not at home. I packed my belongings and moved into the hotel for a time."

"That must have been a very difficult time, Mr. Desmoreau," Kary said.

"Believe me, it was très difficile, monsieur. I left almost all of my momentos behind—family pictures, old sports trophies, and most of the household moneys. I wrote a note to each of my children, but left nothing to Lucy—a decision I regret to this day—despite the years of indifference she had subjected me to."

"There were no notes. He's lying," Julie proclaimed.

Armand was shocked at this revelation. "No notes! But I...." Then hanging his head, he spoke even more softly than before, "Lucy must have found them...."

"With me out of the picture, it didn't take Lucy long to go through with the divorce. Frankly, I think it was something she'd wanted for years; but, I was stubborn, no one in my family had ever before been divorced. In those days, it was rare for Habitant families to divorce. You just stayed together, living as strangers. These days, the young people have children without even marrying, and if they do go before the priest, they don't stay together very long. Back when Lucy and I split up, you could only get a civil divorce, and you were scorned by the church. Your friends never spoke to you about what you had done. I suppose living way up here out in the woods, the sanctions were not as strong. At least we were able to ignore them."

Kary was next to speak. "Monsieur Desmoreau, please explain to me why you keep referring to your daughter as Laureli, while Ms. Woods just called your daughter Lori."

"Laureli is my younger daughter's given name, Monsieur. She was born Laureli Antoinette Desmoreau."

"I understand, sir."

"But following my departure, my wife filed for a civil dissolution of our marriage."

"When was that approved?"

"In 1985, when Laureli was but eight years old." Kary could see that Armand was fighting back tears. He was a private man and this was a particularly difficult matter for him to dredge up, particularly in front of his boss and the young woman who blamed Armand for every sad moment in her best friend's life.

"Immediately, the Desmoreau family was divided up much the way a butcher cuts meat," Armand said sadly. "My son and I were the only ones who retained the family name. The Desmoreau name dates back to the middle ages in eastern France," he said. "By my selfish act, all that was changed."

"So your son continued to use your family surname?"

"Oui, he was already a man, and he was not as much affected by the divorce."

"What did the rest of your family do?" Kary asked.

"Lucy was, as you would expect, furious with me. Because she and Sara were so close, they both chose to use Lucy's family name, which is Dutton. Lucy and I were from two different worlds. She is the daughter of Irish immigrants, while my family—obviously—is French-Canadian."

"And what about Laureli? What did she do?"

"Laureli and her mother remained distant. Despite the fact Laureli lived with her mother, Lucy only seemed to have time for Sara. Once Sara had left for college, Laureli and Lucy lived like strangers in the same house. Contrary to this young lady's opinions," he said while pointing his long, arthritic index finger at Julie, "even though I no longer lived in this house, Laureli knew she could count on me. I even got Laureli and this one over here their first jobs at the resort. Of course, Laureli and I had our differences. We still do as a matter of fact. The thing that hurt me the most is I wanted her to keep her family name. I knew she wasn't interested in changing her last name to Dutton. She always wanted an English name. It wasn't so much that she was ashamed of her French-Canadian heritage, it was more a matter of, how do you say, expediency."

"Expediency?" Chief Brown asked.

"Yes. My daughter was always ambitious. She wanted to be somebody, a bigwig politician. When she used to watch television, she would hear the newsman talk about how difficult it was for an immigrant to be elected to office."

"So she changed her name to Lori?" Kary asked.

"Yeah, to Lori Dark," Julie cut in.

"Such a macabre name, why would she choose that?" asked Joe Crandall.

"It's the translation from the French," Armand answered. "Desmoreau means 'of the dark.' Laureli decided to keep her name while disguising its origin, you see."

There was complete silence in the room. Neither Tom Capstone nor Joe Crandall fully understood what this news meant to the investigation and, more importantly, to Maya Lassiter. So Kary quickly explained to them. Then turning to Armand, he said, "I think that is all the information we need from you, Monsieur." But before Armand Desmoreau could leave the room, Kary stopped him. "Two more quick questions, if you please."

Armand nodded his assent.

"When did you last see your daughter?"

"I spoke with her for several minutes right after her announcement."

Kary nodded. "And do you have any idea where she is right now?" he asked.

"No idea whatsoever, Monsieur. My understanding is she left the resort after the press reception for the economic summit. At least that was her intention. However, if you want to know anything about my daughter's whereabouts, you'll need to ask Miss Woods. After all, they were best friends as children and, as far as I know, they still are."

Before he could leave, Armand was cautioned by the men in the room not to discuss anything that had transpired with anyone. He was to contact Chief Brown or Sergeant Crandall immediately if he heard from his daughter.

As Armand left the room, Julie Woods stood up with the intention of doing likewise.

"Not so fast, young lady," Tom Capstone said. "We have a good deal more to talk with you about."

Sighing audibly, Julie took her seat again.

64

Tom Capstone spoke first to Julie Woods. "From our perspective, young lady, you're in a great deal of trouble right now."

Julie just sat there looking only at Kary. Not realizing he was leading the investigation of Dana Cerone's death, she still considered him her only possible friend in the room. Finally, Kary came closer to Julie. Using the kindest, softest voice he could muster, he said, "There's a good deal you haven't told us, isn't there Julie?"

Julie began to sob again. "All I did was cover for my friend."

"Unfortunately, you've unwittingly done much more than that. Why don't you let me tell you how this looks from our perspective?" he added. Julie looked at Kary then nodded, so he continued. "For starters, it looks to us as though you knowingly kept information about an on-going murder investigation from us."

"Murder investigation?" Julie was silent. She realized she already said too much. She finally spoke. "Lori couldn't have done anything like that. She wouldn't. She couldn't. Besides, she left here the night of her announcement."

"Now, you and I both know that isn't true," Kary replied while somehow maintaining his easy-going demeanor.

Sergeant Crandall knew from experience this was a good

time to play the role of bad cop to support Kary's good cop performance. "I've heard about all of this I'm going to put up with." It was a performance worthy of an Oscar nomination. "Young lady, that was the last lick I'm going to listen to from you." Then looking at Kary he said, "We've tried playing this your way, Dr. Turnell, but this woman's a hard case. She's looking at twenty-five years as an accessory to murder. I'm going to arrest her and bring her over to my station. Believe me, Ms. Woods, when my men get finished interrogating you, you'll wish you had cooperated with Dr. Turnell and Chief Brown." For effect, he unhooked the handcuffs from his belt and moved toward Julie Woods while beginning to read her rights.

"No, wait. Please, Dr. Turnell," she cried. "I'll talk to you. I promise. Just don't let him arrest me."

"I'm not sure there's anything I can do for you now, Julie. I was trying to be helpful, but you refused to be honest with me, and now Sergeant Crandall has decided to assert his jurisdiction."

"Please help me," she cried.

Kary looked at Julie's pitiful face. He turned toward the advancing Joe Crandall. "Sergeant, may I have a word with you out in the hallway?"

"Look, Dr. Turnell, we have a belligerent witness here and I see no choice in the matter but to bring her in, book her, and interrogate her." Then for effect he added, "The electric shock always loosens them up." Over his shoulder, Kary heard the sobs of Julie Woods.

"Please, Sergeant, just hear me out."

The two men left the room while Chief Brown and Tom Capstone kept silent watch over their suspect. Once Kary and Joe Crandall had closed the door and moved away from the security office, they immediately slapped each other five.

"What a performance, Joe. You even had me fooled."

"Thanks, Kary. Those high school drama classes have paid a number of dividends over the years. She needed a good hard kick in the ass, if you'll pardon the expression."

"That she did. We should get some straight answers out of her now. But what if she isn't forthcoming?"

"Then I won't have any choice but to arrest her and bring her in."

"For electric shock treatments?" Kary asked with a smile.

"No, those things are illegal."

"So, what will you do if she doesn't tell us what we need to know?"

"We'll talk with her, then we have to turn her over to the State Police. While there may not be any electric shock treatments in Julie Woods's future, she's leaving herself open to some very unpleasant experiences."

"Let's see if we can avert that, shall we?"

Crandall nodded his agreement and the two men returned to the room.

"Julie, thanks to Sergeant Crandall, I've just bought you about five minutes to tell us all you know about Laureli Hopkins, AKA Lori Dark. But let me warn you, one misstatement or withheld fact, and you're on your way to the Carroll Police Station. Do you understand, Julie?"

Julie nodded. She understood.

65

"Where should I begin?" Julie asked. She was back in control of herself with only the occasional tear welling up in her left eye.

"Why don't you tell us when you first learned Laureli or Lori was coming to the Mount Washington to announce her candidacy," Kary said.

"It was only about a week ago," Julie replied. "Lori isn't a big planner. She tends to do things on impulse. And once she makes her mind up to do something, she does it." Then she added with a smile, "It's one of the things I like best about her."

"And did you have any plans to see Laureli while she was here?"

"Oh, sure," she smiled again. "She needed to have some time to hang out with her father," she said with a frown her face, "and her mom and sister. Of course there was that economic conference she needed to attend. But she told me she wasn't going to stay long, just long enough to have a photo op with the press."

"She planned all along to leave the summit?" Tom Capstone asked.

"Yeah, Lori said she wanted to have fun while she was up here on account of all the years she spent working in the kitchen and—"

"And what, Julie?" Kary asked.

"Because her marriage wasn't doing so hot," she replied.

"Did she tell you what was wrong with her marriage?"

"Not much, really. I think she suspects her husband is having an affair. We didn't get a chance to meet that night. Mr. Kizer said he needed me to stay late in the kitchen, so I didn't catch up with Lori until the next morning."

"Are you dating Mr. Kizer, Ms. Woods?"

"Oh, no. He's just a friend, or was until recently."

"What's happened recently?"

"Lately, he's all over me. The only reason he kept me late the other night was he got it in his head that I'd like to have sex on one of the kitchen counters after everyone else left. But he was wrong."

"Where were you and Laureli Hopkins supposed to meet?"

"In her guest room. I know there's a rule against hotel staff fraternizing with guests, but Lori said that was about men and women fornicating."

"I'm afraid not, Ms. Woods. The rule applies to all forms of interaction in the guest rooms," Tom Capstone reprimanded her.

"I guess that's strike three for me, huh, Mr. Capstone?" she said while repressing another flow of tears.

"Do you know what Laureli did that evening?" Kary asked.

"I—I—I do now," she replied.

"When I saw her the next morning, Lori told me she had dinner delivered to her room and then went for a walk at about nine o'clock or so. She told me there was something on her mind, something she had to find a way to deal with."

"Did that make you suspicious?"

"Not really. I figured something happened during her conference meeting that really upset her."

"So what happened next?"

Julie sat and considered her response to the question. As she did, she began to cry with such intensity that Chief Brown suggested they take a break. Since there were no women on either the Carroll police force or the resort security force, Joe Crandall and Boyd Brown agreed it was best not to continue until they could bring the resort's nurse into the room

66

The break from interrogating Julie Woods was exactly what Kary needed. He was becoming increasingly agitated as the minutes passed. Kary rather liked the mind games one used to get a suspect or a witness to talk. The little game of good cop-bad cop he and Joe Crandall had just played so well normally would have invigorated him.

It wasn't the process of interrogation that was bothering him. Kary was worried sick about Maya. He walked rapidly through the hallways, peeking into dining and meeting areas, then along the porch. There was still no sign of her. Again he went down to the terrace level. This time he walked around the pool, down to the tennis courts, then around the circumference of the hotel. He went up a stairway that lead into the back of the Sun Dining Room, then made his way the full length of the Main Dining Room, peered inside the Ammonoosuc Dining Room, and looked through the windows of the Princess Room. Next, he dialed Maya's room on the house phone and waited until the answering machine picked up. In desperation, he waited outside the women's rest room to see if Maya would appear. After several minutes of pacing back and forth, he stuck his head inside the doorway and called her name. All he got for his trouble was a dirty look from a seventy-something year old woman whose effort to relieve herself he had just interrupted.

With the impending arrival of the resort's nurse at the security office, Kary reluctantly made his way back toward the interview room. Had he known what was in store for Maya, he would have reconsidered that decision.

PART V
CONFRONTATION

67

At the very moment Julie's interrogation began to bear fruit, Maya's day was about to be changed, and not for the better. After she left the poolside area, Maya walked around the circumference of the hotel. Her timing could not have been worse. By walking in a counterclockwise direction she barely missed running into Kary. Finally, having circumnavigated the base of the main building, Maya elected to walk up the steps toward the main entrance. Wanting to take in as much fresh air as possible, she decided against entering the foyer, instead electing to take a right turn and walk toward the southern end of the porch. As she neared the point where the porch turned to the east, she felt a presence. It felt like she was being watched. She turned and looked back in the direction from which she had come. Seeing the porch was empty save for one elderly gentleman asleep in one of the red rocking chairs situated every hundred feet or so, she shook her head and silently mocked herself for being paranoid. Had she peered through the window closest to the ballroom along the west wall of the hotel, Maya would have known she was indeed being followed.

Looking for a spot where she could find some solitude and be able to move into and out of the sun's rays with a minimum of effort, she sat down at the center-most part of the porch on the southern end of the hotel. Behind her she could see the great maroon curtain had been drawn. She suspected this might be the case as she noted earlier that a large wedding reception, with a full orchestra in the ballroom, was scheduled for late that afternoon. As Maya sat in one of the white wicker chairs, she could hear the lead saxophonist blowing the chorus of "In the Mood." Sitting down, she smiled at the thought of Stan and her coming back to the resort, hopefully with Nya and Kary. This time, though, there would be no investigating, only lots of laughter, dancing, and relaxing, as long as she never again had to go near the area where Dana died.

Maya closed her eyes and felt the heat of the mid-afternoon sun on her face, arms, and feet. Suddenly she was in shadow, a chill falling over her. Maya remembered seeing a small puffy cloud hovering in the area of the sky where the sun shown down on her, so she sat with her eyes closed, expecting the warmth to reappear in a few moments. After a minute, when the sun did not reappear, she sat up and looked to determine the sun's progress. It was then that she realized the shade was not being caused by a cloud. A form was hovering over her.

Maya looked up to see what—or who—was blocking her precious sunlight. She could not make out the person's features, for the shadow on the latter's face was in stark contrast to the bright sky behind her.

"Excuse me, please, but would you mind moving over a step or two. You're blocking my sunlight and I've been looking forward to this all day." Maya could now make out that the person standing so close to her was a young woman. Rather than move away, the woman moved even closer.

"Ciao Signora," she said. Maya said nothing in response. She adjusted her position so she could see who was speaking to her in Italian. She half expected to see one of the other women from the AP meeting who, like Maya, had elected to stay at the resort after the conference concluded. That she did not recognize Lori Dark immediately was understandable. After all, the Lori who Maya knew had been eighteen years old, whereas the woman standing next to her looked to be in her early thirties, and the white kitchen outfit was not like any clothing Lori Dark ever wore in high school. The physical contrast between Lori and this woman also was significant: Lori's hair had been dark and cut in a near bowl-like fashion, while this woman's hair had honey blond features and was stylishly coifed. The greatest contrast, though, was that Lori Dark's complexion had always been pale, almost ghost like, whereas this woman appeared tan and healthy, reflecting either time spent in subtropical sunshine or excellent makeup.

"Do I know you?" Maya asked lamely.

"Ciao Signora," the woman repeated.

Maya rose from her chair and lowered her sunglasses. She stared at the younger woman for several seconds before the realization struck Maya that standing before her was the former student who nearly destroyed Maya and Dana's faith in their own senses of judgment. Because of what the Dark girl had done, future generations of students would never again be given the unbridled affection the two teachers had shown to Lori.

Maya's initial response was surprise followed quickly by anger.

"What do you want, Lori?" she asked through gritted teeth.

"Aren't you happy to see me, Signora?" Lori asked.

Throughout her long teaching career, nothing made Maya feel warmer inside than the sound of a student calling her Signora, but she held such animosity for Lori Dark that hearing her say "Ciao Signora" made Maya's stomach turn over.

Maya normally would have gone to any length to disguise the fact that she couldn't remember a student's name or, as in this case, simply did not like her. Lori Dark was a different case entirely: Lori Dark had deceived the two teachers; Lori Dark had taken advantage of their nurturing ways; Lori Dark had feigned dying of cancer. Maya didn't know whether she felt more like vomiting or punching Lori in the face. Physical violence had never been Maya's way. She avoided it at all costs, and did nothing to encourage that behavior in Stan when the two had been a young couple.

One time, when Stan and Maya had been going out for nearly two months, Stan had taken Maya to dinner at a popular watering hole of Dartmouth students. They had enjoyed a nice meal together and were getting their coats on when several inebriated Dartmouth students came over and started making a play for Maya, who looked particularly delicious in a flower print dress that hugged her attractive legs at mid thigh. When one of them placed his hand around Maya's shoulders, Stan reacted by pushing him to the floor inside a coat rack. When the couple arrived at Stan's car, he expected Maya to have an admiring glance on her face. Instead, he had been admonished for risking injury while interfering in a situation "I had a handle on." Stan was to learn an early lesson that Maya, who was fearless in the face of verbal confrontation, despised it when people resorted to physical force to settle their differences. Despite Maya's disdain for Lori Dark, the younger woman was in no danger of being physically accosted by her former Italian teacher. Unfortunately, Lori Dark had no such reservations about using physical force if it served her purpose.

68

"I asked you once, Lori, what do you want from me?"

"Why, Signora, I thought we could be friends, just like before." Maya didn't have any intention of ever being friends with Lori again. Besides, there was something decidedly menacing in her former student's tone.

"That's a laugh, Lori, after what you pulled on Mrs. Cerone and me."

Lori seemed caught off guard. Whatever the reason, she dropped her friendly façade.

"Oh, grow up, Signora. You and Mrs. Cerone weren't a couple of school girls. You'd dealt with a lot tougher kids than me before I came along."

"True, Lori, but never anyone as ruthless and dishonest."

If Maya's words had any effect on her, Lori didn't show it. "My life wasn't easy, you know."

"Of course I knew. So did Mrs. Cerone. You came from a broken home. Obviously your mother was going through a rough time and wasn't giving you the time you or any girl your age needed. We understood that. Why do you think we wanted to help you out in the first place?"

"But, but there were so many other girls—"

"Yes, there were other girls. The Martin girl had just lost

her father in a car accident. She was probably even more needy than you really were. But you saw to it that we only paid attention to you, didn't you, Lori?"

Lori ignored Maya's rebuff. "Mom was never at home. She was dating a bunch of different guys. But the worst was when she moved in with one of them and cancelled the house phone to save money."

"Yes, that was a terrible thing to do to a teenage girl. But other teens have to deal with worse."

Lori's eyes were tearing. "Maybe they were stronger than me."

"That's stronger than I, Lori. Have you forgotten everything you learned in school?"

"Stronger than I," Lori repeated absentmindedly.

"Those girls weren't any stronger than you. They were a hell of a lot more honest, though. Tell me, what caused you to make up such a horrible lie? How did you even think of such a thing?"

"It was one of the soap operas. My favorite character, Maggie, was supposed to go to jail, but she made up a story about a faulty heart valve, even found a way to document it. The judge sentenced her to house arrest because he was convinced she'd die in prison."

"Those damned soap operas," Maya cried out. "I was always telling you not to watch them. That story is a bunch of crap, Lori. There's no way any judge would just let someone stay at home eating bon bons because of a heart ailment."

Lori ignored Maya's criticism. "At any rate, that's where I got the idea to pretend to be sick, so sick that you and Mrs. Cerone would do anything to help me."

"Yes, we did anything all right, including putting not only other students, but our own families' lives on the back burner."

"Come on, Signora, we had a lot of good times together. All three of us did."

"Is that what you thought? Did you think we were just joyfully giving up time we could have been spending with our husbands and children to spend evenings with little Lori. We were sick to death about you. Mrs. Cerone and I cried ourselves to sleep worrying about you."

69

As Maya dealt with her surprise visitor, Julie was telling her four interrogators everything they wanted to hear. She admitted that on the night of Dana Cerone's death, Lori asked to meet Julie in the storage space that overlooking the corridor to the Main Dining Room. Lori was tearful, an emotion Julie rarely saw. Lori said she'd screwed up everything. When Julie asked her what she meant, Lori made no eye contact. She held up her hand as if to say don't go there. After a few moments of reflection, Lori turned to Julie. She took her two hands in hers and said, "I need your help." Julie said she would. "You need to hide me," Lori implored. Julie said she tried to convince Lori to simply return to her guest room, but Lori convinced her that wasn't a good idea because she said, "Someone is after me." Julie recommended they talk with either Chief Brown or Sergeant Crandall, but Lori rebuffed the suggestion.

"Sometimes you're such an innocent, Julie. If I go to those guys they'll just turn me over to the people who are after me," Lori said.

Julie questioned her further. Lori was ready. "I'm such an idiot. I should have realized that as soon as I announced my candidacy there would be people waiting to frame me."

"Frame you? Frame you for what?" Julie had asked.

"Never mind that, Jules," she had said. "Just trust me and do as I tell you, please."

As she did time after time when they were in their early teens together, Julie took the necessary risks to make certain her trouble-making friend didn't get caught. There was the time when Lori stole a bottle of wine from a New Hampshire Liquor Store. It was Julie who attempted to return the bottle unopened and it was Julie who was caught.

As she had done many times before, Julie looked after her best friend's welfare. She borrowed a set of kitchen pants and a jacket in Lori's size and took them to Lori's hiding place in the South Tower. She took the money Lori gave her and bribed one of the housekeepers for a pass key to the guest rooms on Maya's floor. For a hundred dollars and Julie's promise that the housekeeper wouldn't get into any trouble, Julie had "rented" the key for an hour at dinner time. When the housekeeper saw Julie leaving Room 317 with a pillow and a blanket, she confronted Julie, who explained to the young Slovakian that she was doing work for the CIA. The naïve housekeeper had believed Julie and promised never to repeat anything about the key or the bed linens to anyone, not even to Erma Hearns.

"It was you who broke into Maya's room," Kary stated. "Other than the pillow and blanket, what exactly did you take from the room?"

"Lori wanted to know for sure if it was Signora Lassiter who was here at the resort. If she'd only waited another few hours, I could have told her that Signora was here. But Lori was always too impatient."

"You removed a letter and a room receipt from Signora Lassiter's registration packet?"

"Yes, but how did you know that?"

"You weren't very careful to cover your tracks," Kary replied. "You moved her things around so much that Signora Lassiter was on to you the minute she walked into the room. A quick check was all we needed to confirm what was amiss."

"After you brought proof that Maya, Signora Lassiter, was staying in Room 317, what did Lori say?"

"She became very mysterious."

"Mysterious? How?"

"She told me to stay out of her way. There were things that needed doing. She told me not to get involved or I could get in a lot of trouble."

"Quite a friend, that Lori," Kary muttered.

"She's the best," Julie replied. Capstone and Crandall sighed audibly. Once a sucker always a sucker, they were thinking.

***

"Gentlemen, if you'll excuse us," Tom Capstone said. The chief, Crandall, and Kary slowly walked out of the security office in single file.

"What do you suppose that's about?" Kary asked.

"I'd say he wants to fire Ms. Woods in private. I'm certain he's also going to have her check in with Joe before she leaves for her quarters."

"Yeah," Crandall agreed. "I'll be telling her not to go very far." A master of understatement, Crandall added, "Something tells me this isn't the last interview I'll be doing with Ms. Woods."

Julie Woods was going to find herself charged with at least one count of burglary, two counts of breaking and entering, along with being a possible accessory to murder.

Kary was anxious to renew his search for Maya. Chief Brown offered to help, then placed a call to Officer Lonny Goss to use his pass key to check Maya's room. Crandall told Kary that he, too, would join the search as soon as he finished talking with Julie Woods. He sent two of his men in golf carts to cover the perimeter of the resort's property. Chief Brown and Kary split up. The chief was to search the east side of the hotel, then make his way to the north wing, the kitchen, and the guests' parking lot. Kary would inspect the lower level, then the west porch, the ballroom, and finally the south side of the porch. All knew timing was of the essence.

***

Armand Desmoreau was mortified by what he just learned. He returned to his station at the entry to the Main Dining Room and asked that his assistant replace him. He took some resort stationery and an envelope and immediately wrote a letter of resignation, placed it into the envelope, sealed it, and wrote "Mr. Capstone, General Manager, Personal and Confidential" on the front. He walked slowly to the general manager's office and requested permission from Tom Capstone's secretary to leave the envelope on the GM's desk. Being a long-time, dutiful employee, Armand returned to the dining room where he intended to do his job until his resignation became official.

70

While Julie Woods felt as though she had just been through the proverbial ringer, the tension in the air on the south end of the patio was even more palatable. For her part, other than her physical appearance, Lori Dark hadn't changed very much from her high school days: she was still the same manipulative, self-absorbed person she had been. One of the most shocking aspects of Lori's high school ruse, the part that had shocked both Maya and Dana most, was that she was able to keep her secret about feigning cancer from her sister and her best friend. Julie never knew Lori was deceiving her two favorite teachers. In every other aspect of her relationship with her Signora and Mrs. Cerone, Lori had seemed like an open book. She would tell them when she was having her period, which boy she wanted to sleep with, even whether or not she had showered that day. As Lori hovered over Maya, it came as no surprise that Lori was ready and willing to talk about her favorite topic, herself.

I need to keep Lori talking, Maya thought. I've got to stall for time until Kary, or somebody, gets here. Besides, how else will I learn what she's been up to the past twelve years, and especially the last forty-eight hours? It was true that every minute Lori was kept talking improved Kary's chances of finding the two women before something terrible happened.

Maya was well aware that Lori had not stalked her just to sit down for high tea. "Next time, I should rethink this hiding in plain sight business," she thought to herself.

Although Maya would have preferred to be anywhere else at that moment, she was having success encouraging Lori to discuss her whereabouts during the last decade. Things went smoothly enough until, at one point, she tried to casually stand and stretch her legs. The younger, stronger woman reacted by silently blocking her escape route. Not wanting to risk arousing Lori's ire, just yet, Maya casually returned to the white wicker chair as Lori said, "Please don't go away, Signora." Maya knew Lori meant that she had better not try to do that again.

Lori told Maya how she had met and married Bob Hopkins. Feigning interest in what her former student was telling her, Maya said almost absent-mindedly, "Lori Hopkins has a nice ring to it."

"Not Lori, Signora!" Lori snapped at her. "Lori Dark ceased to exist once I was married. I use my given name these days," she said. As Laureli said this, her eyes looked menacingly at Maya, whom she probed for a hint of recognition. It was still a moment in coming.

"Given name?" Maya asked. "But the name you used on all of your papers, in fact, the name on your diploma, was Lori."

"Yes. I became Lori Dark after my parents divorced. But I was born Laureli Jeannette Desmoreau."

"Laureli Desmoreau." Maya repeated, her mind trying to make sense of what she had just heard. Dana's death had deprived Maya of the opportunity to share what her friend had learned; and, she wasn't involved in that afternoon's discussions between the chief and Kary. What she realized next came as a shock.

"So you married Bob Hopkins and became—"

"Laureli Hopkins," Maya said with a sardonic expression on her face.

The words caused the hair on Maya's neck to stand on end again. Suddenly all made sense. Lori Dark, the queen of connivers, had married a wealthy, influential industrialist to use his money and her own powers of persuasion to position herself as a candidate for U.S. Congress. Not knowing about the metamorphosis of Lori Dark into Laureli Hopkins, Maya had not followed her former student's career. Quite the contrary, she steadfastly avoided any mention of her former student's name or whereabouts, a decision she was regretting.

Someone else might have been unnerved by what she had just learned. But Maya drew upon a reserve of emotional strength that had been passed on to both Maya and Nya through parents who escaped atrocities at the hands of the Soviets. Those parents, Csaba and Mietta, had traveled thousands of miles and made a new life for themselves and their twin daughters in the United States. Maya knew well about their sacrifice and she was determined that her part of the story was not going to end here. But where was Kary?

It was vital for her own survival that Maya continue to keep Lori, nèe Laureli, talking. Her former student was standing so near, and was capable of doing almost anything to protect the reputation she had contrived. The realization hit Maya. Obviously, Dana Cerone learned about Laureli's dual identity. Therefore, she had to die.

Maya would have to do something about her own dilemma and it needed to be done soon. She considered screaming but the band in the ballroom was at full swing. Her voice wouldn't be heard inside the building. Looking as casually as she could, Maya saw there was no one else walking or sitting at this end of the porch. The grounds below them were deserted as well.

As if reading Maya's mind, Lori had come to the same conclusion. "The fact that I pretended to be dying of cancer in high school doesn't seem all that important right now, does it, Signora?"

Maya said nothing as she thought, "There's no time like the present to do away with the only other person who has direct proof that our Lori, or should I say, congressional candidate Laureli Hopkins, once pretended to have cancer."

Lori was no fool. She knew if word of her deception leaked to the press her political career would be dead before it started. She weighed the choices: What awaited her was either a rosy future or one she was not willing to accept.

On the silver screen, many a hero or heroine has survived a similar set of circumstances by stalling. It was working thus far for Maya. She had to keep Lori talking about herself. Maya quickly considered there were two ways to engage Lori long enough to allow rescuers to arrive: Act like the curious but compassionate quarry, or take a more assertive approach. Maya knew her captor well enough to realize that while the latter approach was chancy, the former would not work. Lori was tiring of the conversation and growing more anxious to get Maya out of her way. Maya reasoned that if she were able to put Lori on the defensive, Lori would feel compelled to present her side of the story before she finished off her Signora.

71

Once Maya decided to take an aggressive, interrogative stance there would be no turning back. She figured, "What the hell, if I'm going to die, I might as well go out with my pride intact." Maya could not believe the next words she heard herself say—talk about placing your head in the lion's mouth.

"When did you decide to kill Mrs. Cerone, Lori?"

Lori just looked at Maya. She couldn't disguise the annoyance in her voice. "You think I'm crazy, don't you, Signora?"

"Why do you say that, Lori? I don't think you're crazy. I do know that you killed my friend. I'd like to know what prompted you to do it."

"I never planned to kill Mrs. Cerone or anyone else, for that matter. Her death was an accident."

"I saw her body, Lori. You'll have a hell of a time convincing me that was an accident."

"You'll go to the authorities. That's what Mrs. Cerone was going to do."

The direction of the discussion was getting away from Maya. She needed Lori to think about what had happened to Dana, not about what she was going to do to add to her body count. Maya was convinced Lori was operating at a high level of paranoia. She had seen something similar in a student at the inner city high school where she taught briefly. A young African-American student had been pushed too far by some of her peers. It appeared she might do something to harm one of her tormentors who stepped too close to the fifteen-year-old girl. Maya had been able to diffuse the situation by drawing the confused girl's attention away from her target using a well-timed compliment. Once the mood was broken, Maya lead the potential murderer to a chair in the empty classroom next door.

Maya was fortunate on that occasion. She needed to change Lori's mood quickly or Maya was going to be taking flight off of the patio, a flight she would not survive.

"You haven't told me how you were able to make Mrs. Cerone fly so far through the air," Maya said, while appearing to marvel at Lori's accomplishment.

"Tai chi," she responded almost absent-mindedly. It appeared she was reliving the entire episode in her mind.

"Tai chi? What does tai chi have to do with anything?"

"Mrs. Cerone attacked me."

"Attacked you? Mrs. Cerone was half your size. She wouldn't attack you!" Maya replied. In truth, Maya suspected Dana may well have attacked Lori. Both of the teachers were sickened by what Lori had done to them. Perhaps, by not discussing it all those years, Dana was carrying around too much rage to contain. Dana was an aggressive one, that was for certain. How many times, Maya asked herself, had she warned Dana to channel her aggression before she hurt someone or was hurt herself.

"She attacked me," Lori said. Remarkably, Lori appeared sad about what had happened.

"Please tell me what happened, Lori. I want to know everything that was said between Mrs. Cerone and you."

Lori told Maya how her announcement for U.S. Congress had gone very well. She had been mobbed by well-wishers and the press. It took at least twenty-five minutes for her to accept the congratulations of everyone who was there. She had answered questions from a few members of the press. It was then that she spotted Dana Cerone in the crowd. Dana was walking several feet away from Lori, trying to get a glimpse of what she looked like. When their eyes locked, Lori immediately recognized her former teacher.

"She hasn't changed much," she told Maya. "I didn't recognize you, Signora. You've lost a lot of weight and your hair color is different. That's why—"

"That's why you sent Julie to my room to find out if I was traveling with Mrs. Cerone."

"Yes. But that was after—"

"After you'd already killed Mrs. Cerone." Maya took the silence that followed as affirmation of what she had surmised.

"But let's get back to Mrs. Cerone. Is that when you decided to murder her?"

"NO!" Lori cried, grabbing her head as if she could shake away the image by doing so.

"I never wanted to kill Mrs. Cerone. I tried to call her room from the house phone but I had to hang up when a couple reporters approached me. I tried again after they left, but I became scared."

"Then what?"

"I had to go to that economic summit meeting. My head was spinning. I was trying to think of how I could talk to Mrs. Cerone and get her to—"

"Keep quiet?" Maya guessed.

"Yes. I didn't eat dinner in public that night. I kept walking around the grounds trying to think of how to get Mrs. Cerone alone without attracting attention, and what I was going to say when I did."

"Is that when you decided to kill her?"

"You keep saying I decided to kill Mrs. Cerone. I never planned to do that."

"Then what went wrong?"

"I was walking by myself downstairs along the lower terrace. I spotted Mrs. Cerone coming out of the door from near Stickney's. I waited behind a column until she came walking near the outdoor pool. I shouldn't have started with a wise crack. I said, 'fancy meeting you here, Mrs. Cerone.'"

"And what did Dana do?"

"She said, 'I guess they'll let anyone run for Congress these days.' At first I thought she was kidding, but I was wrong. She said she'd sooner see Jack the Ripper in office than see me there. She said she was going to let the press know about my past. She was going to tell them everything about what I did in high school. I couldn't believe she would do that to me, her former student and all. So, I became frantic. I asked her, 'Why are you doing this to me?' But, she just stood there shaking her head and glaring at me."

As she listened to Lori's story, Maya recalled how the two teachers had long carried a great deal of animosity toward Lori. Maya wanted nothing to do with Lori Dark. Dana did have a burning desire to "cold cock that bitch." Maya imagined what must have transpired during the moments leading up to Dana's death. She knew her friend so well. Maya was sure Dana was biding her time waiting for the opportunity to smack Lori. If only Maya had been there to calm down her friend, things might have ended differently. Dana was like the little engine that could. Only on this occasion she couldn't. Lori was more than a head taller than Dana. Unlike the out-of-shape high school girl she had been, Lori was a physically active and fit thirty-year-old woman.

"I swear to you, Signora, she swung at me first."

"You didn't do anything to bait her, did you, Lori?" Maya could feel her own blood pressure rising. Lori said nothing for a moment, then went back to her story. It sounded strangely like a news reporter telling her viewing audience about the aftermath of a murder.

"She grabbed for the front of my pants suit jacket. Then she made a fist and was about to take a swing at me. I just reacted."

"Reacted? You knocked her fifteen feet into the air! Jesus, Lori."

"It was tai chi," she said with a little too much pride in her tone.

"You keep talking about tai chi. What does that have to do with anything?"

"I've been taking tai chi for the last five years. I'd never used it for self defense. Tai chi is a wonderful way to deal with the stresses of life. I use it to help relax; it helps me to temporarily forget my troubles."

"You mean troubles like killing a fifty-year-old woman?" Maya asked. "So, you took a beautiful, meditative, art form and used it as a killing tool."

But Lori was on a roll. She described in full detail how she had used tai chi. Throughout her account, Lori spoke as if she were completely detached from what had happened, not describing a violent act she perpetrated. The more Lori talked, the angrier it made Maya. She forced herself to remain calm, as this could have been what Lori was trying to do, lure Maya into a fight she could not win.

"I fended off her blow by using a movement called 'brush knee'." As she spoke, Lori slowly pantomimed the movement. "Next, I unconsciously performed a beautiful movement called 'grasp the bird's tail.' Master tells us that by keeping the right heel firmly planted and drawing both hands up and back then pushing forward, it's possible to push someone twenty feet or more. What I did was not intentional, but it was executed perfectly." Lori was smiling dreamily as she reflected upon her performance.

"Executed perfectly! You took a human life, my friend's life. Don't stand there telling me how perfectly you executed the movement. Talk to me about how sorry you feel."

"Oh, I was sorry. I watched and waited. But when Mrs. Cerone didn't get up, I—"

"How long did you watch before you ran away, Lori, ten seconds?" Maya realized she was crying now, tears for the callous way in which Dana's life had been stolen from her.

"Yes, I ran. I couldn't help Mrs. Cerone. My campaign— I couldn't risk being caught. It was an accident but it would ruin everything."

"Ruin everything? You'd just killed a woman and not just any woman. She was your former teacher who, by the way, comforted you when you were supposedly dying of cancer. Yes, Lori, the woman you left bleeding and unconscious in the bushes was the same person who gave you your high school graduation party. That is who you killed, Lori. And once you realized what you'd done, you shrugged it off as though you'd just stepped on a bug."

72

For a fleeting moment, all sense of her own imminent peril had left Maya. For the few seconds it took her to release the frustration she'd felt for more than a decade, a frustration exacerbated by the anguish for Dana's death, Maya felt like she was the more threatening one. That sensation was curtailed when Lori looked menacingly at her and asked, "I don't suppose I can trust you to forget all about this, can I, Signora?"

Forget! Maya repeated the word in her mind. How could she possibly forget the horrible deception Lori perpetrated on Dana and her? What kind of person was capable of pretending to be dying of cancer knowing full well both of her pawns had lost their mothers to the same deadly disease? More than a decade had passed and Maya had not yet reached the forgiveness stage. Now, this self-centered sociopath was standing here asking her to forget what she'd done to them. Even if Maya could somehow find it in her heart to forgive past improprieties, Lori had killed Dana two days earlier and was completely capable of simply brushing the entire episode aside. Worse still, she had been working tirelessly for the past forty-eight hours covering up her misdeeds. Maya was not about to forget anything. To do so would make her an accomplice in Lori's dogged effort to gain a seat in the U.S. Congress. What would be next, President Laureli 'Lori' Hopkins?

There was no correct response to Lori's query. The murderer knew there would be no forgiving or forgetting, which left her only two courses of action. Only one was realistic in her depraved mind. Lori had made up her mind even before she encountered Maya on the porch. For that matter, Lori's course of action was decided before the actual confrontation with Dana on the lower terrace. The wheels had been set in motion when she locked eyes with Dana following her announcement for Congress. Laureli Hopkins was going to be a congresswoman. Two impediments stood in the way: the two women who knew what she had done at Crawford Notch High School. Each of them knew that she had committed an unpardonable act. Both had to die.

***

Kary and Chief Brown moved quickly and breathlessly along their respective routes, searching unsuccessfully for Maya Lassiter. The two men weaved in and out of the lower level and then the lobby of the hotel, one time nearly colliding. At the same time, Sergeant Crandall's men scoured the perimeter of the resort.

As Kary and the chief arrived at the entryway to the ballroom, each man realized he was running out of options. They could see inside the ballroom. A wedding was in progress. The eight-tops with their white tablecloths, the gorgeous ice sculpture, and the wedding guests dancing to the tunes of a raucous jazz band made entering the area unnecessary. Maya was not in the ballroom. Then came the break they desperately hoped for with the squelch sound on Chief Brown's two-way radio.

Stepping away from the loud music emanating from the ballroom, the chief raised his radio to his mouth and said, "Brown here. Whattya have?" The voice coming over the radio was excited. Between the background noise and the static on the radio, Kary could not make out what was being said. Chief Brown had no difficulty.

While Corporal Stanton and Officer Rattner were doing their respective sweeps of the property, the former drove a golf cart within fifty yards of the porch on the south end of the hotel. It appeared to him there was a woman alone on that end of the patio. He became suspicious when he realized she was wearing kitchen whites, and resort employees were never supposed to be out on the porch in uniform during daylight hours. Stanton had the presence of mind to bring his binoculars with him. He stopped the golf cart and focused his glasses on the woman in white. He could see the uniformed woman was hovering over a second woman seated in a wicker chair in front of the ballroom's large picture window.

"I think I've found them," he had told Sergeant Crandall. Once Stanton reported what he'd seen to Crandall, the latter had immediately radioed Chief Brown. Crandall ordered his men to converge on the patio.

"Maya's been spotted on the patio outside the ballroom," the chief told Kary. Then thinking quickly, he pushed Kary toward the doorway leading to the east side porch. "Let's split up. I'll take the west side," he called over his shoulder. While Kary had a clear path to the doorway, the short time Chief Brown delayed while calling out strategy would cost valuable seconds. As he headed toward the west side doorway, approximately thirty wedding guests, several of whom were inebriated, unfortunately chose that moment to exit from the ballroom. Seeing Chief Brown's badge, two of the men chose to chide the chief and challenge him to arrest them for being drunk. By the time the chief had extracted himself from the throng, Kary had already arrived at the south end of the patio. The sight before him wasn't pretty.

73

Kary exited the hotel and sprinted the full length of the porch. Fortunately for all concerned that end of the porch was empty. Having been searching for his sister-in-law for the better part of the afternoon, nothing or no one was going to stand in his way. By the time he reached the south end of the hotel his legs and his lungs were in rebellion. Despite the burning sensation in his chest and the steadily increasing pain in his knees, Kary kept running until he made a right turn around the corner leading to the semi-circular south porch. The late afternoon sun caught him square in both eyes, but not before he had a brief glimpse of blood, a great deal of it.

Kary was forced to stop and cover his face for a moment while he allowed his eyes to readjust from the sudden blast of direct sunlight. Kary shielded his face and walked toward the sun's rays. He began to focus upon the carnage before him. He first saw the centermost of the Doric columns. The white paint on the column and one of the connecting balustrades were smeared with bright red blood. The scene looked like a technicolor Rorschach test. Then he saw the body lying crumpled and face down on the porch floor below the large blood stain.

As he ran forward, it occurred to him that Maya had not been wearing a white kitchen suit.

"Kary? Kary, I'm over here!"

"What?" Kary was disoriented. Then he realized his sister-in-law's voice was coming from an area by the large picture window on the south side of the hotel. Running to her side, Kary embraced Maya. Assured she was not injured, he demanded, "What the hell happened here?"

His query was echoed by one chief of security and two Carroll police officers, "That's what we'd like to know, too." Soon the group was joined by Sergeant Crandall and several minutes later by Tom Capstone. In the center of the group, standing quietly by Maya's side was Erma Hearns, the resort's head housekeeper. Several curious guests had gathered on the porch. Tom Capstone quickly instructed Chief Brown and Sergeant Crandall to have their men close off the area. Once the guests had been removed, Maya was asked to recount what had happened.

"I'll be happy to, gentlemen, but will you please get a doctor for my former student. She appears to have been badly injured." Maya nodded appreciatively at Erma Hearns as she said this.

"Of course! Right away, Maya," Chief Brown replied. What was not said by anyone in the group is that no one believed Laureli Hopkins, AKA Lori Dark, was still alive. While they awaited the arrival of the resort nurse and a doctor attending the wedding in the ballroom, Maya began her story.

***

Before Maya could begin, Kary asked her why she disregarded his instructions and settled into such a secluded spot.

"I tried several others. I really did, Kary. Sitting by the pool depressed me. I kept thinking about how Dana died only a few yards away. So I moved."

"Why not go to someplace else on the veranda?"

"I tried four or five places. I just didn't feel comfortable. When I came to this end of the veranda, this beautiful porch felt just right. It was the perfect place to take a little sun but not too much. The views from here are wonderful. And, to be frank, I considered this spot to be public enough as to be out of harm's way."

"So much for that notion," Kary replied.

"How did Ms. Hopkins approach you?" Tom Capstone asked.

Recalling the incident made Maya queasy. "She just walked up and said, "Ciao Signora, "as though we had continued being close for years; however, it wasn't long before the mood of our conversation changed." Sparing the details for the time being, Maya told them how Lori claimed she had never intended to kill Dana, that she was simply defending herself."

"Did you believe her?"

"Lori may have convinced herself of that story, but, no, she didn't convince me."

"What else did she say?"

"She accused Dana and me of ruining all her plans."

"Plans. What plans?" Tom Capstone asked.

"Lori had been planning for years to make something of herself. She set her plan in motion after her parents divorced. Where this was all headed, who knows? Congress may have been only her first political step. Maybe the White House was in her plans."

Tom Capstone and Joe Crandall were aware of only part of Lori's story. This was not the time to bring them up to date, so Maya refocused her comments on what had just transpired on the porch.

"I must confess," she said while looking Kary in the eyes, "I took a terrible chance."

"What do you mean?"

"Within a few moments it became clear to me that Lori

intended to kill me. I realized I'd be dead sooner than later if I just said nothing. So I challenged her."

"Challenged her?" Kary couldn't help but smile at his sister-in-law's moxie, although thoughts of what might have happened made him queasy.

"Look, Kary, I knew this girl well, probably as well as anyone, except for Dana, and probably even better than her own mother. I knew what made her tick. Lori always needed to explain herself to Dana and me. I needed to stall for time until you, or someone, came to help me. The best way to do that was to make her explain how she did everything. And it almost worked."

"Almost? What do you mean?"

Maya raised her head and fixed her gaze on each of them. As she did, she smiled a bit sheepishly. "I went a little too far. Lori was a lousy Italian student. She probably never should have taken Italian four and should have received no better than a D in the course."

"But she didn't?" Kary asked.

"No. I'm embarrassed to tell you she had Dana and me wrapped around her little finger. Not only did I pass her with a C, but Dana and I convinced the principal to give her a special "good citizen" award. Oh," Maya cried out as she held her head in her hands, "what a pair of fools we were!"

"Get back to your story, will you please, Maya," Kary said.

"Oh, yes, my story. Lori was a weak Italian student. She asked me if I could forget about everything that had trans- pired." Then Maya paused and considered aloud, "How inter- esting that she asked me to forget, but not to forgive." All of the men nodded their agreement to this reflection.

"Of course, there was no way I could ever forgive what she did to Dana. As to the terrible thing she did in high school,

I wasn't about to forget about that either, and I told her so. But it was the way I told her," she said with a wry smile.

"What did you say?"

"Ti conoscevo quando . . ."

"Ti con, what?" For all of his education, Kary had always been the victim of a tin ear when it came to mastering foreign languages.

"Ti conoscevo quando. Don't worry, Kary, Lori didn't know its meaning either."

"Even after four years of high school Italian?" Chief Brown asked.

"Nope, and I knew she wouldn't, which is exactly why I said it to her."

Kary threw up his hands. "Does anyone else understand this?" No one responded.

Maya was actually enjoying her own telling of the story. "After she asked me if I was willing to forget what she'd done, I thought I'd blow a gasket. I looked at her and said, 'Ti conoscevo quando.' As I suspected it might, that really pissed her off. Pardon my language. Then she asked me what the hell that means. So I smiled at her and said, "You always were a lousy Italian student, Lori. What I just said is, 'I knew you when'."

"Ouch," Kary said. "What happened next?"

"She attacked me."

Now it was Joe Crandall's turn to ask questions. "Mrs. Lassiter—"

"Please call me Maya."

"Okay, Maya, I'm going to need to hear this part in some detail. I must warn you that you'll be asked to tell your story to me and the state police again."

"I should be careful of inconsistencies is what you're telling me."

"Exactly."

"I understand, Sergeant. Lori took one quick step toward me. She was fast! She grabbed my hair with her left hand and put her right hand around my throat. Her grip was strong and I wasn't ready for her attack."

"Then what happened?" Kary asked. His expression told Maya that he was asking as more than a crime scene investigator. What she saw on his face was the concern of a loving brother-in-law.

"She yanked me to my feet. We were headed toward the balustrade at the end of the porch."

"She was going to throw you over the side."

"Yeah. She said something about snapping my neck. I wasn't sure whether she was going to do that first or if she intended the fall to kill me."

For the first time, Erma Hearn's voice was heard behind them. "But she never made it that far."

"No, she didn't, thanks to you, Erma."

Now it was Tom Capstone who spoke. "What were you doing out here this time of day, Erma?"

"Three in the afternoon every day is when I take my power walk." Then fixing her gaze on Maya she said, "I usually walk down and back up the driveway. I turn around when I reach 302."

"But not today, thank goodness," Maya said.

"Naw. I got a bit of a late start because of a bitchy housekeeper. I figured I'd walk back and forth along the porch a few times. I'd just turned the corner when I heard Missus Lassiter yell. It was obvious to anyone what was going to happen next, so I ran over and yelled at that woman over there to stop." She was pointing at the form of Laureli 'Lori' Hopkins.

"When I got to her, the one over there told me to mind my f'ing business. She said something about martial arts. Well, I've seen that stuff before. It don't impress me much."

"Erma's been something of an enforcer around here for a long time," Tom Capstone smiled and Chief Brown nodded his agreement.

"Then she hit me in the face with something she called cool whip, or something like that," Erma said while touching a small bruise on her nose.

"I think that was 'single whip'," Kary said. Looking at the chief, he continued, "I told you there was something familiar about the way Dana was killed."

"Yeah, well, she single whipped the wrong gal, I'll tell you what," Erma said.

"She sure did," Maya smiled. "Erma grabbed Lori by the back of the neck and dug her left hand into the soft spot on Lori's shoulder. You should have heard her scream. I've never seen anything like it. Lori was helpless. Then Erma took a running start and smashed Lori's head into the column over there. After that, Lori just slumped to the ground." The blood on the column and the balustrade and the position of Lori Hopkins, who was finally rousing with the help of the resort's nurse, corroborated Maya's story. It was evident to all present that Erma had saved Maya's life and Laureli Hopkins had challenged a formidable force.

EPILOGUE

Julie Woods did not have an easy time after the capture of Laureli Hopkins. Initially, the district attorney planned to file charges of at least one count of burglary and was considering filing a charge as an accessory to attempted first degree murder. However, when the public defender assigned to Julie's case proved to the prosecutor that Laureli held a Svengali-like influence over Julie since childhood, the DA was willing to discuss the possibility of a plea bargain. The challenge for the public defender was to convince Julie to serve as a witness for the state by providing evidence against her "best friend."

Julie's relationship with her childhood friend, Lori Dark, had been less than healthy from its inception. While Lori had been no beauty queen, she had gained acceptance from her peers. By contrast, Julie was the proverbial square peg in a round hole.

High school can be a cruel place for such a student, where only the athletic and the beautiful stand out. Because she wasn't a good student, Julie escaped the torture directed at the class brainiacs. The truth is she simply went unnoticed until Lori Dark took her under wing. A perfect match. Julie Woods had needed someone to notice her while Lori Dark desperately needed a worshiper. Throughout their years in high school together, Julie followed Lori around like an obedient puppy. She did everything Lori asked her to do. She hadn't minded in the slightest when she was caught purchasing beer as a minor. The beer had been purchased with money and a fake ID given to her by her best friend, Lori. For Julie, to have been caught while serving her best friend was an act of loyalty. She didn't turn on Lori even when Julie's mother used a strap on her behind, not even when the judge sentenced her to two hundred hours of community service, the first such punishment ever handed down in Carroll. All this time, Armand Desmoreau, the absentee father, blamed Julie for leading his wonderful Laureli down the primrose path.

As a result, it was most shocking to Laureli Hopkins when her dear, devoted friend Julie turned state's evidence in order to save her own neck. Despite the fact Julie had been well prepared by the public defender to give her testimony, she entered the court room undecided whether she would testify against her best friend. Not even the threat of being charged with a Class B felony for burglary, which would have meant three and one-half to seven years in the state penitentiary, had completely convinced her. Mike Fishman, who was assigned to defend her, told Julie that testifying against Lori Dark could reduce the charges against her to breaking-and-entering, which is a misdemeanor offense in Coos County.

"I'm reasonably sure I can convince those guys to reduce your sentence to a couple of months. We could get you off doing some probation time."

"You mean no prison?"

"That's right, Julie, no prison as long as you don't screw up."

Julie was very tempted. The thought of going to jail was very upsetting to her. She had spent years trying to lose weight and had just found a good hair dresser. The thought of those ugly uniforms almost made her nauseous, however, Lori was her best friend, after all.

When Julie arrived in the court room, she was still undecided about how to testify in the case of Coos County versus Laureli Hopkins, AKA Laureli Desmoreau, AKA Lori Dark. Even when Julie heard Signora Lassiter describe how Lori had feigned cancer—without telling her best friend about it—in order to curry favor with her teachers, Julie remained undecided. What finally struck home was when Laureli Hopkins took the witness stand and told the court that it was Julie's idea to burglarize Maya's room and that Julie, not she, was the mastermind of the plot to silence Maya. Thus, it was Laureli's own inability to take responsibility for her actions that worked against her. The jury had been skeptical about Laureli's testimony but still needed Julie to seal the case against the wannabe congresswoman. In exchange for her testimony, Julie was sentenced to two months in the county jail, but her sentence was immediately reduced to two years probation contingent upon good behavior. Julie's employment at the Mount Washington Resort was terminated, before the trial, by Tom Capstone. She soon violated the terms of her probation when she left New Hampshire to marry a Hungarian businessman.

* * *

Laureli's life certainly did not turn out the way she had schemed. Instead of making a run for national office, she was on trial for murder. Ironically, it was her attempt on the life of Maya Lassiter, not the death of Dana Cerone, that proved to be her undoing. Had she simply turned herself in to the authorities following her altercation with Dana, there would have been no case against her. With no eyewitnesses to the actual event and no corroborating evidence to implicate her as a murderer, she could have walked away a free woman. It was not in Laureli's make up to take responsibility for her actions. Besides, had she admitted that there had been a quarrel and Dana Cerone had accidentally struck her head as a result, Laureli's political career would have been tainted. She was convinced the Democratic Party would withdraw its support for her candidacy and Laureli would have resumed being the nobody she always feared she'd become.

While there were no charges filed against Laureli in the Cerone death, the district attorney threw the book at her for her failed effort to kill Maya Lassiter. Several months passed before Laureli's trial began. She spent a week recuperating at the Memorial Hospital in North Conway. Upon her discharge, she convinced Bob Hopkins to pay for plastic surgery to repair her broken nose and an unsightly scar on her left cheek that had resulted from her introduction to the Doric column on the south porch. Hopkins gave Laureli the money as a parting gift, thus marking the dissolution of their marriage.

As could have been expected, the trial was a media circus. Every news outlet in New England, plus the national networks, provided coverage of the first degree murder trial of a candidate for U.S. Congress. Of course, by the time the trial actually began, the state Democratic Party had pulled its support and endorsed Mandy Tomkins, as it should have in the first place. The case was a veritable slam dunk for the prosecution. None of the leading defense attorneys whom Laureli contacted would touch her case after they learned she once pretended to be dying of cancer. Also, Bob Hopkins refused to spend a single dime for her defense. With only a public defender to prepare her case, Laureli Hopkins was convicted of attempted murder in the first degree and given a twenty- to forty-year sentence. Having exhausted her final appeal, the judge gave Laureli a twenty-year sentence of which five years could be suspended once she completed a twelve month drug and alcohol program.

As Laureli Hopkins left the Coos County Superior Court Building for the final time, there was a broad smile on her face. She later explained to her minions in the state penitentiary that things may not have worked out as planned, but she was famous after all.

***

One hour after Armand Desmoreau submitted his resignation, Tom Capstone strode into the Main Dining room and asked to speak privately with Armand. Armand recognized his own handwriting on the letter that Tom Capstone removed from his pocket.

"I regret I cannot honor your request, Monsieur Desmoreau."

Armand was confused. His general manager had addressed him with the respectful term, monsieur, and then refused to accept his letter of resignation.

"I don't understand, Monsieur Capstone."

"There may be some question about whether or not you acted in the best interest of your family long ago, but that's not for us to determine in your place of employ. What matters to me is your record as an employee at this resort has been exemplary. You have never missed a day of work, other than during earned vacation time, throughout your tenure here. Furthermore, I have never received so much as a single negative comment about you from your colleagues. I regret you had to be brought into the nasty investigation of your daughter, but I see no reason to allow one of my most faithful employees to leave because of anything that has transpired during the past forty-eight hours. So, Monsieur, please get back to work."

For Armand, there would be much heartache ahead, but he still had the Mount Washington family that was dear to him.

***

After the police arrested Laureli and Julie, Kary and Maya spent an hour discussing what transpired with Tom Capstone and Chief Brown. Maya was congratulated for her performance during extremely trying circumstances. Both men thanked Kary profusely for the professional manner in which he had accorded himself. As they rose to leave, Tom told Kary he would be dictating a letter detailing his actions during the previous forty-eight hours. He also gave Kary a card containing his private satellite cell phone number.

"If you ever need an immediate reference for a general manager in distress at some other resort, please don't hesitate to contact me. Like your buddy Warn Barson, I'm fairly well known in resort management circles," he said with a wink.

Kary shook hands with both men. Maya kissed each of them on both cheeks and murmured, "Arrivederci." Then they departed.

Once they made their way to Route 302, Maya looked back at the resort and suddenly remembered something.

"Oh no! I left that damned Ford Mustang back at the resort," she cried.

"Not to worry," Kary smiled, "after all you've been through, Chief Brown made arrangements for it to be driven home for you, at their expense I might add."

***

Over the long term, Kary and Nya spent increasing amounts of time with Maya and Stan, something Nya privately wanted for years. Two years later, the foursome visited the Mount Washington Resort, this time for purely recreational purposes. At first, Maya was reluctant to go along. She never wanted to see the site where her dear friend Dana had died. Only after she heard Tom Capstone discuss on television how the entire area surrounding the outside pool was being razed to accommodate the resort's new conference center and spa did she considered visiting. Maya finally was convinced when she learned there was cell phone service.

**

Fifteen years passed quietly. A middle-aged woman packed her prison furlough papers beneath a change of clothes in the cheap, brown, institutional valise that sat open on the cot in her cell. She carefully placed a completed application inside and shut the case. Lori Howard smiled, feeling certain she soon would be deputy campaign manager for the popular Republican congressional candidate from Montana.

AFTERWORD

No one who sets out to write a novel of any genre does so casually, nor does one accomplish such a labor intensive effort alone. Every book necessitates a blending of inspiration, perspiration, and the collaboration of numerous talented individuals. The contributors to each of my previous books remain indelibly etched in my mind. Those who have contributed to this one will be no different. I want to express my sincere appreciation to my publisher, John Greene, and to Rich Kallan, my childhood friend and literary adviser.

Owing to my education as a geographer and experience as a tourism researcher, each of my novels is strongly rooted in place. Settings become leading characters every bit as important as Kary Turnell to the eventual outcome of these stories. I Knew You When is set almost entirely at the Mount Washington Resort in Bretton Woods, New Hampshire. To provide an insider's sense of the beautiful resort hotel, the story incorporates the trials and tribulations of the resort's meetings and conferences personnel, its security staff, and its public relations department. This would not have been possible without the cooperation of six members of the efficient management team at the resort: Dennis Duprey, Lance Baker, Fred Hollis, Martha Wilson, Tim Chapman, and Kim Labnon. I also want to thank my friend Steve Barba, innkeeper emeritus of The Balsams Grand Resort Hotel, for further instructing me in resort operations.

Several others contributed substantially to this author's understanding of elements that were critical to the story line. Arnie Arnesen, a veritable legend on the New Hampshire political scene, hosted me for a delightful and head-spinning afternoon tour of the world of congressional politics. Mark Fischler, a former public defender, provided guidance about likely judicial outcomes. Rossana DiSilvio Woldman advised me about proper Italian phraseology.

Mary Desfosses is my trusted grammar and punctuation consultant, and Sally Stitt is my murder mystery guru. My daughters, Robyn and Elisabeth, advise about character voice and expressing technical observations, respectively. Finally there is Marla, my wife of thirty-six years. Besides being the center of my universe, she brings intelligence and common sense to each of my writing projects.

Books by Mark Okrant

A Last Resort
First in the Kary Turnell Series

Judson's Island
A mystery set in Maine

Sleeping Alongside the Road
Recollections of the motel era

Visit *www.OakManorPublishing.com*
for Mark Okrant books and others.

Mark Okrant has been a university professor and tourism researcher since the mid-1970s, having plied his trade in South Dakota, New Hampshire, Maine, Alaska, Canada and Romania. He is past president of the prestigious Travel and Tourism Research Association.

Mark is the author of A Last Resort, *the first in the Kary Turnell series, as well as* Judson's Island *and* Sleeping Alongside The Road. *Mark and his wife Marla live in New Hampshire. They have two grown daughters, Robyn and Elisabeth.*

Kary Turnell will be back snooping around another resort hotel in the third book of this series.